Also by Geoff Nicholson

Street Sleeper
A Knot Garden
What We Did on Our Holidays
Hunters & Gatherers
The Food Chain
The Errol Flynn Novel
Still Life with Volkswagens
Everything and More
Footsucker
Bleeding London
Flesh Guitar
Female Ruins
Bedlam Burning

a novel

THE
HOLLYWOOD
DODO

Geoff Nicholson

SIMON & SCHUSTER
New York London
Toronto Sydney

SIMON & SCHUSTER
Rockefeller Center
1230 Avenue of the Americas
New York, NY 10020

SIMON & SCHUSTER and colophon are registered trademarks
of Simon & Schuster, Inc.

For information about special discounts for bulk purchases,
please contact Simon & Schuster Special Sales:
1-800-456-6798 or business@simonandschuster.com

Designed by Jeanette Olender

Manufactured in the United States of America

1 3 5 7 9 10 8 6 4 2

Library of Congress Cataloging-in-Publication Data
Nicholson, Geoff.
The Hollywood dodo: a novel / Geoff Nicholson.
p. cm.
1. Hollywood (Los Angeles, Calif.)—Fiction.   2. Motion picture actors
and actresses—Fiction.   3. Children of physicians—Fiction.
4. British—California—Fiction.   5. Fathers and daughters—Fiction.
6. Los Angeles (Calif.)—Fiction.   7. Physicians—Fiction. I. Title.

PR6064.I225H65 2004
823'.914—dc22   2004041666

ISBN 0-7432-5779-0

About 1638 as I walked London streets I [saw] the picture of a strange fowle hong out upon a cloth . . . went in to see it. It was a great fowle somewhat bigger than the largest Turkey Cock. The keeper called it a Dodo.

H. L'ESTRANGE   *in the Sloan Manuscript, circa 1650*

To be rare is to have a lower threshold of collective catastrophe. Any misfortune, even one that would seem small by an absolute standard, is liable to be a total misfortune. A modest-sized disaster can push a rare species immodestly close to oblivion.

DAVID QUAMMEN   *The Song of the Dodo, 1996*

". . . you must, many times, have wished, before this, to be carried back into the past?"

"Oh yes. 'Wished' is a mild word. God! . . . How I longed for it! How I writhed in a bed of nettles, as men scarify themselves for money or women . . ."

JOHN DICKSON CARR   *The Devil in Velvet, 1951*

For Galen imputeth all to the cold that is black, and thinks that the spirits being darkened, and the substance of the brain cloudy and dark, all the objects thereof appear terrible, and the mind itself, by those dark, obscure, gross fumes, ascending from black humours, is in continual darkness, fear, and sorrow; divers terrible monstrous fictions in a thousand shapes and apparitions occur, with violent passions, by which the brain and phantasy are troubled and eclipsed.

ROBERT BURTON   *The Anatomy of Melancholy, 1632*

"But who has won?"

This question the Dodo could not answer without a great deal of thought, and it sat for a long time with one finger pressed upon its forehead (the position in which you usually see Shakespeare, in the pictures of him).

LEWIS CARROLL   *Alice's Adventures in Wonderland, 1865*

Consider the train of events that led to his passing: an avian, possessing the power of flight, finds himself without predators on a luxury island in the Indian Ocean. He no longer needs to fly so he doesn't bother. If I could fly I'd keep on flying, whether I needed to or not.

Laziness is not attractive even in a handsome creature and the dodo was no oil painting—there are oil paintings to prove it.

PAUL SPOONER   *Museum of the Mind, 1992*

If I'd been fucked by my husband as much as I was fucked by Warner Brothers, I'd still be married.

CHER   *1988*

The Hollywood Dodo

one Hurry Sundown

The movement is westward, racing along the swarming freeway, chasing the sun, accelerating towards the sea, in your painted wagon, in your rental car, further, west of here, west of your life, toward some old dream, some new darkness, away from the old world.

It's a race we always lose. We move too slowly. We can't outrun the gathering dusk. The sky turns carotene orange. The palm trees turn into cartoon silhouettes. You settle for the next best thing. You find somewhere to park, you briefly stand in line, buy your ticket, step inside.

You're glad you made it, but it's not quite as you imagined. You were deceived. You believed the word of mouth. The scenes you saw in the trailer had other, lesser meanings when seen in context. There was less than you expected, less of everything, fewer explosions and car chases and sex scenes. The exposition was clumsy. The dialogue was flat, the performances wooden. You got restless and thought of walking out before the end.

The light at the end of the tunnel is the light from the projector. Someone a few rows back seems to call your name, so you turn your head. You're staring into the source, but what do you see? Motes, beams, shapeless light. The images are now behind you, being thrown over your shoulder. The light's nothing till it hits the screen. And perhaps it's nothing much even then: ghosts, shades, chemical traces, digital enhancements, special effects that aren't so special.

You move through the museum, steady as a Steadicam, through the waxworks and the hall of fame. You preserve memories that may or may not be your own, memories of big names and has-beens, shooting and falling stars, the holy and the wholly corrupt. It all decays: the body, the film stock, the remembrances. In the theater and the VIP room and the pet cemetery, the operations of nature continue: a constant fading, a simplification, the crumbling of structure.

In the cinema of your imagination you run the only movies you own. You are the lone viewer here, the only customer and one who's not easy to please. You watch the pterodactyls and the winged dragons, the mutant slime, the things from the lab, the girls in the fur bikinis. You watch the cartoons and the newsreels, the shorts and documentaries and stag films. It all passes before your eyes like a life, yours, and it all looks so old hat, so last season. Was this really the blockbuster you awaited so eagerly? Was this the hot ticket you'd have killed for?

The house lights are always dimmed, the aperture is always contracted. There's always a twist in the final reel. You settle down, kick back. You close your eyes and wait for the next movie to start.

two **Doc Hollywood**

William Draper walks through the stew and babble of London's Alsatia: a place named after a war zone, the quarter for squatters, criminals, cutters of purses and throats, for whores of various hues, for fencing masters, for writers and artists (the less pecunious sort). Above all, Alsatia is the place for mountebanks, for those who profess an arcane knowledge of physic and surgery, for charlatan alchemists, for the hawkers of astrological tracts and prophetical almanacs: a home to all manner of natural philosophers and Empericks, of seventh sons and circulators: in a word—quacks.

William Draper is a student of physic at Oxford University, where he should be now, but he has come here instead, supposedly visiting his recently widowed father in Holborn. For all his belief in science and good sense, he is nevertheless drawn to the exotic, disreputable men he sees about him: the Italian physician in his gold-braided livery, the oculist from Silesia in his ink black suit, these would-be serious men of science with their capes and their bone-handled canes, their black cats and their monkey skeletons.

The air is full of smells and noise: camphor and mint, tobacco and bad eggs, a drum being beaten, a badly played flute, and then there are the voices: persuasive and arresting, crying for attention, making competing and contradictory claims, promising good health and long life, potency and fecundity. Some make comparatively modest promises of clear skin and white teeth, the revelation of mysterious yet frivolous beauty secrets. (Or perhaps beauty is not so frivolous.) Others claim infallible cures for ulcers and scurvy, for dropsy and ague, for the stone and gout and distemper and plague: anything and everything that might ail a body. Others, yet, speak of salvation and hint at immortality.

It might be a contest for the sweetest lies or the glibbest tongues, and sometimes the voices break into song or Latin or what sound like invented languages. But these voices are not raised in spontaneous celebration: they are here to sell. They speak only in the service of their owners' merchandise: pills and powders and potions, noble medicines, tinctures and cordials, elixirs and volatile spirits, Balsamick Essences, fumigants, cure-alls.

And young William Draper is bewitched. He can see that there is a swirl of brimstone about this place, that many of its inhabitants are fearsome and corrupt, and yet he does not fear them. He feels protected and charmed. Even though he does not trust any of these people who surround him, he cannot bring himself to despise them. Somewhere in this coming together of science and art, of common sense and nonsense, of gullibility, scepticism, and eternal optimism, he can imagine a possible future for himself, though the form it might take is utterly mysterious to him, and that is not why he is here in Alsatia today. He is here for what seems to him a much higher purpose.

He is on his way to a tavern, the Three Cranes, but he is not seeking admission to the tavern itself. Above a side door is suspended a painted sign showing a gigantic footprint, the sort that might be made by a monstrous, mythical thing: a griffin, a basilisk, something unheard-of or unimagined or simply unspeakable, and below the image are written the words, "The world's most disgusting bird."

The man tending the tavern's side door, a sickly, white-bearded character of vaguely naval or perhaps piratical appearance, calls to everyone who passes, telling them that the great, hideous female fowl that can make such a terrifying footprint is to be seen in a private upper room of the tavern, if anyone has the nerve and stomach to set eyes on it and is also willing to pay what he assures them is the very reasonable price of admission. He also tells them they must hurry. He is a traveling man. He will soon be gone and it will be a long time before he comes this way again.

William has heard all this patter before, many times. He has become something of a regular here. He has tried to reason with this man, the bird's keeper, whose name he has discovered to be Moxon, a good Yorkshire name, saying that he is misrepresenting the poor creature. William has told Moxon that the fowl which dwells within is far more curious and wonderful, much more of a marvel than his lurid description allows. She is quite a sweet creature, he insists, and Moxon has displayed an extravagant lack of attention.

William reaches into his pocket for a coin to pay the entrance fee once again, but this time he is waved inside for free. This is a new development. Until now Moxon has groaned and cursed at each of William's arrivals and then willingly taken his money, treating him like a simpleton or dupe. Now at least he has learned tolerance or perhaps he has simply learned how to be amused by him, as if William has become part of the sideshow rather than merely a member of the audience. William hopes this bodes well for his plans.

He goes in through the doorway, then up a familiar splintered staircase to a small, low-ceilinged room. There is sawdust deep on the floor, burlap drawn across the windows, some candlelight for mysterious, theatrical effect, and at one end of the room, on a low platform, there sits a rough but sturdy bamboo cage, strewn with half-eaten apples, and inside it is a creature to which William has already grown strongly, incomprehensibly, attached.

It is a bird, a great fowl indeed, though clearly rather a young one, and neither hideous nor disgusting in William's opinion, nor in fact nearly so large as Moxon has implied, in no way capable of making the huge footprint on the sign, and more than one customer has complained of dishonest aggrandizement.

The bird is about the size of a young swan, but whereas a swan is white and regal, this creature has a clumsy, ash gray lump of a body, darkening to black along its flightless, flaplike wings. The legs are short, braided with yellowish scale. The tail consists of nothing more than a few trifling, curled gray plumes.

But it is the face—naked, without feathers—that draws and fixes William's attention. It seems to poke out timidly from under a cowl of folded skin. The beak is large and dangerous-looking, a horned, hooked thing. And then, set high and far back, are two tiny circular eyes, dim, distracted, proud yet confused.

The bird is flightless, charmless to most tastes, songless, habitually taciturn, though not quite voiceless. From time to time she emits a low, pigeonlike sound, a sort of cooing, two repeated syllables, *doo-doo,* which no doubt has inspired the name: the dodo.

William stares at the creature, not with the vacant curiosity of most of the visitors and gawpers who come there but with scientific fascination and what he takes to be a superior sort of compassion. The dodo looks out of place here, out of joint, and in itself misconstructed, as though made out of the left over parts from other, more elegant birds, an abandoned piece of apprentice work from God's workshop. But William finds this very inelegance appealing too, and brave and noble in its way. He responds to something in the bird's ruffled demeanor, in its melancholy, its earthbound plight.

William has heard all Moxon's stories regarding the provenance of the bird, a set of intermeshing yarns involving shipwrecked sailors, some of them Dutch, some Portuguese, assertions of the bird's stupidity, its uselessness, the repellent taste of its flesh, its failure to find a place in the schemes of either God or man.

Even in his innocence and willingness to believe, William is unsure how much, if any, of this information is to be trusted, but he has nevertheless learned it all verbatim, understudied Moxon, and he has been known to repeat the stories to willing, or less than willing, listeners. But today he is alone, the only visitor to the upper room. This too seems propitious. Having viewed the bird again for just a few minutes, having assured himself that she is in good health, if not noticeably good spirits, he goes down the stairs, finds Moxon, and takes him aside.

"Mr. Moxon," William says, in a voice that sounds somber and businesslike, at least to his own ears, "I should like to make you a monetary proposition. I should like to purchase your dodo."

Moxon laughs. Why would he not? "And how much would you be offering, sir?" he asks.

It seems to William that the bird is worth a fortune, a king's ransom. Nevertheless, modestly, a man beginning a negotiation and not wishing to reveal the true depth of his desire, he says, "Two guineas."

Moxon laughs again. He obviously considers his bird to be worth much more than that, as indeed does William. He had imagined he might have to go as high as five and would have done so, but Moxon is not about to haggle.

"You are what, young man, seventeen years old?"

"Indeed," William says, impressed by the accuracy of Moxon's guess.

"And what do you imagine you will be doing with your life?"

"I am training to become a physician," William says, with some pride.

"Then come back, sir," Moxon says, "when you have made your physician's fortune. The price of the bird may have increased by then, but your means will no doubt have increased more so."

It is a most insulting and unsatisfactory answer, not least because William has little idea how long it might take him to make his fortune and even less idea of how long a dodo might live. He suddenly feels very green, and humiliated by the coarse mysteries of the world.

"Will you be still be here?" William asks.

"Not precisely here, no," says Moxon. "As you can see, I am a man who makes his living by dealing in small wonders, and it is in the nature of things that those who are wondrous in a certain place may be common as muck in another. And there is nothing in the world so wondrous that it will not lose its luster through overfamiliarity. In short, I find it pays to keep moving."

William feels his own hopes departing with this mention of Moxon's departure.

"In the meantime," Moxon adds, "here's a feather to put in your cap."

From inside the sweaty leather folds of his jerkin Moxon produces a short, gray tail feather that had once belonged to the dodo. William hopes it molted naturally and that Moxon has not plucked it painfully from the poor bird's rump. A plucked feather he would be most reluctant to take, so he thinks it best not to inquire. He accepts the feather and says he will prize it always. Moxon laughs at him once more.

As William leaves the Three Cranes, achingly disappointed yet somehow undefeated, he still imagines a future in which, perhaps after the death of Moxon (something violently bloody and not without poetic justice, he envisages), the bird will become his.

And he says to himself, aloud yet barely audibly, though in the clamor of Alsatia nobody would hear even if he were to shout it at the top of his lungs, he says, "One day I will have a bird such as this, my very own dodo, perhaps a breeding pair, perhaps many of them, a flock, a colony. I will populate an estate, a kingdom. I swear, solemnly, that I will fill the world with dodos."

three Panic in Year Zero

I was sitting with my twenty-one-year-old daughter, Dorothy, on a Boeing 777, London to Los Angeles: a Thursday in October, the skies more than usually turbulent. We were traveling in business class since we were indeed going to L.A. on business of a sort, or at least my daughter was, and also because, given my size and shape and great bulk, I have some difficulty fitting into the narrow confines of a coach class seat. Shameful but true. And I was thumbing through the airline magazine to see what movies were going to be available on my "personal in-flight entertainment system," and I was thinking of some of the many things I hate about the movies.

The thing I was hating most at that moment was the way that aeroplanes in movies are always so pleasant. They're spacious and airy, so well lit, so quiet, the passengers have so much leg room, the aisles are so unnaturally wide, it's so easy to get a drink. In the real world it is never like this. Even in the ruinously expensive business class none of this, in my admittedly limited experience, is ever the case.

I'm not a fool. I realize there's a perfectly good reason why movie aeroplanes don't much resemble real aeroplanes. Moviemakers want their movies to look good. They need lots of light. They need quiet so that the dialogue is audible. And I suppose the gangways have to be unnaturally wide so that the crew can wheel the camera up and down between the seats. But these rational, practical considerations weren't making me hate movies any the less at that particular moment.

Now, I know you could say that the above was no reason to hate the movies. In fact you could say that it was actually much more of a reason to hate real life, and at that time I certainly thought I had every reason to hate *my* real life, but in the circumstances, I decided it was preferable to hate the movies instead. It seemed to me they were in business to deceive and trick us, to make us believe that the world was a more glamorous, colorful, and desirable place than it really is. Does this seem like enough motivation for hating movies? Perhaps not.

Actually there was a much more local, much more personal reason for my hating movies on that particular day. You see, I was flying to Los Angeles with my daughter (whose real name, the name I gave her—Dorothy Cadwallader—had been abandoned for the stage and screen, in favor of the infinitely more prosaic, though allegedly far more commercial, Dorothy Lee) because she had ambitions, indeed an opportunity, to become a movie actress, possibly even a Hollywood actress, conceivably even a Hollywood star, and frankly this was worrying me a great deal.

Her opportunity was coming via a Hollywood agent she happened to have met in London, a man named Bob Samuelson, who had invited her to come to L.A. to get the feel of the place, to meet some people, chat with producers and casting directors, perhaps do some auditions, possibly have a screen test. He had sounded enthusiastic and confident about her chances of success. I had talked to him briefly on the phone and he had sounded perfectly plausible and professional, if a little manically upbeat for my tastes, and he had assured me that he saw a fabulous future for Dorothy. Be that as it may, he had not offered to fly her out. This trip was at Dorothy's own, or in fact *my* own, expense.

As far as we could tell (I mean we're not complete idiots, we did do a little research via Dorothy's drama school and the few people she knew in the business in London), this Bob Samuelson was bona fide. The agency he worked for was small but respectable, he had a good reputation, at least by Hollywood standards, and that was all some relief, though it was hardly enough to entirely dispel a father's worries.

I was concerned that whatever his reputation, Samuelson might still turn out to be a crook, a liar, a seducer, a user. I was worried that he might hurt my daughter, and I was aware that he might do that even if he was perfectly honest, decent, and honorable. Sometimes things just don't work out despite everyone's best intentions. Basically I was worried that my daughter might be flying all this way simply to be disappointed.

Much as I love my daughter, much as I thought she was talented, beautiful, gifted, determined, and so forth, I was well aware that a father's judgment isn't the most objective in these matters. And so I was concerned that Dorothy might not be talented, beautiful, gifted, and determined *enough* to succeed. And even if she *was*, I didn't know that this would necessarily be a good thing for her.

We all know what Hollywood does to people. It changes them, and very seldom for the better. It makes them vain, glib, fake, embittered. And this seems to have nothing much to do with actual achievement, with how well or badly they're doing. Hollywood success and Hollywood failure can be equally corrupting, though presumably in different ways. Forgive me if I talk as though I knew about these things. The fact is, I only knew what I'd read or imagined or—let's face it—seen in the movies. (Now let's see if it's true.)

And I kept thinking of what somebody once said, that for an actress to be a success, when you see her on the movie screen, "You've got to want to fuck her," and this is not a comfortable thought for a father. It's not the way he wants to think about his daughter and it's not the way he wants anyone else to think about her either. The very idea made me want to lock Dorothy in some fairy-tale tower and threaten to slay any man who so much as glanced toward the drawbridge.

But I knew I had to keep these worries to myself and not share them with Dorothy. My role was to be supportive, to express oceanic confidence in my daughter, to be a cool dad: a role that I thought I'd played more or less convincingly over the years. I thought we had a good relationship. I thought she liked me. I thought we were pals.

All the same, I was aware that it was rather peculiar that a daughter should be taking her father along with her on a trip like this. And in fact Dorothy was less than thrilled by the arrangement. There had been a few arguments and tantrums about it, about my not trusting her, about my treating her like a child and so on. I wouldn't say that I had won these arguments exactly, but given the circumstances and the traumas we'd been through recently, it wasn't too hard to convince even Dorothy that there were good reasons for my not wanting to be alone in England. It's a long story, and one that I do eventually intend to tell, but not at this moment. I now understand that in the world of movies this is known as backstory, and my own backstory was not without its cheap drama, mostly regarding the recent death of my wife, Caroline, Dorothy's mother, but we all know there's no value in revealing too much too soon.

My personal in-flight entertainment system was offering twelve channels of movies, a notional something for everybody, includ-

ing a classic channel showing *Rear Window*, which seemed surprisingly cineast of them. It's one of my favorite movies. Don't
ask me to tell you the others. I hate people who make lists of their
favorite movies, and I despise even more those who make lists of
the greatest movies *of all time*. Above all, I despise people who
then go on to debate these matters, who criticize other people's
lists, who demand to know how you could possibly leave off *Juliet
of the Spirits*.

Perhaps this confession will confirm what you may already
have guessed, that I don't really hate movies at all. I love them
passionately and if not exactly unconditionally and uncritically,
then at least with an essential generosity. If they sometimes let
me down, well, that's the way love is.

The truth, sad or happy depending on your point of view, is
that I'm a movie buff. But that's all I am. I never wanted to be
anything other than a spectator sitting in the dark having his
hopes, dreams, and fears played out, exploited, and sometimes
confounded and just occasionally exceeded. And it seemed that I
had passed on my love of the movies to Dorothy, and I was
pleased by that, but Dorothy wasn't content to be merely a spectator. She wanted to act. She wanted to star. I think you can see
why a father would be worried. I think you can understand why
there might be a moment on the aeroplane when he thought he
hated the movies.

I had never been to L.A. before, except in my dreams, except in
the movies. I knew it was full of cars and freeways, palm trees and
sun and salads. I knew there was ocean and beach and some extravagant shopping centers. I knew it also had pollution and

poverty, gangs and drive-by shootings. But that seemed acceptable. If some parts of the experience turned out to be seedy and
threatening, well, that was very much as promised too. I felt I
could cope with anything the city threw at me.

How Los Angeles might cope with *me* was a different matter.
I was a fifty-year-old Englishman: not slim, not fit, not tan, not
buff, with a tendency to wear tweeds and corduroy. I suspected I
might not be laid-back enough, not glittery enough. I feared that
L.A. might find me too down-to-earth and insufficiently health-
conscious, that I might stick out like a sore, plump Englishman. I
had managed to put the matter in abeyance by telling myself that
all this would be L.A.'s problem rather than mine, but whether
this approach would work on the ground remained to be seen.

And what, as my daughter had asked me more than once, was
I going to do while she saw various movers and shakers of the
movie world? "I'll be a tourist," I said. "They have museums and
art galleries in L.A., don't they? They have sights. I'll go to Universal Studios, I'll go and look at Grauman's Chinese Theatre.
I'll go on one of those 'death tours' where they ferry you around in
a Cadillac hearse to see where celebrities died. If the worse comes
to the worst, I'll go and watch a movie."

You see, I had done some research on L.A. And my daughter
had done a little of her own. I wouldn't say that Dorothy had
ideas above her station, but she certainly had financial aspira-
tions that were well outside my budget. She wanted to stay at the
Chateau Marmont. She wanted us to hire a vehicle from Exotic
Car Rental; I think she envisaged a pink convertible with fins and
a leopard-skin interior. She wanted us to be seen at the Polo
Lounge and the Viper Room and Trimalchio's, although I was
well aware that in these places she'd have rather not been seen
with me.

I did my best to rein her in a little. There was a certain amount of sulking, from both of us possibly, and her sulking skills are much more finely honed than mine, but we did come to a compromise: a good, moderately priced hotel, a sensible car, and a promise that we would upgrade both should Dorothy's meetings start to look promising. She may still have felt hard done by, but at least she stopped sulking.

How long did we intend to stay in L.A.? Well, we had told ourselves we were going for just two weeks; after that I had to return to work in England regardless. This was just a holiday for me. As for Dorothy, she'd heard stories, as who hasn't, about people who go to L.A. for the weekend, find that fortune smiles on them, and end up staying for the rest of their lives. If that happened to her, then so be it. I would be very, very happy for her.

Two weeks was clearly not enough time to succeed to any great extent, though it was certainly enough time to fail. In any case, I thought it ought to be enough to give Dorothy, and me, some sense of whether it was going to be worth her while to stay any longer. If things were looking good, if she was doing well and wanted to stay on, then she'd have my blessing. If failure looked imminent, I would be there to assure her that there was no shame in our both getting on a plane back to England. Did this all sound far too sensible and rational to be true? Possibly.

We had been in the air for a couple of hours. Dorothy lolled beside me, dead to the world as far as I could see. She had headphones over her ears, a sleep mask over her eyes. She seemed neither as excited nor as nervous about this trip as I expected her to be. Perhaps my fatherly presence was dampening her natural high spirits, or perhaps I was having a soothing, calming effect on her. I was prepared to accept either explanation.

I had scarcely started to watch *Rear Window*. Jimmy Stewart had only just started to discover the joys of his telephoto lens, when I became aware that an air hostess (stewardess, flight attendant, whatever they call themselves these days) was standing beside me, leaning over, whispering, "Excuse me, Dr. Cadwallader, but are you a *medical* doctor?"

I confessed that I was. I know I don't look like one. In lots of ways I look like anything but, which is fine by me and to an extent intentional. "Physician heal thyself" has always been the rule, and some patients do indeed like their doctors to be pictures of perfect health. But others think that's somehow unfair, like, for example, taking piano lessons from someone who's a natural, who has perfect pitch and wonderfully long, flexible fingers, who doesn't see what's so hard about playing the piano at all. How would he cope with the recalcitrant, the ham-fisted, the untalented? He just wouldn't understand. Similarly, doctors who, through a combination of good luck and good genetics and (all right, I'll admit it) good diet and exercise and so forth, have never had a day's illness in their lives can be intimidating to a lot of patients, and intimidation is what a lot of doctors strive for and wallow in.

Perforce this is not my way. Patients who look at me, sweating a little, breathing too hard as I tote my bulk around the surgery, limping slightly if I'm in one of my gouty phases, think, well, at least here's a man who understands what it is to be unhealthy. Anyway, I could see the reason for the stewardess's doubt and hesitation.

"Yes," I said to her, "I'm a doctor, but that's no reason to trust me."

She looked at me vacantly and humorlessly and said, "There's a young man in coach class who needs some attention."

"What kind of attention?"

"He thinks he's dying."

Reluctantly I left my seat and Jimmy Stewart and dragged myself toward the back of the plane. Coach class was surprisingly empty, which was frankly a little annoying. Having paid so much to fly in business class, I would have been delighted to see that the plebes were packed in like clams. They weren't. The young man to whose side I'd been summoned had three seats to himself, in which he'd constructed a sort of lair, surrounding himself with blankets, books, movie magazines, a laptop, a professional-looking digital camera, and what looked like the manuscript of a short novel or long short story. I could see that the title on the front of the manuscript was *The Restoration of the Dodo*—a name that meant nothing to me at the time.

I looked him over. He was a young blond-haired man, tanned, lean but muscular, what I thought of as a typical Californian. He could have been a surfer or a rock musician, a lifeguard or a pool cleaner. I supposed he was twenty-five or so; he was wearing a hooded sweatshirt with some Japanese illustration embossed on the front and a pair of shorts that must have been extremely chilly in the autumnal London we were leaving behind. He looked terrible. He was trembling, sweating, panting: symptoms I've been known to share. He also looked terrified.

"How are you?" I asked, in my best seatside manner.

"Either I'm dying or going crazy," he said in his soft, noncommittal West Coast drawl.

"Or both," I said, and rather wished I hadn't.

I felt his pulse, which was fast and irregular. I put my hand on his forehead and detected a raised temperature.

"Experiencing nausea?" I asked.

"Yeah."

"Feel like you're choking?"

"A little, yeah."

"Chest pain?"

"Sure."

"Feelings of unreality, strangeness, detachment from the environment?"

"You bet!"

I could see his alarm mounting. The fact that I could guess his symptoms only distressed him even more. He looked around in a panic, as if he was going to make a run for it. I had an ugly vision of trying to wrestle with him, as he in turn wrestled with the handle to the plane's emergency exit.

"Talk to me," I said. "What's your name?"

"Rick. Rick McCartney."

"OK, Rick, so what were you up to in London?"

"Losing my mind mostly."

"Yes, that can happen in London. Were you there for business or pleasure?"

"Neither, in the end."

"Did you get a chance to do any sightseeing?"

He didn't answer, and I had the feeling that I was losing him again.

"Come on, I'm only making conversation. You must have seen something while you were in London," I said.

"Yeah," he agreed. "The horror! I saw *the horror!*"

And then he started to laugh. You'd have to say there was a fair amount of hysteria in the laughter, but at the same time it signaled that he recognized some absurdity in his situation.

"You're having a panic attack," I said.

"You sure?"

"Either that or you're having a myocardial infarction, and I really don't think you're having a myocardial infarction."

"Good," he said, obviously not knowing what I was talking about but still glad not to be suffering from something with a name like that.

The stewardess produced the aircraft's sealed medical kit with its dire warning that it was only to be opened by qualified medical staff. (It's because of the morphine.) I think that she, and indeed some of the passengers who were gawping at me, hoped I was going to do something dramatic and doctorly, something involving blood and drugs and syringes. I was not.

"So, I'm not going to die?"

"Well, not for the next fifty years or so," I said, although I knew it was generally foolish to predict these things.

"What should I do?" he said.

"Have a drink," I said. "Watch a movie. *Rear Window* is rather good. It's one of my favorites."

"Yeah, mine too."

He smiled sadly. I smiled neutrally. We were both relieved, he because he wasn't dying, I because I hadn't had to deal with someone who was. I had done as much as I could. I had done what I do for most of my patients: listened, talked, been reassuring. This is generally as much as any doctor like myself, a general practitioner, can do.

Later in the flight I went back and checked on him. He was sleeping, with the manuscript clutched tightly in his fist. Later still the chief air steward brought me the captain's thanks, which I thought might have been expressed a little more concretely, say in the form of a bottle of duty-free gin, but it was not to be. Nevertheless this was still one of those all-too-rare moments when I could see that being a doctor had its uses and compensations.

Dorothy and I were waiting for our luggage to come down the carousel, and I was thinking of another thing I hate about the movies: weight improbability. There's often a scene in a movie that requires an actor or actress to be shown struggling with something heavy and cumbersome: large quantities of luggage or shopping bags or packages. But movie actors and actresses are apparently far too delicate to heave weighty objects around, and so in the movies you can see that the things they're pretending to struggle with aren't really heavy at all. The performers load huge cases into the boots of cars, swing them up into luggage racks, as though they weighed next to nothing, and that's because they *do* weigh next to nothing. The suitcase is empty; the package is just a wrapped cardboard box. Thus the performers are left with the job of having to mime the weight of the luggage, and being movie actors rather than mimes, they can't do it at all convincingly.

It's even worse when it comes to dead bodies, especially if they're in body bags or rolled in a carpet. You know there's nothing very much in there, certainly nothing with the weight and mass of a dead body. Trust me, I know a little about the weight of dead bodies. You think I'm being too literal and nitpicking? Well, possibly, but isn't that what we're constantly being told moviemaking is all about: precision, thoroughness, the deadly eye for detail?

Dorothy and I continued to wait. I had imagined that traveling business class might mean that our bags would come swiftly off the plane, and in fact my own battered leather suitcase did. However, the wait for Dorothy's many, huge multicolored bags was a good deal longer. I had known better than to try to persuade Dorothy to travel light. It was not in her nature, and besides, this was going to be an important, possibly a life-changing trip for her, and therefore she obviously needed her supplies: a whole conglomeration of outfits; evening clothes, sportswear, high heels and sneakers; the hair dryer, the travel iron, the small trunk of makeup. I had managed to talk her out of bringing her weights with her, but it hadn't been easy.

As we stood, staring at other people's circulating luggage, I saw the young man who had suffered the panic attack on the plane. I hadn't mentioned the episode to Dorothy. She had been asleep throughout my ministrations and by the time she'd woken up there seemed little point dwelling on it. The young man still looked to be in a bit of a state, and I was hoping he wouldn't see me. What could we possibly have to say to each other? But he came pounding in our direction, and when he was twenty feet or so away he shouted out, "Thanks, man, you saved my life."

When he had got within what I considered conversational range, I said quietly, "No, I really didn't."

"Well, it sure felt like it."

"Yes, that's the nature of a panic attack."

"Well anyway, thanks a lot, Doc."

I hate it when people call me Doc. Then he saw that I was with Dorothy. "And is this your wife?" he said, apparently in some disbelief.

I was momentarily tempted to bask in this Hollywood moment, to pretend that I was indeed the sort of man who had a trophy wife, but I couldn't be so untruthful.

"Daughter," I said, in what I took to be a proud, fatherly manner.

"Right," he said, his face showing that he was slowly shuffling a whole pack of assumptions.

I saw no reason to introduce him to Dorothy, and fortunately two of her bags were now on the conveyer belt and she moved off to grab them.

"Well anyway, I owe you one, right?"

"All I did was tell you you weren't dying," I said.

"Yeah well, there are days when that's something you need to hear. Look, I'm still a little out of it right now, but later I'll gladly buy you a beer, or a smoothie, or an English muffin, or whatever it is you people eat."

There seemed to be no reason to argue about it. I assumed that even if he meant it at that moment, his offer would nevertheless come to nothing. It was just one of those things you said to some-body you'd met on a plane. So I gave him my name and that of our hotel and said we had a very busy schedule but he could phone us if he wanted to. He in turn handed me a business card that reminded me his name was Rick McCartney and that his title was "Auteur of the Future." I hoped he was being ironic.

I wondered whether I should do the proud father act and tell him that my own daughter was a wonderful and talented actress but decided against it, fearing that he might want to seize her for some improbable, auteurish project that involved lots of impro-visation and nudity.

After a needlessly formal handshake he was gone and Doro-thy was beside me, her face deadpan, her eyes still hidden behind dark glasses.

"Who's he?" she asked as she saw Rick McCartney disappear-ing and giving me a final, distant wave.

"Just another satisfied patient," I said glibly.

She stared after him, at the shorts, the hooded sweatshirt, the blond hair. He looked very much at home in L.A.

"Is he for real?" she asked.

I said that I had absolutely no way of knowing.

four Sweet Movie

I don't know if you've been to many pitch meetings, but pretty much what always used to happen in *my* pitch meetings was this: I'd finally get to see some movie producer, and I'd go along to his office and park my shitty old Toyota around the corner where I hoped nobody would see it, although in fact I kinda suspected they had security cameras trained on me, and I was being judged on my car instead of anything I might actually have to say.

So I'd go into the building and announce myself to some receptionist who thought she was too good for her job, and who's to say she wasn't? and then I'd wait a while. Being made to wait a long time was obviously bad, but being seen right away wasn't necessarily good.

So sooner or later I'd go into the guy's office and he'd look no older than me, although cooler and richer and with that weird, unmistakable sheen of money and success, and there'd be a yes-man with him, and he'd say, "Hi, Rick, good to see ya. Mind if Carter sits in?" and what was I going to say? "Well, I do mind, actually. I don't want to drop my pearls in front of some talentless asshole like Carter"? So I'd say sure. And then the guy would make a big deal out of telling the switchboard to hold all his calls, but you know what, one or two always somehow managed to seep through.

And the office always had two big posters on the wall. One of them would be for some really great, undeniably significant, classic movie like *La Strada* or *La Grande Illusion,* to show they really cared about movies. And then on some other wall there'd be a poster for the last movie the company made, which you could guarantee was going to be something like *I Spit on Your iBook: 4.*

So they'd look me up and down, and what did they see: a dude, a movie brat, an all-American boy, an auteur? Or none of the above? The fact is I know I don't look like what I am. Inside this tan, buff, blond, Californian shell, there's a little bespectacled geek just itching to get out.

If they'd looked at the material I'd given them (and I had to assume they had, otherwise why would I be there at all?), then they knew that I wasn't there to pitch a remake of *Slaughter's Big Rip-Off,* but the fact that I was actually trying to sell them a historical costume drama which was basically a meditation on mortality and loss, well, that still seemed to take 'em a little by surprise. But that was OK. Surprise is good. Right?

So they'd always say they really liked what they'd heard so far, but now they wanted to hear it from the horse's mouth, and in more detail, check out my "vision," and if they liked what they heard, then they could "guide the project along a little." This always sounded as though it might involve them pushing money in my direction, but that's not necessarily what happened, believe me.

So then the yes-man would wake up out of his coma and say, "This is the dildo movie, right?"

"Dodo movie," I'd say. *"The Penultimate Dodo."*

"That's the title you're going with?"

"For now," I'd say.

Something would get jotted down on paper at this point,

probably it was a note to ask some underling to look up the words *dodo* and *penultimate*, "Oh and while you're doing that, look up *the* as well, so we've got full coverage."

Sometimes they'd ask me to say what the movie was about in just one word, and I'd say, "Extinction." And other times they'd ask me to sum it up in one sentence and I'd say, "It's the story of a man who owns what he fears may be the last dodo on earth, and he's trying desperately to find a mate for it before the whole species dies out."

"So it's like an ecological thriller."

"Ticking clock."

I'd say sure. And if they gave me the chance, I'd go into more detail and explain that the central character was an English dude in seventeenth-century England and when he's young he sees a dodo and gets kind of obsessed with it, then later he gets one as a pet, and he knows it's an endangered species (although they wouldn't have had that phrase at the time, obviously) and he has a dream of filling the whole world with dodos, if only he can find a mate for the one he's got. And he searches and searches—

And the flunky would cut to the chase and ask if he finds one. "Well, no," I'd say. "The species dies out. You know, as in dead as a dodo."

"Sounds like you could have your title right there."

"And this is happening when exactly?"

"Well, David Quammen says the dodo was extinct by 1690 at the very latest. But the last credible sighting was 1662."

They'd ask if I was definite on this. I'd say pretty much. And they'd say OK, OK, no problem, like they didn't really believe me, that maybe I hadn't done my research and there must be a dodo somewhere, maybe stashed away in a private zoo in Pasadena, and they'd put one of their people on it.

Once in a while some guy who liked to think he was an intellectual would say to me, "So give me a rundown on the dodo's backstory," and that's when I'd really spring into action.

"Basically," I'd say, "the dodo—or *Raphus cucullatus* as some like to call it—is a poster bird for extinction. It obviously wasn't the first creature ever to disappear from the face of the earth, but it was the most visible, and the one in which mankind had the biggest hand.

"Dodos lived perfectly well on the uninhabited island of Mauritius. They had no natural enemies and so they lost the ability to fly. Then mankind arrived: first a bunch of shipwrecked Portuguese sailors, who were hungry enough to eat anything, including the dodo, which they say tasted pretty bad, but I guess if you're shipwrecked . . .

"Then the Dutch tried to colonize the island. They probably killed plenty of dodos for sport, but what really finished them off was the livestock. The settlers kept pigs, dogs, monkeys, and some of them escaped, went native, and wiped out the entire dodo population. The colony failed, the Dutch left, and the island was uninhabited again but it was too late for the dodo.

"There's a really sad story about the last sighting of a dodo. A party of Dutch sailors were marooned on Mauritius in 1662, after the colony had gone, and they reported that there were no dodos anywhere on the island. But they did see a few stragglers sitting on a islet just off the coast, separated from the mainland by a thin band of water that kept predators at bay. But it didn't keep the sailors at bay. They waded across, captured a few dodos, and ate them. The sailors were rescued a few days later, and at that point there were still one or two dodos left sitting on that little piece of land, surrounded by water, waiting for God knows what. Nobody has ever seen a live dodo since."

I told the story as well as I knew how, but I'd always lose them about halfway through. Then they'd ask me some questions, which I guess they always ask, whether you're trying to pitch *The Penultimate Dodo* or *I Spit On Your iBook: 5:* questions like, Who are we rooting for here? Where's the jeopardy? What's the character's arc? Is there a part for Jennifer Lopez?

I'd gotten pretty good at answering this stuff. We're rooting for the dodo *and* the guy. The jeopardy is that they both *might* die. The arc is that they both *do* die.

"The guy dies too?"

"Everybody dies," I'd say, trying to sound deep and philosophical and a little bit tortured. "But sometimes something lives on. Like here we are talking about a bird that hasn't existed for three hundred fifty years, so that's a kind of immortality. And sure, I can see Jennifer Lopez as . . . as a female quack."

And the other question I always used to get asked, which it took me a long time to think through, was "So this dodo in the movie: we're talking animatronics? Computer generation? Hand puppets? What?"

I always used to say, "Sure, something like that."

"How about cloning?"

"Sure. Cloning would work."

The meeting always ended with smiles and handshakes and how it had been good to meet at last, and there'd be a promise to keep in touch. Sometimes they might even have meant it, but the movie always remained at the "idea" (i.e., penniless, unfunded, entirely theoretical) stage.

Actually the cloning idea wasn't quite as dumb as it might sound, at least in a futuristic, science fiction, Jurassic Park kind of a way. Fact is, I always knew there were a few bits of dodo still lying around the place, mostly in Europe, including a head and a foot

in Oxford, England. And in the nineteenth century they exca-
vated some swamps on Mauritius and found various dodo body
parts preserved in the mud. And there was a time a few years back
when scientists talked about recreating a dodo from the preserved DNA. I was kind of relieved when they found out that the
genetic material was damaged and they couldn't do any cloning.
In one way it might have made my movie easier to pitch, but I'm
sure the big boys would have muscled in and pushed me out.

Bad pitch meetings were by no means the only thing wrong with
my life at that time. My girlfriend had thrown me out, which I
could understand, given my inability to pay rent, and so I was
sleeping on the couch belonging to a friend of mine, a guy called
Tom Brewster. Tom was a special effects dude, worked on second-
rate sci-fi and fantasy and horror movies. Of course what's second-
rate today would have been state of the art only a couple years ago,
so it's not like he was some total loser. If you wanted exploding
spaceships or exploding heads, he'd give you what you wanted and
do the job at a price you could afford.

Tom must have been, what, forty-five, a black guy, mixed race,
whatever, and he lived in this weird, windowless industrial building in Lincoln Park. I don't know what the place had been used
for in the past but whoever built it really wanted to keep people
out. Having no windows was a good start, and then there were
metal doors and steel security shutters. The place was impregnable and Tom liked it that way, and I could sort of see why. It's
not like this place was his workshop or anything, 'cause he
worked for a company that was in an even weirder, even more
impregnable industrial building in Culver City, but he was a guy
who liked to take his work home with him.

So the place was full of stuff, though I don't think it was the kind of stuff your local criminal pachucos would have had much use for. It was all special effects: robot hands and arms and prosthetic breasts and ray-guns and models of space stations and Martian volcanoes and jet packs and wrist-mounted TVs. Some of it was work in progress and some of it was more like souvenirs. I didn't know how he could stand it, and I don't know how I did either. It was like living in a cross between a prop house and a chamber of horrors, and it would just drive any sane person nuts, and maybe that's what it had already done to Tom and probably what it was doing to me.

This was not a place you could bring a woman back to, not unless you wanted her to think you were a weirdo. "Want to come up and see my deformed Venusian embryo?" "Want to be seduced in the shadow of alien Siamese twins?" There are some weird babes in L.A., but I'd never met one *that* weird and neither had Tom Brewster as far as I could tell.

But having all this mutant technology around did start to give me ideas. I said to Tom, "Wouldn't it be cool if next time I go into one of these fucking pitch meetings I could take a big bird cage along with me, and there'd be a black cloth over it and when the moment was right I'd whip the cloth away and there'd be a dodo inside the cage?"

"Well yeah," said Tom, "anybody'd have to be impressed."

"It wouldn't be a real dodo," I said, just in case he thought I was a complete moron. "It'd be like a windup, clockwork automaton kind of thing. Obviously. But totally lifelike. And the guys in the meeting would be fooled for a second, and they'd be amazed. And they'd see what I was trying to do. And then they'd give me money. And then I could make my movie. Wouldn't that be cool?"

"Yeah, bitchin'," said Tom.

"Think you could make one of those for me?"

"You need a clock maker and/or a taxidermist," he said.

"What's a taxidermist going to do for me?" I said. "It's kind of tough stuffing a bird that's been dead for three centuries."

"Point taken," he said. "The thing is, you always read about how these latest special effects are so high-tech and computer-generated and totally next-generation, and some of them kind of are, but half the time the things don't work like they're supposed to and they're behind schedule, so in the end it's just some guy screwing around with a piece of rubber tubing and a coat hanger. And a lot of the time I'm that guy."

He'd said this kind of thing to me before and I knew he was probably right. A lot of special effects aren't nearly as special as people want them to be.

"If you want a dodo just dye a turkey," Tom said. "Who's going to know?"

"Boy, I bet you wish Ed Wood was still alive and hiring, don't you, Tom?"

"All I'm saying is don't get hung up on the props. Write your story, write your characters. Do your research. If it ain't on the page, blah, blah. Then if somebody likes it enough to hand you some money, give me a call."

"And you'll dye a turkey for me?"

"Then I'll make you a reasonable working facsimile of a dodo. OK?"

I said, "Sweet, dude," but I was only quoting from a movie.

I knew Tom was basically right. My dodo movie wasn't really developed. I'd got my file cards. I'd got a pile of notebooks full of late-night ramblings. I'd gone and done some research, read some books, watched the appropriate movies *(Cromwell, Restoration, Vatel),* and I'd come up with a few ideas for characters, and I had some sense of where the plot might go, and obviously I'd written a sort of treatment, otherwise I wouldn't have had anything to pitch. I'd even doodled some storyboards. But the fact was, one way or another I knew, and everybody else knew, that it just wasn't happening. It wasn't really there. And I didn't know how to get it there. I wouldn't say I was "blocked" because that sounds a bit too fancy and dignified, so let's just say I was stuck. Tom told me to think laterally.

What I knew I hadn't got was the detail, the atmosphere, the look, the sounds, and maybe even the smells; all the good, vital background stuff. And I thought the totally perfect way to get it would be to have a time machine and go back there and experience some local color at first hand (which is maybe a movie in itself—cool L.A. dude goes back to uptight England in the seventeenth century and introduces them to snowboarding or some crud like that). But on the assumption that I might have to wait a few more millennia before the technology became available, I was looking for a shortcut and I did what Tom told me to do, I thought laterally and I came up with a totally great, totally insane idea. So then I did what anyone in Hollywood might do. I went to see a past-life therapist, right?

five **The Shining**

It is during his early days as a student of physic that William Draper is first afflicted with the symptoms that will change his life utterly, and in so many ways for the worse.

He was young when he arrived at college, though this fact owed more to his father's ambitions and connections than to any precociousness on his own part. And besides, his father evidently wanted him off his hands. After the death of his wife he had little time for his son and threw himself into the dull necessities of his business as a London paper merchant.

William has always been a pale specimen. His skin has always had an extreme and perhaps unwholesome whiteness about it. He has never taken much pleasure in the sun. Its glare hurts his eyes. Its rays make his skin tighten and itch. He sweats distressingly and feels quite discomposed on the mildest sun-filled day. The sun, for all its mystery and majesty, simply does not agree with him. And yet he feels healthy enough otherwise, and his condition seems not so much more extreme, his sensitivity not so much greater, than that experienced by many others of the general population. William is soon to discover, however, that his own case is most particular.

It is a thick, stifling summer's day. William has been to a lecture on the movement of the planets and their effect upon the humors. The lecture, delivered in Latin, a language with which he is not so richly acquainted as he would like to be, has desiccated his wits. He returns with some relief to his college room, a small, dark, unventilated place, where he arrives sweating and itching and ready to collapse. He peels off his jacket, then his shirt, and he lies down bare-chested on his narrow scholar's bed. Even here the sun reveals its presence. The room is warm certainly, but more than that, a polygonal slice of sunlight is projected in through the room's single slit-like window, down onto the bare boards of the floor. And as William remains on the bed, listless and immobile, he sees that as the sun rises and turns, the polygon shrinks to become sharper and more intense, and he notes that it is moving at a slow yet discernible rate across the room toward him.

The fledgling natural scientist in him is fascinated. He sees that in due course this compressed dagger of light must inevitably mount the bed and reach his chest, its clear-edged geometry becoming less rigid and pure in the process. He waits, disinclined to move. For all his aversion to the sun, he feels happily part of some inevitable, diurnal process, a part of moving nature.

But as the patch of light arrives at his rib cage and begins to touch him, something most unnatural happens to the area of skin that is now stabbed by sunshine. Before his eyes it starts to redden and darken, to become the color of a laborer's or mariner's skin, the complexion of one who lives nakedly and unrelievedly in the elements. The effect is not displeasing at first, but then it darkens yet more. It is like watching a piece of bread left toasting on a fork, becoming singed, then charred, then burned into unpalatable oblivion.

As William watches, with both alarm and fascination, his skin flakes, then blisters, then erupts and curdles into a sort of soft, infernal, living crust. His instinct to move from the light is tempered by his scientific curiosity and by the terrible singularity of the sight. By the time he can bear it no longer and is forced to move his body out of the way of the beam of light, a section of his chest no longer looks like any form of toasted bread, but rather like a piece of chicken skin left forgotten in the far deep corner of an oven.

He knows enough to douse the affected area with water, and then having wrapped his shirt loosely but painfully around himself, he is able to make his way to an apothecary's shop, where he devises some not wholly implausible story about an experiment with phosphor that has disastrously misfired.

The apothecary accepts the explanation without question or any but professional interest. Perhaps he sees this kind of thing all too often. Perhaps he imagines that William is an alchemist in training. He considers the matter, consults a chart and a herbal, then hands over a salve made from onion juice and dwarf elder, which later, in his room, William applies as best he can, with much agony and very little expectation of relief.

He suffers horribly for a week or more, the agony assuaged only somewhat by the essential oddity of what he has witnessed and experienced. It seems to be a unique and inexplicable occurrence, something previously unobserved, something not recorded by Hippocrates or Paracelsus. And yet a part of him also realizes that this is a life-changing moment, one that augurs ill fortune for someone who wishes to become a physician.

Why his affliction started precisely on this day he could not say. For all his uneasiness with the sun, this was scarcely the first time his chest had been exposed to direct light. Nor could he have said why it was his chest that suddenly reacted this way, when his hands, face, and neck, which are exposed to sunlight every day, remained unaffected. But that is about to change too.

In time his chest duly heals, though as with any burn, a mark remains. An area on the left side of his torso remains as a thick patch of ugly scarring. More is soon to come. In the days that follow he begins to notice flaking and redness on his cheeks, burns and rashes on the backs of his hands, blisters forming around his eyes and throat. Mild at first, these symptoms soon became violently conspicuous, and even though they heal, they too leave their deep traces. William's face becomes a chart of former injuries, like a table top on which a heedless, negligent cook has placed hot pans straight from the fire. In a student of medicine this marking can scarcely go unnoticed. His fellow students begin to keep their distance, to place William in an unstated but carefully delineated quarantine.

However mysterious his condition, both its immediate cause and the immediate remedy are obvious enough. William protects himself from the light. Staying indoors in his room or in the recesses of the college library helps somewhat, but his ambit necessarily extends beyond these confines. He has to venture out sometimes, and when he does so, he takes to wearing gloves and a turned-up collar and a broad-brimmed hat. He is aware that he looks absurd, not least because it is still high summer. He looks like a fop or a cavalier or worse, but what other remedy is available to him?

Before long he is summoned by his director of studies, a certain Dr. Clayton, a good, knowledgeable, and most honorable man and a good doctor too, qualities that William has already learned are all too rarely found in the same person.

Dr. Clayton stares hard at William, then asks if he knows what ails him, and William repeats that although he does not know its name or its prognosis, nor certainly its cure, he can readily understand its direct cause and its manifestations. Dr. Clayton finds this a wise answer but it does not wholly satisfy him.

"I fear," he says, "that your condition may be having an adverse effect upon your studies."

This strikes William as monstrously unfair and untrue. It is affecting his body, his face, his life, his peace of mind, but in other ways it is making a better scholar of him. It has driven him toward books and study and isolation. It has made him more philosophical and thoughtful, more a man of science, less susceptible to the distractions of society. It has even led to an improvement in his Latin. William states his case as forcefully as he thinks advisable, and Dr. Clayton appears to be listening sympathetically.

"And yet," the doctor says, "there is no doubt that your alarming appearance is having a marked effect upon your fellow students."

William cannot deny it. Few of them can even tolerate being in proximity to him anymore. They treat him like a leper, like a source of infection. It is with great feeling, and a sense of hurt rectitude, that William says, "Surely they above any, if they are to become even passably good physicians, should be able to tolerate their fellow man's infirmities."

"No doubt they should," Dr. Clayton agrees, "but they are also human, and I for one would prefer not to have my physicians any other way."

"Indeed," says William, "but still I do not see why their human frailty should drive out their common fellow-feeling toward me."

"No," Dr. Clayton says, "nor do I, but there is another difficulty too, and one that will lie in wait and must surely ambush you before so very long."

"Sir?" William says.

"Patients are human too. If you should become a doctor, and your condition persists, what in the world will your patients make of you? A physician who comes to them suffering from a troubling, indeed disfiguring, condition? A physician who cannot heal himself?"

"I would be most content to be healed," William says, "by my own agency or by any other."

"Then, as a first step," says the doctor, with compassion and a certain professional glee, "let us try to heal you."

six The Man in the Glass Booth

 Dorothy and I were staying in Hollywood (where else?) on the better end of Sunset Strip at a hotel that stood within shouting, or at least viewing, distance of the Chateau Marmont. Dorothy now regarded this proximity as something of a provocation but I declined to argue about it.

After we'd parked, registered, and examined our rooms—identical in every way and separated by a decent length of corridor—we went to a rather bland Thai restaurant for dinner, although as far as I could see, Dorothy didn't actually eat anything, just pushed squid and noodles around her plate until our waiter, who was called Chip and who looked like an actor playing the part of an actor playing a waiter, took them away again.

We went back to the hotel for an early night. Tomorrow, Friday, was bound to be a difficult day. We would both no doubt be suffering from circadian dysrhythmia (jet lag) and in the afternoon I would have to drive Dorothy to her meeting with Bob Samuelson. I'd suggested that we come a couple of days in advance so Dorothy could acclimatize but she was having none of that. She said she wanted to hit the ground running. So be it.

I realize I'm not the very best judge of these things, but come the next day I really did think Dorothy was looking absolutely gorgeous: bright-eyed, pert, quite the English rose. I was very proud of my daughter, and I felt full of confidence on her behalf. How could she not succeed?

In due course I dropped her off at Bob Samuelson's office, located in a black glass building in West Hollywood. Neither of us had the slightest idea how long this meeting might take, but we agreed that we'd meet up in an hour's time at a coffee shop we could see on the corner a block away. If the meeting went on longer than that, I'd simply wait. Fathers are very good at waiting. I tried to give Dorothy a goodbye and good luck kiss but she held me at arm's length, afraid I'd smear her makeup.

I found myself thinking about Marilyn Monroe, a woman who, in general, I don't think about all that much, but now I was recalling the story of when she was discovered by Ben Lyon, head of casting at Twentieth Century Fox. He met her and liked what he saw, so he sent her out to do the rounds of studio executives and he gave her letters of introduction to each of them. In every office the same thing happened. Each executive welcomed her, looked her over, read the letter, then walked round his desk, opened his fly, and put his cock in her mouth. The "letters of introduction" merely said that Marilyn gave a great blowjob.

Who knows if the story is literally true? I'm inclined to think not. If Marilyn was so willing to perform oral sex on all and sundry, then why would there have been any need for the letter? And even if Ben Lyon needed to tip off the other men, wouldn't he have just phoned them in advance rather than messing about with the written introduction?

Nevertheless, you're bound to feel that the story is symbolically true. Or perhaps we just want it to be true. The moral, I suppose, is that even a goddess like Marilyn Monroe had to degrade herself before she got a break in the movies. The corollary, perhaps, is that degrading herself is the *only* thing an actress needs to do in order to get a break in the movies, that even the best of them are sluts who connive at their own exploitation.

And I wondered what Dorothy was up to. Would Samuelson be as enthusiastic on his home turf as he had been in London? Would he write letters of introduction? Would there be requests, demands, for oral sex, and if so, how would my poor baby react? The worse scenario I could imagine was that she'd just shrug her shoulders, say OK, and get on with it. This outcome did not bear thinking about, and I had a modest plan to distract myself. My guidebook told me there was a movie memorabilia store not too far away, a place called the Beauty Vault, a name that managed to sound simultaneously like a hairdresser's and a sex club, but the book assured me it was not to be missed and that it contained a "trove" of desirable merchandise.

I must say I've always had some ambivalent feelings about movie memorabilia. Back in England I had, if I say so myself, rather an impressive library of videotapes—slowly being upgraded to DVD—and they were a great source of pride and pleasure. But I didn't consider them memorabilia; they were the thing itself. Equally, I'd read and indeed owned my share of film histories, reference books, some movie star biographies, even a few books of the saner kind of critical theory. These were secondary materials but they didn't seem too far from the source. And I suppose I could see why people might want movie posters to decorate their rooms, or even framed portraits of their favorite movie stars, even though personally I had no desire for these things at all.

But actual memorabilia, that seemed to be something else completely. The desire to own, say, Jane Russell's bra, or a prop ray-gun used in *Starship Troopers,* or the raincoat Robert Vaughn wore in *The Spy with My Face:* this I thought was pretty odd. It made movie stars into saints, and the things they'd owned or even merely touched, became holy relics. This fetishism was surely not a good thing.

Yet I couldn't absolutely condemn it. I could see the appeal these objects had, even if I didn't want to. I solved the problem somewhat by telling myself it was all right to *look* at these things, just so long as you had no intention of acquiring them. And that was why I was going to the Beauty Vault.

Judging by the outside, I felt that my guidebook had over-stated the charms of the place. It was a grubby one-story shop tucked in between a dry cleaner's and a shoe store. Some movie posters, for *Breakfast at Tiffany's, Psycho,* and *Attack of the 50 Foot Woman,* had been stuck over the door and windows to prevent anyone's looking in and perhaps also to deter and intimidate the less determined browser, but I was damned if I was going to be deterred or intimidated by some shop that called itself the Beauty Vault.

I parked in a sort of yard round the back of the store, which was even less impressive than the front: bins, ducts, an aban-doned car—backstage paraphernalia. A Mexican family, the wife heavily pregnant, appeared to be living there, in the back of a rusted white van. For a moment I wondered if they were likely to steal my car but decided I was being unnecessarily wary, to say nothing of racist.

I entered the Beauty Vault. It was bigger than it looked from outside: a long, deep, high-ceilinged space arranged with shelves and cabinets, books and posters, and a museum-size vitrine down the far end that no doubt contained suitably fetishistic items of movie memorabilia. I appeared to be the only customer.

There was far too much to take in at once, and so my eyes

searched for some focus and fell on the nearest thing, a display arranged along one wall of the shop. Mounted there were a hundred or so framed photographs of female movie stars: Rita, Marilyn, Brigitte, Raquel, Lana, Hedy, Ava, Farrah, all the iconic ones who can be identified by first names only. Then there were ones who were less iconic though certainly no less beautiful: Fay Wray, Pam Grier, Gloria Grahame, many others, and then some younger ones whose attractions are obvious and yet who frankly (and I know it's entirely because of my age) leave me rather cold: Salma Hayek, Cindy Crawford, Demi Moore, Jennifer Lopez. There were certainly one or two I couldn't identify. I have never denied that my movie buffdom (buffery?) has its limits.

The immediate impression was of having walked into the den of some poor little rich teenage boy, and the keeper of this display *was* in some sense boyish, though he was actually white-haired. He was up a ladder rearranging some of the framed photographs. I could see he was slight and trim, a dapper little character in sharply creased aquamarine slacks and a black bowling shirt. His skin was a blanched, papery white and he wore sunglasses, a ridiculous affectation in this cavern of artificial light, I thought.

"Be right with you," he said. "Just putting the ladies in order."

"Do they need that?" I said.

"Oh, they most certainly do."

He straightened Sophia Loren and gave a beam of exaggerated satisfaction before he came down from the ladder with a balletic jump. Then I saw that the sunglasses were less of an affectation than I'd thought. It appeared to me that the man was suffering from erythrohepatic porphyria, a dominantly transmitted Mendelian genetic disorder, basically an enzyme deficiency, characterized by acute photosensitivity reactions and, in some patients, serious liver damage.

It's one of nature's uglier little diseases. Onset is usually around adolescence. Once the condition's established, even a few minutes' exposure to light will make the patient's skin erupt into burns, swelling, puffiness, and blisters which scar when they heal. It gives rise to what the literature calls a "cobblestone effect" on the exposed areas.

Treatment is a fairly unsatisfactory business. You pump the sufferer full of beta-carotene and that increases tolerance to light, but it also tends to turn the skin orange, so I was assuming my man in the Beauty Vault wasn't taking it. But beta-carotene or not, there's no treatment available to prevent the liver disease. Other than that, all you can do is tell patients to the avoid sun, wear sunglasses, and smother themselves in sunblock.

How strange and self-punishing, I thought, that a man with this condition should choose to make his home in the relentless sunshine of Los Angeles. Having made such a choice, he would have to live his life in the shade, in the darkness of movie theaters, in this shop where sunlight wasn't allowed to penetrate, Of course there is nothing so very unusual about choosing self-punishment.

Another clerk, a younger man, sat behind the shop's counter. He too wore sunglasses, this time of the inscrutable wraparound sort, and for all the activity he displayed he might have been a waxwork.

The man from the ladder said, only partly for my benefit it seemed, "I've just had to move Catherine Zeta-Jones down a couple of places. I couldn't really tell you why. She's lovely, but I guess I'm just not in a very CZJ mood today. Whereas I'm suddenly feeling very, very upbeat about Sally Kellerman, so she's moving up into the lower reaches of the top twenty. With a bullet."

I hate people who make lists of the best movie stars even more than I hate people who make lists of the best movies.

"But I'm still having trouble with my top three," he said. "I don't know why but today I just feel like moving Rita Hayworth up into the number one spot, even though that would obviously mean moving Marilyn down. What do you think?"

"Rita Hayworth's one of my favorite actresses," I said in what I thought was a noncommittal way.

"Well, that's good enough for me," he said, and he made a camp little moue that I chose not to interpret. Either way he didn't get back up the ladder to make any further adjustments.

"So, what are you looking for?" he asked.

"Well, I'm just looking," I replied.

"Mmm," he said, "not very fond of customers who just look."

The temptation to say "Well, sod you and I hope you go out of business very quickly indeed" was strong and yet I thought I could have more fun with him than that.

"How about a photograph of Peg Entwistle?" I asked.

"Before or after she jumped?"

"How about while she was falling?"

His features gave a shimmy of appreciation. Perhaps I was a man he could do business with after all.

"How about Jayne Mansfield's dog?" I asked.

"Alive or dead?"

"How about stuffed?" I suggested.

"Now that *would* be a collector's item."

You probably know that Peg Entwistle was the woman who committed suicide by throwing herself off the Hollywood sign. You perhaps "know" that Jayne Mansfield's dog was decapitated in the car crash that killed her, though I'd never been sure that this was actually the case. Peg Entwistle and Jayne Mansfield's dog weren't the most obscure names in movie history but apparently my interest in them was enough to convince the man in the Beauty Vault that I was someone worth talking to.

"My name's Perry Martin," he said. "Welcome to my world. And this is Duane."

"Charmed, I'm sure," said the assistant in the wraparound shades.

I've never understood what it is that goes on with gay men and female movie actresses. I know that whole library sections have been filled with books on the subject, but I've still never quite understood it. No doubt it has something to do with genuine admiration, a shared desire to be sexually attractive to men, along with a touch of misogyny (sublimated or not), and no doubt some unresolved feelings about their mothers, yet quite why these things should turn an otherwise sane person into a fan of Liza Minnelli still escapes me.

At that moment the phone started to ring.

"Well, you can look around," Perry Martin said, "but . . . oh well, whatever."

So for a while I looked around the Beauty Vault, at the books and posters and lobby cards, at film scripts and press packs, at framed autographs and signed photographs. In the vitrine at the far end there were props and small personal items that claimed to have been owned or used or at least touched by movie stars: Ronald Colman's cufflinks, Bob Hope's putter, Errol Flynn's cocktail shaker.

Perry Martin finished his phone call and I half expected him to come over and tell me I'd already had enough browsing time, but as he put the receiver down the other assistant, Duane, said, "Actually Jayne Mansfield had *four* dogs. Two survived the crash, two died. Emerald and Precious Jewel went with Mommy. The survivors were called Cow and Dorothy."

I thought Dorothy was a most inappropriate name for a dog. "I didn't know that," I said.

"It's forgivable," said Duane. "They were Chihuahuas."

There seemed no answer to that.

"Now, what can I tempt you with?" Perry Martin said. "Are you by any chance in the market for a little memorabilia?"

"I don't think so," I said.

"How about this?"

He produced an envelope from under the counter and pulled out a sheet of transparent plastic, an animation cel, something quite crude and colorful but cleverly drawn, a cartoon image of a dodo. Naturally I thought this was a bit of a coincidence, given the manuscript Rick McCartney had been reading on the plane, but not an overwhelming one. Life's like that, isn't it? You spend decades not thinking about dodos, then suddenly you come across two in two days.

"Any idea what it is?" Perry Martin asked.

"An animation cel," I said, not very brightly.

"I know *that*. The question is, what movie? Who? When? Why? And more to the point, worth how much?"

"No idea," I said.

"I didn't think you did. I don't suppose you want to make me an irresistible offer for it either, do you?"

"No thanks."

"You know," Perry Martin said, "I'm a pretty good judge of character, and although you say you're not looking for anything in particular, I think that's wrong. I think you *are* looking for something, something very specific, but perhaps you don't know what it is yet."

I grunted at this display of amorphous intuition, suspecting it was just a sales pitch.

"When you know, then you should come back again. I may

have something for you. I don't touch porno, but there's plenty of very intriguing stuff that isn't porno."

He nodded toward a door in a rear corner of the store. It was covered in green baize. I wasn't sure I'd ever previously seen an actual green baize door outside of a movie. He seemed to imply that anything I was looking for might be found behind the door, if only I could name it. But of course I couldn't. At that moment I didn't think I was looking for anything at all.

Dorothy was already waiting for me when I arrived at the coffee shop. She was nursing a cup of black coffee and a glass of iced water.

"How long have you been here?" I asked.

"About an hour."

"What?" I thought we must have done something stupid, arrived at the wrong time, the wrong day, the wrong address.

"They sacked Bob fucking Samuelson first thing this morning," Dorothy explained. "It was one of those 'you've got five minutes to clear your desk' numbers apparently."

"That's terrible. So what happened? They told you to go away?"

"Not immediately. Samuelson's boss agreed to see me since I'd come all this fucking way."

"Well, that's good."

"No, not so good actually. According to Samuelson's boss I'm fat, my hair is mousy, my teeth are yellow, and I have the kind of broad, wholesome English face the camera is never going to love. Apparently I should go back to England and spare myself a lot of grief."

"I've a good mind to go in there and punch the bastard on the nose," I said.

"Bob Samuelson's boss is a woman," Dorothy said.

"Oh," I said, sounding disappointed, though I don't suppose I'd have actually gone and punched Bob Samuelson's boss even if it had been a man. "Poor baby. What shall we do?"

"I don't know what *you're* going to do, Dad, but I'm going to go back to the hotel and weep hysterically for the next twenty-four hours or so."

So I spent my Friday evening alone in Los Angeles, while Dorothy spent hers in her room. No doubt a man alone might get up to all sorts of California mischief in such circumstances but I settled for an early dinner and a browse in a book shop and I was back at the hotel well before any conceivable bewitching hour. I walked past my daughter's room where the Do Not Disturb sign was in place. I knew better than to knock. Dorothy's sulking and weeping had always had a heroic grandeur to them, and I knew that a premature attempt at consolation would only make things much worse.

I returned to my room, where I attacked the minibar. I lay on the bed swigging from tiny bottles of wine, delving deep into a tub of cashews, while watching TV, flipping restlessly through the channels, hoping to find a suitable movie. Watching a Hollywood product while actually in Hollywood had its appeal, but I couldn't concentrate. Even the porn channel offered nothing. I watched five minutes of a bizarrely disagreeable movie called *Age Gap*, in which a man of very much my age and build had sex with two very young and pretty girls. I supposed it was designed to appeal to men like me, but I found it powerfully unerotic. In fact the channel that turned out to have most appeal for me was a local station showing end-to-end ads for a real estate company, something called the Barbara Scott Agency.

It wasn't exactly sophisticated marketing, just an endless series of still photographs of Los Angeles houses and apartments, while a female voice-over extolled their virtues in vague but enticing terms. There was much mention of designer dream homes, gourmet kitchens, spas, sunken living areas, media rooms, sunset views, and yet the pictures on the screen, the faces that these properties showed to the world, looked surprisingly modest. There would be a palm tree here, a Spanish arch there, a swimming pool perhaps, but in general there seemed to be very little that justified the million-dollar prices that were frequently attached. Yet for some reason I found it all rather compelling and likely to reveal far more about the city and its values than any guidebook ever could.

However, the woman doing the voice-overs was trying far too hard, sounding overdramatic and needlessly poetic, but I wondered if perhaps in Los Angeles people were always auditioning. Perhaps doing voice-overs could be considered a showcase. You never knew who might be listening, so you had to give it all you'd got. I wondered if this was how Dorothy might end up. I could certainly imagine worse fates for a failed actress.

Early Saturday morning the phone rang in my hotel room and it was Dorothy. Her weeping had lasted less than the promised twenty-four hours and she sounded surprisingly cheerful. She was now commanding me to get up and meet her in the lobby. I went down and there she was, posing languidly by a fake plaster column, examining her image in one of the lobby's many mirrors. She didn't appear to be much enjoying what she saw.

Before I could say hello and ask her how she was feeling, she said, "I've been thinking. I know what I'm going to do. I'm going to go on a crash diet, get a new haircut, buy some tooth whitener, rent a fancy convertible, and then grab this fucking town by its balls."

seven

Another Country

You know what past-life therapy is, right? It's when, allegedly, you get taken back to your past reincarnations so you can remember and relive all the stuff you went through back then. Does that sound simple enough?

So I called up some past-life therapists and told them I was a successful screenwriter/director (OK, I was lying) and that I had this really great idea I wanted to talk to them about. And in L.A. you'd think this would get a very positive response, because everyone wants to get into the movies, right? But no, they didn't go for it at all, none of them. They didn't want to know. Like they thought I was some trashy investigative journalist or something and I was going to expose them for the frauds I assumed they probably were. But exposure wasn't what I had in mind at all.

Fact is, I knew even less about past-life therapy than I did about seventeenth-century England. I mean, I was only guessing, but somehow I didn't really believe it put you in touch with the memories of your reincarnated selves. I figured, at best, it was some kind of hypnosis that tapped your imagination and made you "remember" stuff you'd read or heard or dreamed or even just seen in movies. But something about the process made it all seem totally vivid so you thought you were really there.

It was a complete illusion in other words, but I had no problem with that. I like illusion. It didn't matter to me if it was fake or not. I didn't have to "really" go back there, I just needed to be able to write a script that could give the *illusion* of having been back there. "A movie so real you can smell the dodo."

So that's what I wanted to say to these past-life dudes when I called them up. "You just do what you do. I don't care how you do it or if it's for real or whatever, just send me back there, or at least give me the sensations of having been sent back there, let me soak up the vibe, let me have the memories, and then I'll go away and write my movie. You got a problem with that?"

You bet they had a problem with that. What I found out right away is that these past-life therapists should really learn to lighten up. They take themselves way too seriously. None of them even let me get to the end of my pitch. They gave me a lot of crap about how serious and important their work was and how it wasn't some sort of party trick. It was for people who had serious unresolvable problems in their present lives and they had to go back to their past reincarnations and release a blockage. I mean, I just wanted to say, hey, relax, take a Xanax.

So I saw that in order to do this thing, I was going to have to lie a little. Next therapist I called, I said I seemed to have these unresolvable problems in my present life and I was wondering if I needed to go back to a past reincarnation and maybe, you know, release a blockage. She said, "Come right on over." I said, "How much?" She said, "Rates are flexible, based on ability to pay. Nobody is ever turned away for financial reasons." So I went right over.

I guess I always have a problem when I consult so-called professionals, people like lawyers and doctors and agents and producers, and obviously therapists. Now, I don't want them to look like complete losers. I don't want to find them operating out of some crummy storefront in a strip mall. But then again I don't want to see them living like boy princes either. If I see they have a suite of offices on Rodeo Drive and they're running a fleet of classic Bentleys, I always think, wait a second, I'm *paying* for all this fucking lifestyle.

The past-life therapist I'd made the appointment with operated out of her own apartment in Venice Beach. That seemed about OK. And when I got there, I saw that the apartment block was a little bit funky and run-down, which is how Venice Beach is, and the building was painted duck egg blue and it had balconies that gave kind of a sideways sea view. And I thought that was all OK. It looked like the kind of place a more or less honest past-life therapist could set herself up without having to bleed her patients too much, if patient was the word, and if you believed there was any such thing as an honest past-life therapist, which I guess I didn't.

Her name was Carla Mendez and on the phone she sounded friendly and smart and only moderately flaky, and I guess you'd also have to say that she sounded like a woman who had two legs, which she did not. She only had one, at least one whole one. When she opened her apartment door I was confronted by this really great-looking Hispanic woman, with olive skin and festoons of black hair, and dark eyes and lips. She looked kind of gypsyish, but I think that had less to do with any real ethnicity than with the paraphernalia: a lot of clanking jewelry, a few cosmic-looking tattoos, a flower in her hair. I could have done without all this stuff. If you'd peeled it away you'd have had the kind of woman who might have been starring in some Spanish soap opera, the hot older woman, apart from the fact that she was using crutches, so that only one lean, bare foot poked out from underneath the hem of her long, gray silk dress. My face must have shown some surprise, but she wasn't interested in acknowledging it.

"Hello, Rick," she said, and she led the way into the apartment, which looked like a one-stop, satisfy-all-your-New-Age-quasi-mystical-quasi-spiritual-requirements-under-one-roof kind of deal. I'd have found it hard to imagine anywhere more cluttered than Tom Brewster's studio, but this place gave it a run for its money. There were glass balls and tarot cards, astrological charts, lumps of mineral and crystal, plaster Buddhas, wind chimes, dream catchers, wall hangings with suns and moons and mandalas, and kitschy framed photographs of waterfalls and mountain tops. More was definitely more.

We managed to find a couple of gaps to park ourselves in, and as Carla Mendez was sitting down she started to fold her legs up and under herself, and for a second the gray silk of the dress clung to the outline of her stump, what remained of her left leg. I could see that it ended just above where the knee should have been. I tried not to stare and more or less succeeded, I think. And once she was sitting down she looked perfectly natural and elegant, kind of posed and glamorous, and I hardly thought about the stump at all.

Now that she was settled she said, "I know you must have a lot of questions, Rick. Questions such as, if I was a homosexual in a previous life does that mean I should adopt a homosexual lifestyle in this one? Is it possible to be reincarnated as a being from another planet? What about Siamese twins?"

I guess it would have taken me quite a while to come up with questions like these, and I noticed that she wasn't making any attempt to answer them. Instead she started to explain what she called "the intellectual underpinnings" of past-life therapy, though she said she preferred to call it regression.

"That means to make progress by going backwards," she said.

These underpinnings seemed to stem from the fact that sometimes you go to a new place and you feel right at home, or you meet someone for the first time and you establish an instant rapport, or you've never played whiffle ball before but you give it a shot and there you are whiffling with the best of them. And so on.

"The truth is," Carla Mendez said, "we've all lived a whole lot of lives, and somewhere in one of them we're almost certain to have experienced some major trauma. Perhaps you were hung, drawn, and quartered. Maybe you were one of the slaves who built the pyramids and then got buried inside along with the Pharaoh. Maybe you were one of those guys who got crucified next to Jesus. Well, you're not going to get over something like that in a hurry, are you now? Not in one lifetime. Not even in two or three. We call this the activating event."

I wondered if I ought to be making notes, but then I thought she was probably just making it up as she went along anyway. She kept intense eye contact with me the whole time, and I kept looking back at her, and I kept thinking, how can this great-looking, intelligent-seeming, charismatic woman really believe all this shit?

"And so here you are in your current incarnation," she said. "What do you do for a living, by the way?"

I said I was a pool cleaner, because I couldn't tell her I was a filmmaker, right?

"OK, well, I guess you must go into a lot of other people's spaces. Something in one of them could very easily have triggered a disturbing memory from a past life. And you need to deal with that. Find closure, right?"

"Right," I said.

"You know, Rick, I sense some skepticism in you. And it's OK to be skeptical up to a point. But I'd like to tell you a story about a client of mine. Let's call her . . . Maxine. She was suffering from weird pains behind her eyes, headaches, visual disturbances, flashes, kind of like migraines but not exactly. And she went to a great many doctors and they did all the tests, but you know what conventional medicine is like, and they couldn't find anything wrong with her.

"So, very wisely, she came to me and we went back into her past lives. And guess what? It turns out she was a French foot soldier at the Battle of Waterloo, and she killed one of the enemy soldiers, I guess they'd be English, right, killed him stone dead by bayoneting him in the eye, left eye, all the way through to his brain.

"Well, you don't need me to tell you that's a whole lot of bad karma to be toting around with you through the ages. But once Maxine knew this, once she'd had what we call a Recognition, then she was able to make amends and move on."

Carla Mendez stopped and smiled triumphantly, as though that was the end of the story and everything was now revealed and that my skepticism must surely be blown to the four winds.

"How did she make amends?" I asked, because it seemed to me that if somebody told *me* that I had to make amends for having stabbed somebody in the eye a few hundred years ago, I'd have been kind of at a loss to know where to start. Get a job in an eye hospital? Become an ophthalmologist? What?

"Maxine got a job teaching yoga to pregnant mothers," Carla Mendez said.

"And that was enough to lift the bad karma?"

"It was a start, Rick. It was definitely a start. Although, of course, the real start was coming to see me in the first place. The real start was wanting to get in touch with the source of her pain."

If I'd been taking any of this seriously I'd have had to ask myself, even if not her, what terrible karmic screwup I must have committed in a previous life that was forcing me to become a failed moviemaker in this one. Maybe I wasn't getting my movie made because I'd pillaged some Indian encampment back in cowboy times. Or was that the plot of *The Searchers*? And what would I have to do to make amends? If Maxine's story was anything to go by, the act of atonement could be pretty oblique.

But since I thought it was all crap anyway I didn't ask these questions, at least not aloud, at least not in any way that demanded an answer. Nevertheless, Carla Mendez was continuing to smile smugly at me. It was a smile that said she'd got my number. I'd come to her, hadn't I? I obviously wanted to get in touch with the source of my pain. Her smile also seemed to be trying to tell me that I'd come to the right place. Maybe I had.

Meanwhile, of course, I couldn't stop myself thinking about her leg, her nonleg, her partly absent leg. Was that evidence of karmic disaster? Well, if you believed this stuff, how could it be otherwise? And I did keep thinking how good she looked, and you know, I reckoned I could imagine dating a woman with one leg. It would be a little strange but it wouldn't be a complete turnoff. And it wouldn't be a specific turn-on either, not like I was attracted *because* she had only one leg, and that had to be a good thing. Anyway, these were no doubt wildly inappropriate things to be thinking, and they also meant that I was missing some of what she was saying, although I was guessing that wasn't any big loss.

One way or another it took her about forty-five minutes to get to the end of these damn intellectual underpinnings. I guess I'd never thought it was going to be quite as easy as just walking in there and having her snap her fingers and instantly I'd be back in London in the 1640s, but all the same I hadn't expected this first session to be quite so theoretical.

We were obviously getting to the end of the session: a past-life therapist's hour is apparently the same length as any other kind of therapist's, i.e., about fifty minutes. I hadn't even had the chance to explain any of the more or less imaginary problems I'd invented specially for the occasion, and it was pretty obvious she wanted it that way.

"If we're going to proceed," she said, "I have to tell you that regression therapy is no quick fix. It takes time and commitment and it can result in a lot of distress for the client. Just like any other therapy. You understand?"

"Well sure," I said.

"And are you ready for that?"

"Ready as I'll ever be," I said, and I realized I might be sounding way too casual.

She said, "In our first proper session we'll do our best to find your activating event. I'll conduct a life review, take you through the death experience, and then you can start to learn the lessons of previous incarnations in terms of your present situation. Got it?"

"Got it," I said.

I still didn't want to think she was dumb enough to believe what she was saying. So maybe she was a true charlatan, a quack, and she thought I was the dumb one for listening to her, and I realized I didn't want her to think I was dumb either.

At the end of the session, as she was seeing me out, leaning somehow sexily on her crutches, after I'd handed over quite a large chunk of money, I said, "About the skepticism . . . does it matter whether or not I believe?"

"It doesn't matter to me," she said.

"But if I don't believe, does that mean you can't regress me?"

"If you don't believe, then why are you here, Rick?"

"I do believe, I guess, but you know, I have . . . certain doubts."

"Yes, you do, don't you?"

Maybe she was already realizing I was a bit of a fake, but so what? I mean I thought she was a *lot* of a fake, and I was still there, wasn't I? I didn't see a bit of fakery as any reason why we couldn't do business.

She said, "You'll find some therapists who'll tell you it doesn't matter whether these 'memories' come from past lives or not. They'll say they're 'symbolic scripts' that can help resolve life problems regardless of their authenticity.

"Well, I say phooey to that. If you just want to read a script, then go to a library. If you want symbolism, go watch early Bergman. What I do is for real. And you'd better believe it, buster."

She looked very intense and a little scary, and just for a second I think I did believe it, or at least I definitely wanted to. In any case, I made an appointment to go back there the next day at the same time, and then she'd send me back into my (or somebody's) past.

eight

The National Health

For the next several months William Draper continues his studies while attempting also to study his own condition. At first he is called upon to stand in a crowded lecture theater, to bare his chest or back or legs and then position himself in a beam of direct, concentrated sunlight for the edification and education (and undoubtedly also the amused, horrified fascination) of his fellow students. A crowd of young men, not all of them the most earnest or scholarly, gather eagerly to watch as sections of William's skin are made to bubble, boil, and blacken.

Perhaps Dr. Clayton imagined that this public display would afford William some measure of acceptance by his peers. To understand all might be to forgive all. Here, alas, the good doctor is mistaken. William's role as a living specimen only makes him more remote, a freak of nature in their midst.

Then, once the condition has been observed and exhibited, the attempts at treatment can begin. Dr. Clayton's opinion is that the problem stems from an excess of phlegm and blood in William's system, along with a lack of, and an imbalance between, black and yellow bile. He checks William's horoscope and discovers that he is an Aries, therefore in the house of Mars. Consequently the cure shall be a martial one: strenuous, bold, combative. The bleeding and purging and cupping, the spitting and sneezing, the administrations of enemas and emetics shall be unusually warlike. The plasters, decoctions, and syrups will be made from martial herbs, from cardoon, wormwood, madder, bastard rhubarb. Much bravery will be required on William's part, and he says he will try to be a good soldier.

William becomes all too intimately acquainted with clysters, with setons, with suppositories and cantharides poultices. His urine is much examined. Dr. Clayton puts great energy into the production of new blisters on William's skin, although it seems to William that his body is able to produce these well enough without further assistance. These contrived blisters fill with their necessary poisons and expulsions and then Dr. Clayton fiercely, cheerfully lances them. He devises a special diet for William, one involving fungi, foxes' lungs, and crabs' eyes. William has tasted worse. At least he is allowed to wash it down with all the ale he wants.

One day, in a moment of inspiration, Dr. Clayton reasons that since the sun is the cause of William's condition, ice might be the perfect antidote. Consequently William endures many long, afflicted hours submerged in a trough of iced water. Afterwards, shivering, close to delirium, swathed in a chrysalis of blankets, he spends twenty-four hours in a darkened room and feels profoundly guilty when Dr. Clayton at last comes by and examines his body to find it unimproved.

And yet there are satisfactions, and some consolation, to be found in simply doing anything at all. William is grateful to Dr. Clayton for that. He wants to be helped. He wants to help himself. He wants to be cured. Above all, he wants to *believe*, perhaps like those people he saw consulting the quacks and mountebanks in Alsatia. The fact that these dupes believed nonsense while he believes in science is, he thinks, an important difference, but he can see it is not an absolute one.

In need of solace, in any form, William waits for the night and heads for the nearest tavern, finds the darkest of dark corners, and drinks himself into robust, defiant impregnability. The taste of ale is good, its effect is better still, and the young woman who serves it to him is indifferent to the scars and traces on his face. Her manner seems to imply that she has seen many faces more fearsome and grotesque than his.

In these dark regions he feels briefly content, feels that his condition is tolerable. He would rather be here, drunk, hidden, numb but his own man, than anywhere else he can think of. Certainly it is immediately preferable to being the subject of another of Dr. Clayton's experiments, and he thinks he might tell him so and rebel. But then he realizes the consequence of resistance would be too terrible. It would signal the end of his ambition to be a physician, and that seems unendurable. So the next morning, sober, begrimed, thick-headed, no longer brave, William once more submits.

This time Dr. Clayton brings a natural philosopher to meet him, a gaunt and impressively austere man by appearances, though his suggestion of a cure is extravagant enough. He offers the opinion that gold is all that is needed to cure William. He envisages covering William's entire body in gold leaf, effectively gilding him. Since gold is the most precious, powerful, and holy of metals, it must surely be efficacious in renewing and restoring the skin.

Dr. Clayton appears to find this reasonable, but William suggests they begin modestly, with a small piece of gold leaf, perhaps a couple of inches square, placed on an area of his cheek. If this proves useful, then possibly, with much begging and borrowing and throwing himself on his father's mercy, he might just be able to afford to buy the vast quantity of gold required to cover his whole body. But the philosopher is adamant; it must be all or nothing. And it must be soon. Now. William smells a rat.

"Tell me, sir," he says, all apparent innocence, "and what would happen to this gold after it had served its purpose?"

"Why," the philosopher replies, "it must be got rid of, since it would be tainted, suffused with the evil that besmirched your skin. I should dispose of it for you, using certain secret and infallible processes."

William is incensed. He rises from his chair as if to give the man a thorough box about the ears, and when the villain scurries out of the door, calling after him, "Some men do not deserve to be cured," William turns to Dr. Clayton and says, "Perhaps he is right. Perhaps I am an undeserving man."

Dr. Clayton will have none of it. Indeed, William is surprised to find that the doctor is looking at him with some admiration.

"That man was evidently a scoundrel," Dr. Clayton says. "You were right to dismiss him. I should have seen it from the first. I should not have troubled you with him. My apologies."

William finds this show of modesty a touch embarrassing. "But he may have had a point about my undeservingness," William says.

"I do not believe that," Dr. Clayton says. "I am by nature an optimist. If the cure comes not today, then it will surely come before long. We live in an age of hope and discovery, an age of miracles. The exploration of new territories brings endless new blessings. In America, for instance, there are daily discoveries, wonderful plants and drugs that must surely be all for man's benefit: quinine, ipecacuanha, tobacco. God constantly shows us new wonders. And if it is his will, then he will show us a cure for what ails William Draper."

William wants to find comfort. He still wants to believe. But when he goes to Dr. Clayton's rooms a couple of days later and finds him brandishing a sack of leaves, and when the doctor announces that he has been contemplating the theory of resemblances and has seen that the jagged edges of some of William's scars correspond to the shape of stinging nettles, and since the nettle is a plant under the dominion of Mars, he thinks it would be a fine idea to bring the one in contact with the other, i.e., rub the entire surface of William's body with nettles, then William finally turns.

He is tired, weak, fearful. He feels ill in all sorts of ways that he never felt before. He cannot face any further cure. He finds the improbable strength and courage to say to his mentor, "Dr. Clayton, I know that God has made everything for a purpose, not least the stinging nettle, yet I cannot believe that the Almighty would be so perverse, so cruel and mysterious as to make that purpose the rubbing of my poor, afflicted body."

Dr. Clayton stares at William with some pity and rather more alarm. William fears he may have uttered some terrible blasphemy. Quickly he adds, "Dr. Clayton, I respect you as a doctor and a man, but this nettle business is simple madness. In this matter if in no other, I trust my own instincts in preference to yours."

He gets up and shambles from Dr. Clayton's study and hastens away before his natural cowardice takes him by the collar and drags him back to beg for forgiveness and further treatment. But then the street itself is a form of torture. The sun is shining and it hits him like a cataract of light. He hunches, covers his face. He needs shelter. He needs escape. Half an hour later he is on a coach departing Oxford, and not so many hours after that he is back in London.

He supposes he is running home, going back to his father's house, though he knows this is not a place where he will receive much of a welcome. And perhaps that is why he does not go directly there but instead walks to, where else? Alsatia.

It is a while since he was here, and he fears that he may be misremembering the place's high color and drama. The reality may be drably quotidian. But in the event he is not disappointed at all. Today the quacks seem more lurid and ridiculously compelling than ever. His woefully incomplete education in physic is already more than enough for him to see through the majority of these impostors. Many of them are peddling nothing more than air and lies. And even the ones whose products seem sound enough are employing a wheeling and unnecessarily florid rhetoric to sell them.

Here in Alsatia the streets are cramped and the shadows are long. The sun does not penetrate. He is grateful for that. He feels secure, and he turns down the nearest dark alleyway, between a printer's and a pie shop, and there he sees a painted sign, showing a gigantic avian footprint and the words, "The world's most disgusting bird." Moxon and his dodo did not leave town after all. William fears he is about to swoon with emotion.

nine Housesitter

No father wants to associate his daughter and testicles; he just doesn't. Equally, even the most doting of fathers would surely be reluctant to accompany his daughter while she went clothes shopping, visited a hair salon to perfect a new look, and so on. Consequently I spent my Saturday alone and rather bored. In the early evening I went back to the hotel and decided I'd sit in the bar for a while. In movies these are always the places where adventures start. And true to form, an adventure looked about to unfold when a tarty young blonde sidled up to me and said, "Looking for a good time, Doc?" and for a second it crossed my mind that a good time was very much what I was in need of, but a second later I realized the tarty young blonde was Dorothy.

Chiefly I suppose it was the hair that had confused me, now dyed and cut very short and lubricated in some way, so that it resembled an aluminum bathing cap. But it wasn't just a matter of the hair. There was something about her face, or I suppose more precisely about her makeup, that gave her a tougher, harder, and probably sexier look. It made her seem different, like a different kind of person from the one I knew as my daughter.

The clothes too signaled a change in character, or at least in persona. Like many men I tend only to be aware of the general effect of women's clothes, not the specifics, and I expect this is healthy. In Dorothy's case, however, the individual items stood out rather forcibly. Certainly she was wearing jeans of a sort, and I don't suppose they were actually made of either metal or alligator skin, though they gave a fair impersonation of both. Her T-shirt was a skimpy little purple nothing, though not quite so insubstantial that the maker hadn't been able to find room to attach a few sequins in the nipple areas. The look was accessorized, I believe that's the word, with high-heeled mules, rhinestone sunglasses, and a beaded choker. Overall, the look was undoubtedly eye-catching, perhaps head-turning, but even for a Saturday night in Los Angeles I couldn't help feeling it might be a little excessive.

"You're looking very pretty," I said.

"Pretty?" she said, as though I'd accused her of having scurvy.

"Well, very something," I said, and that placated her a little. Being indefinable appealed to her.

"Ready for dinner?" I asked.

I may have sounded tentative. I wouldn't have said that I'd have been embarrassed to be seen out in public with Dorothy, but I did feel that at best we would have looked a tragically ill-matched pair. At worst I might look like the most pathetic, Emil Jannings–ish, would-be sugar daddy, exactly what Rick McCartney had thought I was.

I needn't have worried. Dorothy flapped a hand dismissively, as though dinner was a thing she'd vaguely heard of, some quaint habit from the old country that only the ancient and the feeble-minded indulged in.

"No," she said, "but I'll show you my car."

One didn't seem like much of a substitute for the other, but I went down to the hotel's subterranean car park to see what she'd come up with. I like cars well enough, and actually I was rather impressed with the one Dorothy had rented. It was an open-topped Corvette, not one of the very early ones with the snarling teeth in the grille, but a very serious, eye-catching, all-American classic car nevertheless. Above all else it looked very expensive.

"How on earth can you afford to rent something like this?" I asked.

"I did a deal with the guys at the car rental place. I could probably have made a better one if I'd waited until after I'd had my hair done."

And then she got into her car and showed every indication that she was about to drive off.

"Where are you going?" I asked, trying to sound concerned but not *too* concerned.

"Off to circulate, network, make contacts . . ." The rest of her sentence was cut off as she fired up the car's engine. "I've been invited to a party," she yelled.

"Where?"

"Laurel Canyon," she said, these unfamiliar words dropping very easily from her tongue.

"Whose party?" I was aware that I might be sounding like the heavy father, and yes, there was some paternalistic concern involved, but more than that I was amazed that a girl who not so very long ago had been despairing in her hotel room was now on the party circuit. Perhaps this was exactly the kind of resilience a person needed in Hollywood.

"The guys from the car rental place," she said blithely.

No doubt my face displayed some dubious fatherly disapproval.

"They're not really car rental guys. Obviously. They're screenwriters. They're just working there till they get their big break. In the meantime they have a lot more contacts than I do."

I supposed that had to be true. Everyone started somewhere,

and a place that hired out fancy American cars might be better than some. Dorothy reversed her car out of its parking spot and powered up the ramp at the end of the car park before I could even wish her good luck.

When I went up to my room at a tediously decent hour I saw that the Do Not Disturb sign was still in place on Dorothy's doorknob, a not very subtle way of trying to cover her tracks and defuse her father's concern. And it didn't work. My daughter, dressed very much like a tart (although I knew that tarts dressed more or less every way imaginable) was out on the town in L.A. on a Saturday night, going to a party in Laurel Canyon with some men she'd briefly met in a car rental office. It would surely have been dereliction of fatherly duty not to be concerned, so concerned I was, but I also couldn't help feeling a small amount of pride. My daughter, my Dorothy, was out there pursuing her dreams, living her life, being embraced by the city, and I had to admire that.

I ended the evening as I had ended the previous one; wine, nuts, and TV. Having flipped through any number of unsatisfactory old movies, monster truck rallies, and shows fronted by religious zealots, I found myself watching the real estate channel again.

The next day, Sunday, was apparently the day when estate agents, or realtors as they seemed to be called in America, held their open houses, occasions when anyone could go along and wander round properties for sale. The now almost familiar, sexy woman's voice from the Barbara Scott agency cordially invited me, and the rest of the TV audience, along to a million-dollar open house (or in fact bungalow) in the Hollywood Hills. "Stop by. Have some decaf. Have a bran muffin. If you're not there, we'll sure miss you." I decided I didn't want to be missed.

Come the morning Dorothy's Do Not Disturb sign was still where it had always been, and I chose to believe that she was in her room, safe, alone, sleeping off the late night and the mild hangover of the well connected. What else would a good father have chosen to think? I wrote a note, slipped it under her door, and set off to find Barbara Scott's open house in the Hollywood Hills. Ah, the potency of cheap TV advertising.

Of course I was aware that this might seem a rather eccentric thing to do (So what did you get up to in L.A.? Oh, I nosed around in other people's houses and pretended I was interested in buying them), but I was also able to tell myself it would be a cheap form of entertainment, like joining a tour group, and it promised to be more quirky and revealing than, say, a trip to Universal Studios.

The drive up to the house was livelier than I could have imagined; the route involved steep gradients, blind bends, and other drivers who found my caution annoying and unnecessary. There were a lot of high walls and locked gates, and many notices warning of mean dogs and armed response. I eventually found the open house and parked across the street. It looked amazingly modest. There were two other cars parked in front, a massive Jeep and some overdesigned, silver Japanese thing with a wing on the back. My stolid rental car seemed extremely sober and grown-up by comparison.

As I walked up half a flight of steps to the front door a woman in a tight, faintly glistening blue business suit came trotting out onto the porch to meet me; an estate agent rather than the home owner, I assumed, correctly as it happened, because she announced herself as Barbara Scott, shook me by the hand, and gave me a printed sheet describing the house. I could tell immediately that hers was the voice from the TV commercial, although less mannered than when in voice-over mode, and her greeting made me feel like a guest of honor at a party that would be incomplete without me.

"Hello," I said vaguely.

By Los Angeles standards Barbara Scott may not have been excessively glamorous, but by any estate agent standards I had ever encountered, she was positively ravishing. Her age was indeterminate in the way that certain American women (mostly movie stars, I admit) have perfected. They're slim, they look fit, they have no bags or jowls, they don't wear middle-aged clothes or have middle-aged haircuts. You know that they *are* middle-aged but they don't look it. They look just great. And if there's some degree of fakery in the final product, well that's a price most of us are willing to pay.

Looked at a certain way she could definitely have been an older version of a "chilly blonde." The effect might have been intimidating but there was something about Barbara Scott that was also familiar and appealing. I could see this must be an advantage for an estate agent, and I had the funny feeling that I might indeed have seen her before somewhere, but before I could pursue this thought she said, "I'm in the middle of talking to some people right now. They're checking out the media room. I think they're probably just window-shoppers, but I have to be polite. Why don't you walk around by yourself? I'll be with you soon as I can."

She gave me a smile that I found disarming, seductive, intriguing, devastating, reassuring. It felt like a smile that could easily persuade a man to buy a house he couldn't afford, possibly didn't even want, and I suspected it could make him do a great deal more besides. But perhaps I'm being wise after the event. At the time it may well have been no more than a good, pleasant, professional smile.

I walked through the house. It was hideous. The entrance hall had a black marble floor; the living room featured a bar and a granite fireplace big enough to sleep in. I went into the bedroom, which the piece of paper in my hand described as "decadent," which apparently meant mirrors, black satin curtains, and a lot of erotic art that you could only hope didn't come with the house. I reeled into the kitchen, which was poky and dark and looked as though nobody had ever so much as boiled an egg there, and I continued to reel as I stepped outside toward a ridiculously ornate fountain with cracked hand-painted tiles. I was ready to leave, but at that moment Barbara Scott came out to the garden and I saw that a quick getaway was going to be difficult.

"Losers," she said, referring to the now departed house viewers and implying that I was not at all like them. "So how'd you like the house?"

"It's all right," I said.

"You hate it, don't you?"

"Well, it's not quite me."

"Of course it's not. You're looking for something more . . . well, just *more*. You're English, right?"

"Definitely."

"And I'm guessing you're looking for something with character."

"Right," I said.

"But you don't want flashy. You're not Venice Beach, and you're not Marina del Rey. You've probably considered Santa

Monica but decided that was too obvious. You've no doubt looked at Silver Lake and decided the bargains are all long gone."

She seemed so positive, so sure of herself, that it would have been hard to disagree, even if I'd known what she was talking about.

"How long have you been looking?" she asked.

"I've only just started."

"Like a virgin. I like that. I'd be delighted to be your guide through the jungle."

Then she handed me a pamphlet describing her real estate company, along with a business card which had her photograph on it, and as she handed it over she put her hand on my elbow, squeezed it, and said, "You're an actor, right? I've seen you in a couple of things, haven't I?"

She sounded intimate, as though we were sharing a secret. Actors, even English actors, couldn't have been much of a novelty in L.A., and yet I did feel strangely flattered. It made me feel that I didn't look quite as out of place here as I'd feared. And just for a second I toyed with saying that I was indeed what she thought I was. It's not as if anyone swears an oath of fidelity in their dealings with an estate agent. But then I thought no, it sounded like I'd just be setting myself up for some slightly weary comedy of mistaken identity.

"I'm a doctor actually," I said, and then she was *really* impressed.

To describe an estate agent as calculating is, I suppose, only to state the entirely obvious, and is probably not even a criticism. Yet, now that she knew I was a doctor, I could see her assessing my worth, my income, my prospects, possibly even my life expectancy, and she was rather pleased by the result she came up with.

"Look, I'm stuck here for the rest of the day," she said, "but I'd be thrilled if you wanted to stop by my office, like tomorrow."

I said that I would, that I definitely would, but I didn't mean it. Seeing the inside of one unimpressive, overpriced property had told me all I needed to know. I'd had my small L.A. real estate adventure, and it had been small indeed, but I felt it had been enough.

For a second, as I was leaving, it looked as though Barbara Scott might be about to plant a farewell kiss on my cheek. I would definitely have let her do it, but it never quite materialized. I got back to my car feeling mildly flushed and decided it was time to get back to Dorothy and the hotel.

When I was nearly there I found myself driving past a Burger King and saw an open-topped Corvette parked askew at some distance from the drive-through window. It looked a lot like Dorothy's car and there she was sitting at the wheel, eating. I turned in to the car park and pulled up alongside. Dorothy was obviously having some trouble with her crash diet. She was gnawing on a large spongy hamburger, and the wrappers strewn around the dashboard and passenger seat proved it was not her first.

I got out of my car and was about to do a cheery, fatherly, well-isn't-this-a-coincidence sort of number, but was deterred when Dorothy glared and angrily threw the remains of her hamburger at me. She missed. I noticed that she was wearing the same clothes as the previous evening, so presumably she'd stayed out all night, but this didn't seem the moment to talk about that. Then she slumped, seemed to melt and fall like a sad soufflé, and she began to sob. There was mustard and ketchup all over her chin, and she looked an absolute picture of misery, and how (even given the thrown hamburger) could a father not wish to comfort her?

"Good party?" I asked clumsily.

The question caused Dorothy to compose herself a little, to become simultaneously thoughtful and angry, as though she needed to organize some powerful feelings and find exactly the right words to express them. Eventually she said, "It sucked big time, as I believe the locals say."

"No opportunities for networking then?"

"If I'd wanted to network with a lot of thin, fashionable, shallow people, then plenty of opportunities."

If Dorothy was really going to have a career as an actress, then I felt she ought already to have accepted the inevitable presence of shallow people in her life, but I was wise enough not to say that. Nor did I ask why, if it had been such a bad party, she had apparently stayed there all night. Instead I tried to stroke her head and her newly blond hair but she pulled away as though I were coming at her with a cattle prod.

"This is all your fault," she screamed.

"What is?" I asked calmly.

"Everything. It's all because of your genes."

"Excuse me?"

"I didn't ask to be born, did I? And even if I had, I wouldn't have asked to be born with your genes, with fat genes and bad bone structure and a wholesome fucking English face the camera doesn't love."

"Well, your mother also had a bit of a hand in providing you with genetic material," I said.

"But hers was all right."

"I see. So you just wish she'd married someone else."

"Got it in one, Dad." In the circumstances, that was unbearably hurtful, but worse was to come. "I mean, what did she ever see in you?" Dorothy demanded.

It was a question that many people, myself included, had been known to ask. "I suppose she saw the best in me," I said.

"Is that why you killed her?" Dorothy yelled.

I let that hang in the air for a moment and then I said, "Fuck you, Dorothy." It seemed rather an L.A. thing to say, and it took Dorothy by surprise. And when I turned on my heel and got back in my car and drove across the car park with a satisfying yelp of rubber, I think she was probably gobsmacked. As I pulled into the stream of traffic outside Burger King I looked in the rearview mirror and saw Dorothy leaning against the rear wing of her car, vomiting spiritedly.

So another night alone in L.A., but now I was at odds with my daughter and she was even more at odds with me. Nothing so very unusual there, I supposed, and no doubt Dorothy's hatred of me had been stoked by whatever had happened to her at the party, things I could imagine but preferred not to. Even so, being accused of killing my wife, that was a new development, a new low in my relationship with my daughter. I knew perfectly well that we were bound to make up sooner or later, but at that moment I wanted it to be later. I suppose I also wanted to demonstrate that my genetic material wasn't quite so revolting as Dorothy thought. I decided that I'd visit Barbara Scott's office first thing the next day.

ten The Time Machine

Not like I ever really cared about this shit or anything, but it always seemed to me that the objections to reincarnation are so totally obvious that you almost hate to bring them up. Like it seems there's a contradiction right at the very heart of your basic, old-style reincarnation, right? The big idea is that you've lived all these past lives but you don't remember them. But if you don't remember them, then in what sense have you lived them? More to the point, in what sense are they *you?*

At least the past-life therapy people meet the problem head-on. They say that you *can* remember them, you just need a little help, which is obviously a very appealing idea to some people, and it does imply a kind of consistency. They say the past lives are in you, just waiting to be accessed, although I'd want to ask where they're supposed to be located. In your brain cells? In your genes? In your hair follicles?

But then there's still all the other really obvious stuff, like how do you explain population growth? New souls are coming into being the whole time? Well, OK, in that case I'll take one of those new-fangled souls please, one of the ones that doesn't have any of that nasty old previous-life, karmic buildup that's going to make my present life such hell. And in that case I'd have no past life to regress to, right?

And how would you explain population *decline?* That there's some sort of bull pen for souls who are just hanging around, waiting for the right moment to be beamed down? Sounds pretty lame to me.

One thing I did think was pretty funny: if it was true what Carla Mendez said, that straights get reincarnated as gays, blacks as whites, men as women, that was bound to create some real karmic havoc, wasn't it? KKK members being reincarnated as brothers, Bushmen coming back as members of the Kennedy clan. Well, OK, I admit that havoc has its attractions, but *really*.

And reincarnation must also mean that Buddhists are constantly being reincarnated as Christians and Muslims and atheists; the people who believe in reincarnation are bound to be reincarnated as people who *don't* believe in it. What would be the point of that exactly?

Look, I can see that the idea of karma is appealing, and sometimes it feels like you can even see it in action; what goes around comes around. Yeah, I've always been more or less prepared to buy that, but it still brings a truckload of problems with it, like I've never been sure if the laws of karma mean that you're in control of your own life or not.

OK, I'll accept that, say, the captain of a ship who brought a load of slaves over from Africa was probably building up quite a head of bad karma: the whippings, the starvation, the inhumane conditions, and whatever. But in a situation like that, how could those slaves ever have built up any *good* karma? Was it about being brave and stoic? Or just about singing a cool version of "All My Trials, Lord"? Or is being a helpless victim enough to ensure that you're a winner in the next round of the reincarnation sweepstakes? And I don't even want to *think* about Jews and Nazis.

OK, so I knew that most of this stuff was pretty naive and

probably not original and I'm sure somebody somewhere had already come up with smart answers, and no doubt I could have asked Carla Mendez about it all, but for the kind of money I was paying her I didn't really want to get hung up on theory.

I went to her apartment again, and when she opened the door this time I was just overwhelmed by how great she looked, and I knew this was a really bad thing to be thinking. You really shouldn't get a crush on your therapist, especially when your therapist is some flake who believes in reincarnation, regression, and activating events and who only has one leg. So I told myself I was there to do a job and I shouldn't let myself get distracted. That almost worked.

She made us some herb tea, which tasted kind of foul, and we began by doing what she called a "life review," which I guess is pretty much the thing any therapist might do: you know, background, relationships with parents and siblings, sexual orientation, spiritual beliefs, all that stuff.

I had difficulty knowing how far I should make things up and how far I should stick to the truth. Obviously I had to present a few problems because otherwise why would I have been there? On the other hand I didn't want to tell her all the stuff about my movie because then she'd have asked what the movie was about, and then she'd have known that I was up to no good, and then I assumed she'd react like all the other past-lifers I'd called up and tell me to fuck off. So I tried to invent a life for myself, as a pool cleaner with problems that weren't exactly my *own* problems but also weren't too far away from the truth. I wanted to keep it simple. I was planning to become an auteur, not a serious improv actor.

So I told her a lot of stuff about difficulties with my parents, my sister dying when I was a kid, my parents splitting up and marrying other people (all true), and having problems about not feeling wanted, and some sex stuff, and how I was basically straight though I'd taken a few walks on the wild side and although I wasn't like guilty about it or anything, there were times when I did have some issues about not knowing what I wanted, and not knowing the difference between love and sex, and wondering if I was ever going to find love at all, or even if I knew what love was, and if that really mattered, and also that I had recently had a panic attack and a bunch of anxieties about death and extinction and stuff like that. In fact apart from not saying that I was a filmmaker it was all pretty much gospel.

What Carla Mendez did ask me, and this seemed like the moment when we were really getting down to business, was whether there was any particular historical period I was especially drawn to, because this might indicate the area of my "blockage." Well, I tried not to be too obvious about it, but I said that yes, funny she should mention it, I'd always had a bit of a thing about seventeenth-century England, you know, Charles the First, Charles the Second, the Civil War, Cromwell, the Commonwealth, the plague, all that stuff. I could tell she didn't have the slightest idea what I was talking about, and she gave me a very serious, knowing smile, which I guess was supposed to disarm me and cover up her ignorance, which it pretty much did.

But again, I couldn't see that it mattered whether she knew what I was talking about or not. I'd always reckoned that *I* was going to be the one doing all the real work and providing all the historical data here. It wasn't like I was relying on her to project anything or put ideas into my head. So I still wasn't complaining.

And then very casually, like really way too casually, she said, "OK then, let's go back there now." And I tried to sound casual too, but I'm sure I failed, and I said, "OK, sure, why not? If you think so. Really?" And I asked if I should close my eyes or something, and she said sure, if you wanna, so I closed my eyes and suddenly, Jesus K. Christ, there I was.

Where? Well, I was in a stinky, crowded, bustling city street that looked pretty much like a shanty town, the buildings mostly made of wood, like the whole place was falling apart. But I knew it was London in the seventeenth century, and even though the word meant nothing to me at the time, I somehow also knew that the district was called Alsatia. How did I know that? Where did I get that name from? I had no idea.

There were a lot of people around who looked pretty much like authentically filthy seventeenth-century English peasants and there were a lot of horses and horse shit in the street (or maybe it was human shit) and there was an amazing amount of noise (which was strange because I'd always thought the past would be really quiet). And all the people were talking very loud in what sounded like a foreign language, though I guess it was just weirdly accented, old-fashioned English.

This was obviously, in every rational sense, a place I'd never been before, but I didn't get that stranger-in-a-strange-land feeling because somehow I pretty much knew where I was. And I knew my way around. I knew where the streets led and what I'd see if I turned left or right or walked straight on, and that was freaky in itself. In some way or other I belonged there.

So what was the experience like exactly? Was it like watching a movie? Well no, not really, because I was right there in the middle of it all, and nobody was doing anything for the sake of any camera: there was no "point of view," no "shot." But more than that, I was way, way more involved than I ever would be watching any movie, even though there was nothing very dramatic going on. I mean there were people doing things—walking, riding, shouting, eating, buying things, spitting, pissing on street corners (hey man, just like L.A., man!)—but it wasn't exactly plot-driven.

So was it like a dream? Well, it sure wasn't like one of *my* dreams because everything was way clearer than that. There was none of the drift you get in dreams, none of that surreal psychological stuff where things suddenly turn into other things and you know who people are supposed to be even though they don't look like them, or they're an amalgam of two different people; there was nothing like that. And it was even less like a dream sequence in a movie: no blurry focus, no Dalí backdrops, no slurred music, none of that crap. (Man, I hate dream sequences in movies.)

But the one really big, major difference between this and a dream was that I very obviously wasn't asleep. I wasn't unconscious, and I hadn't been transported to some other world. I knew I was still right there in Carla Mendez's apartment, and I could still hear her voice. She was talking to me, asking me questions, and I'm prepared to believe that these were *leading* questions, that she was imposing some sort of visualization on me, but they were only the kind of things anybody would ask. What do you see? What do you hear? Are there any smells? What's the weather like? What are you wearing? What age do you feel yourself to be?

Some of these questions were much easier to answer than others. Like it was easy enough to tell her that the weather was hot, that the air smelled of baking bread and cinnamon and rotting vegetables. And I could tell her that I felt like I had on way too many clothes, that I was wearing some kind of wool shirt and woolen leggings and they were itching the hell out of me.

But when it came to describing who exactly this "me" was,

well, things got a lot hazier. I knew I was a man, about my actual age, about my actual build; physically I felt just like me, but I knew I wasn't. Does that make any sense? I knew that in seventeenth-century London I was definitely somebody else (obviously) but I sure didn't know who. And I sure didn't know my name or where I lived or what I did for a living, or anything that might have been useful.

I could hear Carla Mendez's voice telling me I should do some exploring, so I started walking the streets. And again it was all very clear. I could see the grain in every piece of wood in every building. And I could see all the amazing faces of the people, all the bad teeth and the open sores and the facial deformities, and I thought to myself, where would I ever get extras this authentic?

And I turned a corner and I was in a dark alleyway, a place where the sun didn't penetrate, between a printer's shop and a bakery (I could smell the pastry), and there was a door with some kind of painted sign attached to it, with what looked like the footprint of a giant bird. What was *that* all about? And the lock on the door had been smashed, and it was just a little open, and I tried to look inside, even though something told me this was really unwise. Somehow I knew (though I sure didn't know *how* I knew) that I was going to regret it, that there was something just terrible in there. But I couldn't stop myself. I looked, but it was too dark. I couldn't see anything, and yet I knew I was inches away from some sort of terrible horror.

I started to get really, really frightened, without having any idea what I was frightened of. It was bad. Real bad. It was like the panic attack on the plane, like an acid flashback, like some evil, unidentified critter had suddenly attached itself to my back, as if the devil had opened up his big, black, leathery wings right behind me. I wanted to scream, and maybe I did.

Then I felt a sharp slap on my face and I was being shaken, and suddenly seventeenth-century London had gone and I was back in Carla Mendez's apartment (which, of course, I'd never left), staring up at a poster on the wall of a deeply spiritual beach scene, and she was pressing a cold wet cloth to my forehead and asking me over and over again if I was all right.

"I'm fine," I said quickly. "Fine."

"You sure didn't look fine. You were sweating and trembling and you were trying to speak but you couldn't. And you looked just terrified, like you were having a panic attack."

"Really?" I said. "I don't know why."

"What happened back there? What did you see?"

"Nothing much," I said. "You know, people, horses, buildings."

"What else?"

"Nothing. I mean, if there was anything else I sure don't remember it."

She didn't believe me. She knew something was up. "Something's spooked you, hasn't it?" she said. "We need to talk about this."

I really thought we didn't need that at all. I looked at the clock and I could see we were right at the end of the session, so I started to get up and I said, "There's nothing to talk about. Really."

"No, don't go," she said. "The debriefing is a very important part of the process. You need to talk about what you've experienced."

"Tomorrow," I said. "I'll come back the same time tomorrow. We'll do it then."

I didn't mean it. At that moment I was absolutely sure that I'd never go anywhere near Carla Mendez ever again. Why was I pretending I hadn't seen anything, why wasn't I admitting that I was scared? Because, gorgeous though she was, I thought she might be a witch, or worse. She'd already exerted way too much power over me. I had no idea what this past-life therapy crap was all about, but I felt sure she was fucking with something in my brain, something weird and very unhealthy, and something that was much better not fucked with. I even wondered if she'd put something in the tea. I'd been an idiot to do this stuff. Past-life therapy suddenly didn't seem like such a simple, trivial thing after all. It definitely seemed like no way to get your movie made.

Carla Mendez made me promise faithfully that I'd be back the next day, so I lied through my teeth and said I would, I sure would, and only then did she let me leave. I ran down the stairs from her apartment and headed straight for the beach and the ocean. The freak show that is Venice Beach, with its muscle men and beggars and hustlers and cranks and manic roller skaters, now seemed the sweetest, most wholesome, sanest place on earth. I gave a bum some money, though it seemed to make me a lot happier than it made him.

eleven

The Cutting Edge

William Draper stands in the shade of the alleyway, looking up at the sign with the dodo's falsified footprint, trying to gather his wits, inhaling the smell of pastry and stewed beef. He feels adrift, as though he might be dreaming or having a vision, as though he might have slipped back into his own past. And yet everything here seems real and substantial enough, and now that he examines the sign with the footprint more closely, he can see evidence of wear and neglect. It is nailed to the door of a house, almost derelict, not much more than a hovel really, and only the most intrepid seeker after curiosities would be likely to cross the grim threshold, but fortunately William Draper is such a man.

He opens the door, aware of some viscous residue on the handle, and steps into fetid gloom. There is the smell of dung (human and not human), there is straw and mud beneath his feet. Two pale candles burn in opposite corners of the room, reinforcing the darkness around them. This is no place to see wonders. In fact William can see nothing at all, no sign of life, and then there is something more, at first a presence rather than a face, swimming toward him through the darkness: Moxon.

He is even less presentable than when William last saw him. It appears that he has recently received a beating. His clothes are torn and dirty, his cheek is gashed, his mouth bloody as though he had lost a few teeth, although William would be hard pressed to say precisely how many he had possessed at their previous meetings.

"And how is the world treating you, Moxon?" William asks archly.

"Life has been meager of late," Moxon says, rubbing his jaw in a tender, exploratory fashion.

"And how is your marvelous dodo?"

"A dodo is no longer considered the oddity it once was. Nowadays people will only pay to see monsters: things with many heads and an excess of limbs and eyes, or no heads and no limbs and no eyes. Or creatures that are half human, half devil—"

"Yes, yes," William says. "Public taste is execrable. Where is she?"

Moxon takes one of the candles and moves into further, deeper darkness. William follows, feeling unpleasant solids squash beneath his boots, hearing a distant feathered rustle until he can make out the bamboo bars of the cage, and then the dodo within. She has grown and matured since he last saw her, but now her eyes are even blanker and beadier than he remembers, eyes incapable of expression, yet William cannot help but feel that the bird is infinitely bereft and forlorn.

"She looks a mite thin," William says.

"I can barely feed myself, let alone a growing, useless, ugly bird. Neither of us has eaten in days."

William feels a taut pang of compassion for the underfed dodo, but all he says is, "And yet I feel that this imposed fasting does not entirely explain your present distressed state."

"Debt collectors, sir," Moxon says.

"Did they extract what they were owed?"

"They did not, and so they will find me again, no doubt.

Therefore it has become necessary for me to liquidate some of my assets. And here you are sir, arriving in my moment of need. Fate, some might call it."

So, Moxon is ready to part with his dodo, yet William fears that the man might still be overestimating both the bird's worth and William's means.

"In truth I offered the bird to my creditors," Moxon says, and William feels another pang, this time of anger and betrayal, which is only alleviated when Moxon adds, "but it seems, sir, that when it comes to dodos, you are a market of one."

William allows himself a tiny smile of triumph, yet since he conceives of himself as an honorable man, he determines that he will not exploit too severely his position of monopoly. He will not rob Moxon.

"What then is the current market price for a dodo?" he asks.

Moxon turns a defeated gaze in William's direction and says, "My debt runs to a thousand pounds, sir."

"Good lord!" William says. "A man might buy himself a peerage for that amount."

"It would most surely have been a better way to lose the money, sir."

William is staggered that a man of such lowly appearance would have the ingenuity to amass such a formidable debt. If that is really what Moxon now hopes to receive for the dodo, then the price has risen astonishingly.

"I honestly don't see that we can do business at that price, Moxon," William says.

"The debt collectors are returning tomorrow, sir. If I can pay them nothing, then they have sworn to kill me. My life thus seems to have taken on an all too specific monetary value. If I could pay them five hundred pounds, they would perhaps only half kill me. Whatever fraction of a thousand pounds you can bring yourself to pay me for the fowl, then that is the fraction of my life they will spare."

William feels there is probably a fundamental error in Moxon's mathematics. He thinks too that Moxon must be exaggerating the severity of the case, overstating the murderous intentions of his creditors. A dead debtor is of no use to a debt collector. A token payment will surely hold them at bay for a while, and that is what he offers.

"Fifty pounds," he says. "A year's wages for a lesser physician. That will have to suffice."

Moxon looks disappointed and terrified. "I hope that will be enough to save my skin, sir, or some part of it."

"So do I, Moxon," William says, and he means it sincerely enough.

He promises he will return as soon as he can, just as soon as he has scraped together the money. One or two items will need to be sold. He goes home, to his father's house, and is dismayed at how little surprised his father is to see him. Yes, it is good in one way that his father is not asking difficult questions—why he is in London again and not at his studies in Oxford—but some small show of fatherly concern would not be unwelcome. At the very least he might have passed comment on the most recent blotches and scars that mark his son's face. But no. And so William is free to go about his money-raising activities, filching from the house and then selling a couple of valuable maps, an antique book or two, a pair of enameled miniatures (his father will never miss them), and the watch given to him by his grandfather. It is a lively few days, but three mornings later he is in a position to return to Moxon's quarters to complete the bargain.

On the way he thinks of the dodo, starving according to

Moxon. Perhaps the creature has expired in the night, doubly snuffing out Moxon's hopes of preservation. Or perhaps, William thinks, Moxon had simply been lying. Perhaps there are no debt collectors. Perhaps he had hoped that William, in his eagerness, would simply have handed over some money, and that would have been the last William ever saw of it, and indeed of Moxon and the dodo. But that is surely too naive a scheme for a man like Moxon. Untutored he may be; artless he is not. Then a far worse possibility presents itself. Perhaps Moxon has found someone prepared to offer him more than fifty pounds.

William hurries to the alleyway, arrives at Moxon's hovel. The door is locked this time, but he can hear odd sounds and strainings coming from within. He hammers on the door but receives no reply. He puts his shoulder against it, and only a little effort is needed to break the feeble lock. William steps inside, takes the time to let his eyes acclimatize, and then he sees Moxon. The man is not quite dead, though it might have been better for him if he had been.

The debt collectors must have arrived early and not been much impressed with his promise of fifty pounds to come, or perhaps they simply enjoy torturing a man. They have stripped Moxon naked and bound him, on his back, to the four corners of his own bed. They have then taken the carrying cage in which Moxon transports the dodo, removed its wooden base and found an elaborate means of strapping the cage to Moxon's bare torso, a method that employs rope and wax and strips of cloth, so that the cage forms a barred dome, as it were, on top of him. Then they have simply strewn a few handfuls of seed across his belly, sealed the dodo inside the cage, and left bird and man to their conjoined fates.

The bird, stupid by reputation, without moral sense, raven-

99

ously hungry too, and obeying its nature, has used its dangerous hooked beak to pick at the seed on Moxon's belly. This has caused deep lacerations in the wretched man's flesh. Blood has flowed. The bird evidently lost interest in the seed once it was presented with the enticingly ragged dish of Moxon's guts. Or perhaps the bird is not so much foraging for food as trying to dig its way out through what it takes to be the floor of the cage, tunneling to some imagined avian freedom. Either way, the bird's beak, feet, claws, and feathers are now richly daubed with Moxon's blood and entrails, and the dodo shows no signs of being satiated.

Moxon's mouth is thickly gagged, else his screams would surely be echoing through the whole of Alsatia. His eyes are clenched shut, but when he becomes aware of William's presence in the room he opens them wide and looks at him beseechingly.

Patients expect miracles from physicians, even from quacks, but Moxon's case is beyond anything that physic or faith can address, and Moxon is wise enough to know it. William loosens the gag from Moxon's mouth, and though the man can scarcely stop himself from screaming, he does make one coherent utterance. "For the love of God, kill me, sir." And his eyes flick across to a chair in a murky corner of the room, where a short, bone-handled knife is lying.

The physician's oath to do no harm seems sadly immaterial at that instant. William attempts to do good in the only way that is feasible. He says a short, improvised prayer, for Moxon and himself, and then he does as Moxon has requested, drawing the knife deeply and quickly across Moxon's throat: a swift, precise incision, worthy of one of the better barber surgeons.

The dodo becomes enraged, frenzied. She flaps her short wings violently against the bamboo bars of the cage as though, defying all the laws of nature, she now wants to fly off, carrying both cage and Moxon with her. Only with the greatest difficulty does William succeed in calming her. Then he removes the cage from its place on Moxon's belly and finds a way to reattach the base so that he'll have some means of carrying the dodo away with him.

So William Draper becomes the owner and protector of a dodo. He would scarcely say that it cost him nothing, since the killing of Moxon will cost him much remorse and many nightmares. And although he did what he did for the best of reasons, who knows how God will ultimately judge his action: mercifully, he hopes, as William showed mercy to Moxon, though he thinks God might already have behaved more mercifully toward both of them. Nevertheless, William departs with his fifty pounds intact. He has acquired his first dodo, the first of what he is sure will be a great, great many.

twelve Regarding Henry

Believe me, I did not kill my wife, Caroline. Given the circumstances there are no doubt some men who might have and probably a great many more who would have at least contemplated it. But I did not. I bore her taunts, her provocations, her spectacular infidelities. There were days when this course seemed stoic and sensible, others when it seemed merely spineless. When she killed herself, I wouldn't say that I was glad, but a part of me was certainly relieved that it was all over. If Dorothy chose to believe that I'd driven her mother to suicide, well that was simply untrue. If there's one thing I've learned in my career, it's that nobody can ever *make* another person kill themselves. I realize it's convenient for me to believe this, but if it were possible, then there'd be far, far more suicides in the world.

As I made the short drive to Barbara Scott's office that Monday morning I was trying hard not to think about either Dorothy or Caroline. I really wasn't sure why I was going there. Was I pursuing Barbara Scott? Did I fancy my chances with her? No, I think not. I knew myself. I knew what I was: a fat, unfit, middle-aged Englishman. I knew what I was entitled to, and it most definitely was not someone like Barbara Scott.

I think the truth was much tamer, and probably much more pathetic. Barbara Scott had simply showed some warmth and friendliness toward me. It had been a long time since a woman had done that, and I now realized just how much I'd missed it. I realized too that I was grasping at straws.

"Henry!" she said the moment I walked in the door of her office. "You came. I somehow didn't think you would."

"Why not?" I asked.

"I don't know. Instinct. But I'm glad my instincts were proved wrong."

She shone a high-voltage smile at me, and I returned it, though with rather less in the way of teeth.

"Your timing isn't perfect," she said. "I got a call earlier today from a guy who wants to sell his house. I'm on my way there now. I can't get out of it. On the other hand, it might be the property of your dreams. Hollywood foothills, seller sounds motivated. Want to come look at it?"

"All right," I said. "Why not?"

Many reasons why not, of course, but having come this far, I felt there was no point being timid. We only took one car, hers, the long, low, overdesigned Japanese sports car that I'd seen parked outside the open house. In the course of the short drive, Barbara Scott asked me a number of questions that seemed a little too intimate. Was I married, did I have children, how many people would be living in the house, how many bedrooms would I need, how many bathrooms? Would I require a mortgage? Did I have a house I needed to sell back in England? I answered with a mixture of truth, white lies, and monstrous dishonesty. My answers, in mounting order of mendacity, were that my wife was dead, that I had a daughter who might or might not be living with me, that I was wealthy enough to have no need of a mortgage, and that I'd arranged to rent out my large house in London to a couple of diplomats. She had no problem believing any of this.

We arrived at the house. Once again it looked a modest enough place, on a street with lots of other more or less similar houses with small gardens and neat fences. The property had a certain amount of character, the house painted yellow and blue, with a complicated arrangement of roofs and dormer windows, balustrades and balconies. A small, exotically shaggy dog lolled on the porch beside the front door, and he started to yap benignly as we got out of the car. This in turn brought the owner of the house to the front door.

He was an improbably good-looking man: regular all-American features, a square jaw, big sensitive eyes—an actor, I assumed. He had that kind of neutral, tough, youthful leading-man quality that refused to give away his real age. Above the waist he was naked, and below he was wearing a pair of too-tight jeans.

He held the door open, greeted us, beckoned us in, grabbing the dog by its collar so it couldn't leap up at us. Like the dog, the owner was relaxed and floppy, and it took me only a short while to realize he was completely smashed. My skills in toxicological analysis aren't as finely honed as they might be, but I would have guessed he was flying on some finely balanced combination of alcohol, marijuana, amphetamine, and perhaps a little cocaine.

We walked into the hall, then into the living room, and Barbara scanned the place with her professional eye. "Well," she said, "it's a very well *edited* house." I tried to look interested. There was plenty of space, though not as much light as I might have imagined, and the furniture was bulky and expensive, cowboy-influenced, and there was a vast TV that overwhelmed the living room.

"So you're eager to sell," Barbara said.

"No," the man replied, and he said it rather dramatically and tragically, as though this single word conveyed a whole galaxy of sadness and loss. "My wife wants to sell. My wife wants me out of her life. And the house is in her name. And she's divorcing me. And right now she's in Malibu with her new boyfriend. So . . ."

Barbara gave me a look that said there was nothing remotely unusual going on here, that it was the kind of professional glitch she dealt with all the time.

"Do you guys want a beer?" the man asked.

"Not really," Barbara said.

"How about you?" and he looked at me accusingly, as though I would seriously damage his feelings if I refused.

"No thanks," I said.

"I can tell you want one really."

He went into the kitchen and after longer than seemed necessary returned with a can of beer. He forced it on me, and oddly enough I did think twice about opening it. I suspected he might be up to something. And it turned out that he had given the can a good shake while he was in the kitchen. His idea, apparently, was that I should cover myself in a great spume of beer froth. Hollywood humor. But suspecting this, I opened the can rather gently, while pointing it away from myself, so that his TV screen received most of the gush.

Ever the Englishman, I said, "Oh, sorry," and the man said, "Shit," and Barbara said, "Maybe we should come back later when you've sobered up a little."

"This is about as sober as I get," he said.

"Then I guess we *won't* be back," Barbara said.

This offended him grievously for some reason. "I think you ought to stay," he said. "I think you ought to stick around and party."

For entirely obvious reasons he was keener to party with Barbara than with me. He made a clumsy lurch across the living room and grabbed her by the arm. The move was sudden and very aggressive and it took her, and indeed me, completely by surprise.

"Let go of me," she said, as anyone would, and she pulled away but his hand stayed locked in place.

It was one of those situations that most of us find ourselves in all too rarely, a moment when what we have to do is absolutely, transparently clear. I stood up to him and said, "Take your hands off her," and he did and then squared up and pulled back his fist, giving me plenty of notice that he was about to try and punch me.

I have personally, directly, been involved in very few fights. I've been a bystander at a few more, and I suppose I've seen tens of thousands of them in the movies. However, I have never seen a fight that went quite the way this one did.

I could tell the man was ready to hit me. He'd done all the mental computation and decided it was worth his while to fight. I was not inclined to do anything other than defend myself and I suppose defend Barbara too. I thought this stance, plus my sobriety, might give me a slight edge but you could very easily have calculated the odds the other way.

Then Barbara said, "This is stupid and unnecessary," and the man stepped toward me while staring at her and shouted, "You keep out of this, bitch," and then I did something that at the time didn't seem to be anything at all. I suppose I thought I was keeping him at arm's length. The flat of my hand pressed against the upper part of his sternum. It wasn't in any sense a blow, and it was far from dramatic, but I suppose he was unsteady, and the moment I touched him he keeled over backwards like a toy soldier and he landed on his back with a thick, sickening slam.

I couldn't be sure which part of him hit the floor first, his backside or his shoulders or his head, but once he was down, it was apparent that he was staying down, and the look on Barbara's face suggested that she thought I might have killed him: not an impossibility in that situation but rather unlikely, I thought.

Fortunately my long years of medical training came in handy here. One of the first things we doctors learn is to tell a live patient from a dead one. It isn't always as easy as it sounds but most of us get there eventually. When I found my wife sprawled face-down on the bed in our spare room, for instance, I knew with absolute certainty that she was dead. In the case of the man on the floor of his Hollywood house, I checked his pulse and his breathing and I was absolutely certain he was alive.

I was pleased for him, and for Barbara and myself too. I helped him up off the floor and sat him in an uncomfortable-looking armchair. He seemed a rather pathetic specimen now, and as he came round I wondered whether the conflict was really over. For all I knew he might have had a gun somewhere. My worries were only somewhat alleviated when he said, "I deserved that, man," and then began to weep noisily. "This is my birthday, man. This is my fucking birthday," he added, and his dog came snuffling over to him.

"Come on, Henry," Barbara said. "I think our work here is done."

I certainly hoped so. Once we were in the car, Barbara said, "That's a first. The vendor being knocked unconscious, that's definitely a first. Let's just hope he doesn't remember enough about it to think of suing."

I was aware that my hands were shaking a little. The role of action hero didn't suit me at all. "God, that was awful," I said. "Really awful. I'm sorry. It's so embarrassing."

"Sometimes a man's got to do what a man's got to do."

I wished I knew her a little better, enough to know how many layers of irony she was playing with there. But then she touched me on the arm, and that felt very reassuring and not ironic at all.

"Don't you ever get worried?" I asked. "Going into strange houses? Or when you're doing an open house. You're there all alone. Any kind of nutter might walk in."

"Or someone like you," she said. "So it has its upside as well."

That was the moment when I had reason to believe she liked me. I wasn't foolish enough to think I'd "saved" her from anything, but I had in some way acquitted myself decently. Although I certainly wished that the whole episode had never happened, I didn't feel I had anything to be ashamed about. When Barbara said there was a restaurant nearby where they served pretty good duck sausage pizzas, I knew we were friends, and at some point as we ate lunch there I began to think that we might be more than friends, unlikely though it still seemed.

It was midafternoon by the time we'd finished eating, and I was certainly wondering where we went from here, and in truth I was experiencing a little guilt about what poor Dorothy might have been up to while I'd been enjoying myself, but that didn't burden me for long.

Barbara said, "Come on, there's a property I really want to show you."

We got in her car again and she drove me at high speed into what she assured me were the Hollywood Hills proper. The roads were narrow and steep, a tight curving track between walls, gates, palm trees, parked cars, vertiginous drops. I loved the way she drove.

We came to a house, or rather a high electronic gate, and after some elaborate play with keys that disarmed the security system, we drove into a small courtyard belonging to the house, a house of a sort that I had never seen before, at least not outside of a movie. I suppose you'd have had to call the style mock-Tudor, but the mockery had reached a level of hysterical taunting. There were jet black timbers embedded in gleaming white stucco, bay windows with myriad diamond-shaped panes. The front door resembled a portcullis and the building was topped off with what looked vaguely like a thatched roof, but even a quick glance told you it was made out of plastic. There was also an overgrown rose garden with a thoroughly inauthentic swimming pool.

"Isn't this wild?" Barbara said.

Well yes, it was in a way, but I hoped she didn't think it was the kind of house I might be interested in. I mean, I wasn't in the market for a house at all, but if I had been, surely she couldn't think my tastes ran in this direction. Soon we were inside, in a paneled entrance hall with suits of armor and swords and shields that had been enameled in lurid acid colors.

"Some of this stuff is a lot more authentic than it looks," Barbara said, but that wouldn't have been hard.

And then we were upstairs in a room with a four-poster bed, with animal skins and tapestries on the walls, and Barbara Scott was closing the heavy brocade curtains and stripping off her clothes, and I was beset by two thoughts. One, could this really be happening to me? And two, who on earth owned this house?

The first issue had to be dealt with first. It's not easy to have sex when you're in a state of disbelief, and I did suspect that I had a look of stunned surprise on my face throughout the proceedings, but fortunately the emotion was not wholly incapacitating. Everything went very well. I'm sure you can imagine: bodies, sweat, a certain amount of harmless clumsiness in amongst the tried and trusted techniques.

I've always thought that as a person gets older, age ought to matter less and less to them, and yet we know that very often the reverse is true. People obsess about youth, either their own or other people's. They want to split hairs, split numbers; to be forty-nine is so much better than to be fifty; to be fifty and mistaken for a forty-year-old is supposed to be the best thing in the world. I hate all that nonsense. What's wrong with looking like a fifty-year-old, if you *are* a fifty-year-old? As far as that goes, what's wrong with looking like a fifty-year-old even if you're only forty? There was no doubt that Barbara and I were two middle-aged people having sex, a prospect that would fill many people, including most filmmakers and filmgoers, with distaste, but I must say it filled me with quite the opposite. A rare triumph for life over the movies.

There was, however, no doubt that Barbara Scott was a rather spectacularly good-looking middle-aged woman, and I was very appreciative of the fact. I was extremely glad that she was not fat, not wrinkled, not slack and baggy, glad she wasn't like me. Does this make me a hypocrite? Oh yes, very probably.

It seemed that nature, hard work, and medical art had all played their part in making Barbara Scott look so good. Yes, she'd had good basic materials (I was inevitably reminded of Dorothy's complaints regarding my own genetic bounty), but then she'd obviously had a boob job, a good one, nothing showy; the scars were small and neat, evidence of a skilled hand on the scalpel. And then she obviously worked out a lot. Her body was toned in a way that nobody's body is unless they've spent a lot of time in a gym. She looked great. She felt great. She smelled great. What on earth was she doing with me?

I have never been the sort of man who enjoys looking at himself while having sex. Mirrored ceilings and Polaroids and making dirty home movies has never been my style. I'm sure it has something to do with the way I look. If I were slimmer, fitter, healthier, more "buff," no doubt I'd be more inclined to look. But the truth is I've never much enjoyed watching *other* people have sex either. It's not some moral objection, and I'm well aware that there's an important visual component to sex, it's simply that I find looking at sex somehow vaguely embarrassing. I'm one of the few people who rather welcome visual metaphors for sex in the movies, however corny: the crashing waves, the slow pan away from the bed into the flames in the fireplace, the slow dissolve from the long, newly lit candle to the short, burned-down one.

I became aware of how silent the house was, and in a different kind of movie this silence might have been creepy, creating tension, a prelude to the axe murderer's first appearance. This is probably only to say that there was something distinctly cinematic about the situation. It was impossible not to feel that I was living out a fantasy. It wasn't one that I'd ever consciously indulged or imagined in any great detail, but this definitely felt like a scene that had very little connection with life as I knew it. Perhaps this was the English dream of America, a hope that the new country would embrace the old, that it would not find us as worn out and effete as we feared. The new world would recognize our sober, unostentatious appeal. It would not find us (I suppose I mean me) too tired or ridiculous. I had certain feelings of "If they could see me now," though I couldn't have said who I would have wanted the "they" to be. Not Dorothy, certainly.

"Whose house is this?" I asked.

"Some industry guy," Barbara said vaguely. "It's been on the market for years. I've showed dozens of people round. I don't think it's ever going to sell."

"Not even with your very persuasive sales techniques."

"I know I'm good, but I'm not *that* good."

Later she drove us back to her office, to my own car. "Call me tomorrow," she said. "I've lots more houses I could show you."

It was just about that moment when I realized where I'd seen Barbara Scott before. In the movies, of course.

thirteen Staying Alive

Tom Brewster's studio is really not the place you'd want to be if you were trying to come down from a bad trip. All the severed heads and mutated aliens seemed to be looking at me and laughing. Tom wasn't even there. He was off on some all-night shoot. So I had to try to do my own debriefing; specifically, I tried to get something down on paper. And if that sounds vague, then that's very appropriate, because I hadn't the slightest idea what the something was. Nameless horror just doesn't lend itself to simple exposition. I tried to write a few lines, just a diary entry would have been enough, describing how I felt, but nothing would come. I found myself jotting down stupid disconnected words: *shanty, bones, velvet, black wings, extinction*, which made a sort of sense, but not *real* sense.

Then I tried to do some drawings, like a storyboard of what I'd seen or remembered or imagined in the session, and that was no good either. I filled half a dozen sheets of paper with doodles and cross-hatching, outlines of roofs and badly drawn dodos (not that I'd seen any dodos during the regression, of course). I worked and reworked the drawings until they just disappeared under a hail of dense, black scribbles. And I was still very, very scared.

I was stuck with some big, ugly thing in my head, something I could neither remember nor forget. It was as though some large, dark, ominous lump of knowledge had been dropped into my head, like an ice cube tossed into a cocktail. That was as subtle as I could get with the metaphors, and the metaphor didn't really work because it's easy enough to take an ice cube out of your drink again, whereas this incomprehensible thing in my head seemed to be stuck there permanently. Also you can see an ice cube for what it is, and I didn't know what the fuck this thing in my head was. It was related to something terrible in a room somewhere in the past. That was as precise as I could get. The thing wouldn't go away but it wouldn't reveal itself either, and I wasn't sure I wanted it revealed, but how could I live with it just lurking there?

I went on-line and tried to find out where this name Alsatia came from, and that was revealing in one way. It turns out Alsatia was a part of London in the seventeenth-century, quite a small strip of land along the Thames, between the river and Fleet Street. Apparently it got its name from Alsace—a place that France and Germany had been fighting over for centuries. So basically they were calling it a war zone.

Seems that when Henry the Eighth dissolved the monasteries, he took away all the land and the buildings belonging to the White Friars and handed them to some guy called William Butte, who was the royal physician. Now, you'd think that a royal physician would be smart enough to look after a chunk of real estate, but no. The monastery fell into ruin, squatters moved in and claimed they were exempt from the law because the area was still holy ground, and somehow or other the government more or less fell for it. So there went the neighborhood. All kinds of riffraff moved in, mostly criminals, but also writers, painters, Bohemians, some fencing masters, and especially quacks.

Well, that explained *something*. What it didn't explain, what it couldn't possibly explain, was everything else. Like how I'd even known it was the name of the place I'd regressed to. It wasn't a name I'd ever heard before, and I hadn't come across it in any of my half-assed historical research. So how exactly had it got into my head in the first place?

One explanation, of course, might have been that I'd *really* lived there in some past life, and that Carla Mendez had *really*, miraculously reawakened some ancient memories of the place in her therapy. But as a matter of fact, that was the one explanation I wasn't inclined to accept. I absolutely, positively didn't want to see Carla Mendez again. I was convinced that whatever she'd done to me, or whatever she'd had me do to myself, was very bad stuff. I hated her for it, and I hated myself for having fallen for it.

I had a really bad night. I couldn't tell when I was asleep and when I was awake, when I was dreaming and when I wasn't, and I didn't know which was worse. And in the morning I went back to see Carla Mendez. Sure. Of course I did. You always knew I would, right? Probably I knew it too.

"Look," I said to her, "I think something very weird's going on here."

"I told you it might be traumatic," she said. "Just like any other therapy."

"Yeah sure, but psychoanalysis has you all weepy 'cause your mother didn't love you enough. That I could cope with. This isn't like that."

"So what *is* it like?"

I told her as best I could. There really wasn't much to tell, just something totally terrifying in a dark room somewhere. She listened carefully and I got the feeling she was impressed, like her clients weren't usually this dramatic, like I was a prize pupil.

"I'd guess this room was the scene of your activating event," she said, and who was I to argue with her? "You need to find out more about this event."

"Do I?"

"I'd say so."

"And how do I do that?"

"The only way I know is to regress again, return to this scene of darkness. Confront your demons."

"I don't really do confrontation," I said.

"You just want to walk away from this?"

"Yeah, that would be fine. I do walking away much better than I do confrontation."

"But then the therapy would have been wasted."

"I'd be prepared to waste it if only I could get this damn thing out of my head."

"I can't do that for you," she said. "I can't erase memories. That's not what I do. All I can do is help you go back again, try to take you through it, try to be there for you."

"But you *won't* be there, will you? I'll be there, in history, in the dark, on my own in this terrible, terrible place." I thought I might be about to have a very spectacular panic attack.

"The truth is," she said, "we're all of us alone in a dark, terrible place."

I don't know why I found that consoling but for some reason I did. So I went for it. I went back again. This going-back thing was really way too easy. It wasn't like Carla Mendez had to do much of anything, hypnotize me or anything. I just closed my eyes and there I was, right back where I'd been before, same place, same time, all the same smells and sights, and all the same free-floating terror.

I was in the alleyway again and I was approaching that same door, and this time I could see the painted sign on it a lot more clearly, and I could read the words that I hadn't noticed before, "The world's most disgusting bird." I had no idea what that meant but I didn't like the sound of it. The door was just like before, closed but with the lock smashed, and I knew that something very, very bad was on the other side, but I'd come this far in space and time; I wasn't going to chicken out now.

I pushed open the door and went inside. It was dark in there and it stank. It wasn't totally pitch black because there were a couple of candles off in the corners but they didn't provide much light. And I kept thinking it would be good to have a lighting designer with me and get him to light the place way more artfully. And I also thought there ought to be some music playing, something by Bernard Herrmann maybe, although I could see why you might think that was too obvious. And yes, sure, I knew that thinking all this movie stuff was displacement activity, but in the dark, with nothing to see, and with the knowledge that something terrible was lurking there, I needed all the displacement I could get.

And the smells came in around me; shit, sweat, rancid food. Does blood have a smell? Does torn flesh? I don't know exactly. I stood there for a long time until my eyes got used to the darkness, and gradually I knew where I was and what I was looking at: the crime scene, the murder scene. There in front of me was the victim, or what was left of him, a middle-aged man with white hair, strapped to a thin straw bed, his throat cut and his body cavity ripped open, blood and guts and stomach-lining torn apart. Oh man.

I thought I was going to throw up, and maybe I would have, but suddenly I was being shaken, really thrown around, and I could hear a woman's voice shouting at me, and the next moment I opened my eyes and I was in Carla Mendez's apartment, in fact in her arms, which under the circumstances wasn't as much of a thrill as it might have been, and I was sobbing and shuddering and doing the whole Oscar-winning performance.

"It's all right," she was saying to me. "It's all right."

"No, it's not," I said. "No, it's fucking *not* all right." And I got up and pushed her away and headed for the door.

"Where are you going?" she said.

"I'm going to Alsatia."

fourteen Destiny Turns On the Radio

As William Draper returns by coach to Oxford, he feels, above all, rich. As the owner of a dodo he considers himself wealthy beyond all imagining. The bird seems to have infinite worth, infinite value. Besides which, he also has an unexpected fifty pounds in his pocket.

He feels that he cuts quite a figure among his fellow coach passengers, and he realizes it has much to do with his new sense of purpose, his sense that the world is a place of fulfillment and possibility. He carries himself as though he is a somebody, and people respond to that. They respond too to the caged dodo that sits on the coach seat beside him. A dodo looks like a rich man's novelty, the sort of thing that would hardly be owned by a pauper. His fellow travelers show a welcome interest in the bird: these are university men, after all, and they can see that it is a wonder worthy of attention and study.

Just as pertinent—and this was a factor that had never crossed William's mind till now, and had certainly played no part in his desire to possess the dodo—the passengers pay more attention to the bird than to him. They see him anew. They regard him as the man who owns this curious fowl, not as the man who has that curiously scarred face.

In Oxford, William returns to his room. There is perhaps some college regulation which forbids the keeping of creatures in

121

students' rooms, but he feels sure they will make an exception for him. Today he feels truly exceptional. He sets the cage in a corner, opens the room's shutters just a crack so that the dodo has some light. He paces the room, views the dodo from various angles and vantage points. She is already recovering from her ordeal, and she is certainly looking happier and healthier than she ever did while in Moxon's care.

And then William sees that in all his buoyancy, in all his optimism, he didn't spot that a note has been pushed under the door of his room. The handwriting shows that it comes from Dr. Clayton, and now William feels less buoyant by far, his optimism evaporates, reality beats in around him.

He makes an appointment to see Dr. Clayton the following afternoon. He prepares himself to do much apologizing, much eating of humble pie, to make many promises to submit himself utterly to Dr. Clayton's will and methods.

The doctor is talking to a stranger when William enters his rooms. The stranger's appearance is complex: long hair, a topiaried beard, an elegant costume, with more lace and leather than seems strictly desirable. He is introduced as one Dr. Lloyd of London, and William cannot fathom what his presence means. Is he another physician with a wonder cure? Certainly Dr. Clayton seems to be in some awe of his colleague, and little is clarified by the stranger's first remark, which seems, to William, eccentrically oblique.

"Do you believe in destiny?" Dr. Lloyd asks.

Without much consideration William replies, "I think, sir, that destiny is that which happens to us whether we believe in it or not." William has replied honestly enough but he fears the two doctors may find something offensively flippant in his answer.

Dr. Lloyd then asks, "And do you believe that disease is a manifestation of God's will?"

William replies, "I suppose everything is a manifestation of God's will. Or of man's willfulness." He is not quite prepared to blame God for his condition, yet he is equally reluctant to accept that it is entirely his own fault.

"True physic is indeed the gift of the most high God," says Dr. Lloyd. "This university is not its foundation, nor are written texts, whether ancient or modern. Its foundation is in God's invisible mercy."

William would not dispute this, but he feels it has little to do with his own case. He wishes this learned gentleman might express himself less artfully. He is glad when Dr. Clayton speaks.

"Am I right in thinking, William," he says, "that you are familiar with some of the less healthful areas of London?"

Have they been observing him? Was he followed? Surely not, yet it is disturbing to have them know this about him. It makes him feel much less his own man.

"To an extent," he admits. "I have perhaps, on occasion, found myself in some out-of-the-way places, and yet I would say I was motivated by curiosity rather than by any unwholesome attraction to disease."

"Quite, quite," Dr. Clayton concedes. "But you are familiar with an area known as Alsatia. You have been a disinterested mover among the quacks and mountebanks there, no?"

"Rather, I think they have moved around *me.*"

"And how have you found them?"

William feels he may be defending himself against unstated and perhaps as yet unformulated charges, yet he knows that if he tries to second-guess his interlocutors, he will be lost entirely.

"Some I have found amusing," he says. "Some ludicrous. A few I suspected were downright lethal."

For the first time the two doctors seem pleased by something he has said. They indicate that they want him to continue.

"Some of them, I would have to say, try to do a fair job at a fair price. Some, I would say, deal with their patients at least as fairly as certain practitioners licensed by the Royal College of Physicians."

Dr. Clayton raises a warning hand. He would not have William hang himself. "Dr. Lloyd is a most distinguished fellow of that college," he says, but in truth the stranger doesn't appear unduly insulted by anything William has said.

"I wonder, Mr. Draper," Dr. Lloyd says, "if you have consulted any of these quacks regarding your own singular condition. No doubt many of them would be swift to offer you a miraculous cure."

"No, sir," William says carefully. "I have placed myself in the hands of Dr. Clayton. I believe in him. I believe that if he cannot cure me, then I am most probably incurable."

Dr. Clayton stares at him with sadness and sympathy: an exasperating case, a rare failure.

"And yet Dr. Clayton tells me that you have become an embarrassment to him."

"Embarrassment?" William says.

"I would not have put it so cruelly," Dr. Clayton says, but this makes no impression on his colleague.

"An embarrassment," Lloyd repeats, "an accusation, a flag of our professional deficiencies: a would-be physician who can neither cure himself nor be cured by the best physicians. You see Dr. Clayton's position, surely."

William cannot speak.

"I have failed you, William," Dr. Clayton says, sadly, humbly, "and I am sorry for that, but you can surely understand that I do not wish to publicize my failures."

"I . . . I . . . do not understand," says William, though of course he does.

"So after much consideration and with some regret, we have decided that there is no place for you here at the university. We cannot imagine a world in which you might function as a physician. I am sorry."

William feels hot and angry, a tide of blood thrashes through him, makes his face red, makes his scars throb.

"I can see that you have some knowledge and understanding of physic," Dr. Lloyd says. "It will be useful to you in the future, but you will have to employ it in some way other than becoming a physician."

"Someone will have to explain to me how that might be done," William says.

"We are in a position to do that," Dr. Lloyd replies, and he and Dr. Clayton exchange looks that appear benign enough, but William cannot conceive how these looks are to be reconciled with the sudden destruction of all his hopes and ambitions.

"As you must surely know, Mr. Draper, the Royal College of Physicians is a most noble institution," Dr. Lloyd says. "Among our many duties we are charged with the licensing of physicians in London. Your adventures among the quacks will have shown you the eagerness with which the untutored wish to dispense physic to anyone gullible enough or desperate enough to consult them. This is to nobody's advantage. Believe me, it is not simply for our own narrow self-interests that we seek to weed out the worst sort of the, as you put it, lethal quacks. We act in the public good."

William's thoughts are a shambles. He cannot understand why this doctor is justifying himself and his college in this way. Why now? Why to him?

"Let us imagine," Dr. Lloyd says, "that you returned to some of your old London haunts. There you might seek out the advice of those who pretend a knowledge of physic. You might ask for their recommendations regarding your condition. You might see what pills and nostrums they wish to sell you. And at what price. You would note what claims are made for them. Perhaps your knowledge of chemistry would be sufficient for you to take these substances away and analyze them.

"In any event, your basic knowledge would surely be enough to distinguish the ignorant from the misguided, the merely fraudulent from the truly dangerous. You would be able to do that, would you not, Mr. Draper?"

"Of course," says William. To say otherwise would be to deny everything.

"We are not vindictive men," Dr. Lloyd says. "Those who do no serious harm may be quietly dealt with: a stern word, a firm suggestion that they shut up shop, seek other ways of making a living. The more serious cases you will report to me at the Royal College and the culprits will be dealt with by the church courts. We may choose to make an example of some of them. We may decide, say, to hold a public burning of the worst, most useless elixirs and remedies. As a last resort there is always jail."

"So you see, William, " Dr. Clayton adds, "the role you are being offered is not such a noble calling as that of physician, but it is still a most useful one. You would not be one of us, but you would certainly be on our side."

With as much tact as his disarrayed wits and emotions allow, William says, "The task seems, sirs, to have something in common with being a spy and an informer."

"By no means," Dr. Clayton says. "We are asking you to play Doubting Thomas, not Judas."

"Besides, Mr. Draper," Dr. Lloyd says, with what all three of them know is complete finality, "what else can you possibly do with your life?"

fifteen The Party

It was early evening as I drove away from Barbara's office, and a modest orange sunset was staining the sky. A part of me wanted to hurry back to the hotel and patch things up with Dorothy, but a somewhat larger part didn't want that at all. Let the little cow suffer, I thought. More persuasively I now had an urgent desire to find out more about Barbara Scott. I returned to the Beauty Vault.

As before, there were no customers. Perry Martin and his assistant were behind the desk, and Martin greeted me as "the Englishman who doesn't know what he's looking for," and I said this was no longer true.

"Did you decide you couldn't live without an animation cel of a dodo?" Martin asked.

"Not exactly," I said, and I handed him Barbara Scott's business card with the photograph on it.

"Do you know who this is?" I asked.

"I'm assuming you don't want me to say it's Barbara Scott the realtor?" he said, reading the card.

"She's an actress, isn't she?" I said. "Or used to be. But I don't think that was the name she used. I'm sure I've seen her in movies; I'd like to know a little more. And I thought that you with your encyclopedic knowledge—"

"You thought what? That I might like to turn myself into a public information service?"

"I thought you might like a challenge," I said.

He gave a cough of derision. "Go and browse," he said, and as I withdrew he started taking down reference books from the shelves behind him. I noticed that the assistant didn't help at all.

I went slowly to the back of the shop where the big display cabinet was. The animation cel had now been placed in there, along with a card that said, "Very rare. Make us an offer." I couldn't quite stop myself sniggering. It seemed that Perry Martin had more of a sense of humor than I had given him credit for. He gradually moved on from his reference books to his computer and I heard him tapping away enthusiastically.

Occupying myself as best I could, I found myself looking at the green baize door that, in Perry Martin's account, promised so much. What was really beyond it? An inner sanctum? A private screening room? An actual, as opposed to a metaphorical, vault? Or in reality nothing so grand, just a storeroom with a needlessly fancy door? All these seemed perfectly possible.

At last Perry Martin called out to me, "Well, we're not talking Hollywood legend here. Your Barbara Scott was better known—to the extent that she was known at all—as Bibi Scott."

The name still sounded unfamiliar.

"Biographical info is a little scarce," Martin continued. "I'm afraid the official biography is still waiting to be written. She was born in Baltimore apparently. You can choose from quite a few different dates of birth. Started out as a dancer. Married and unmarried a few times, no children apparently, no awards, no Oscars. No spells in rehab that my sources are aware of.

"Her earliest masterworks include such treasurable classics as *A Matter of Fiction*, *Acid Sky*, and *The Fricatrice*. Then she appears to have had a brief continental phase, some Italian movies, *Il*

Robot, L'Estremità dell'Amore. Then a few late-period master-pieces, including *The Jacuzzi Killers* and *Suicide Planet.*"

He handed me a list of films he'd printed out. I'd never heard of any of them, though that didn't necessarily mean that I hadn't seen one of them at some point.

"We're talking about a good-looking actress," Perry Martin said, "but not quite good-looking enough. The kind of actress who gets work so long as she takes her clothes off. As long as people want to *see* her take her clothes off."

I thought of various things I might have said about Barbara Scott, with and without clothes, but that would have been giving far too much away.

"Where is she now, I wonder?" Perry Martin asked grandly. "Oh, I know, at a real estate office in Hollywood. Some I'm sure would say this was an excellent career move."

I couldn't see why he was being so nasty about her. It was easy to mock a second-rate or second-division actress, but the difference between second and first is often so slight, so arbitrary, such a matter of luck, of being cast in the right film at the right time, of having an affair with the right director, that I thought mockery was hardly appropriate. I couldn't see what Perry Martin, or anyone else, had got to feel so superior about.

"Well, thank you very much," I said coldly.

"Yes, well, knowledge is power. Use it wisely. And before you go, don't you think you ought to buy a little something?"

I must have looked rather surprised at this suggestion.

"There's no such thing as a free public information service," he said.

"What do you think I ought to buy?" I asked, powerfully reminded that most things in this shop were both undesirable and ruinously expensive.

"How about a signed portrait of Bibi Scott?" It wasn't Perry Martin who said this but his assistant, Duane, who had unexpectedly come to life.

"Hmm?" said Perry Martin, suppressing what was evidently real surprise.

"Second filing cabinet on the right, third drawer down," Duane said.

I went to the drawer as directed and found a stash of photographs of actresses whose surnames began with S: Susan Sarandon, Romy Schneider, Hanna Schygulla, et al., and before long I came across a film still of a young-looking actress who was obviously an earlier incarnation of the woman I now knew as Barbara Scott. She was more or less naked, or at least topless, but you couldn't see much of anything since she was sitting behind the wheel of a car. She looked good—big bright eyes and dark lips and shaggy permed hair—and yet for my tastes she looked considerably less interesting and appealing than the older woman I had actually met. Today she had more style, looked more engaging and sophisticated. She was, I suppose, more my own age.

"We even went to that movie," Duane said. *Suicide Planet*. It was OK. I mean, what can I tell you, it was a movie."

Perry Martin was a little ruffled by the realization that the gaps in his knowledge extended as far as his own stock, but he was prepared to shrug it off for the sake of a sale. So I paid rather more than I wanted to for a signed photograph of Barbara—or Bibi—Scott, although I had no idea what I would have considered a fair price. Then again I suppose a fair price is whatever some poor sucker is willing to pay.

Perry Martin took my credit card for payment, and as he checked it, he said, "Are you a real medical doctor?"

"Real enough," I said.

"Would you do something for me?"

I assumed he was going to ask my advice about his porphyria, but I was quite wrong.

"The pregnant Mexican lady living out back in the van," he said. "Would you take a look at her, make sure she's OK?" As I hesitated he added, "You're the only doctor she's ever likely to see."

So Perry Martin and I went out to the car park and he introduced me to the Mexican couple in the van, Carlos and Elisa. The circumstances weren't conducive to a very thorough medical examination, but as far as I could see, Elisa was in rude good health, just as well if you were living in a van, I supposed. I knew nothing about American prenatal care but I asked whether there wasn't some local heath services that would help her. She and Carlos looked at me as though I'd suggested there was a place where money grew on trees.

For reasons that I didn't wholly comprehend, I drove away from the Beauty Vault feeling rather more ready to confront Dorothy, but in the event, it was hardly a confrontation at all. She was in her hotel room watching TV, and she was good enough to turn the sound down when I came in.

"Sorry about that," we said more or less simultaneously.

"I know you didn't really kill Mummy," Dorothy added.

"Yes, I know you know that."

"I was pretty unhappy after the party."

"Yes. Want to talk about it?"

"No," she said, and I was greatly relieved.

"So what did you get up to today?" I asked.

She gave a melancholy shrug. "Not much. I went for a drive. I found a gym. I had a massage, a facial, a manicure, did some thinking."

It all sounded commendably L.A., apart from the thinking, though it didn't seem quite to amount to taking the town by its balls. And so, somewhat to my surprise, Dorothy and I spent the evening together. We ate, we drank, we talked, we expressed affection, though I suppose I did rather more of all these things than she did, but that was all right, that was only to be expected. Dorothy showed no interest in how I'd spent my day, and no doubt that was just as well.

I know there are families who have no secrets, who tell each other everything, but ours had never been that sort of family and it suited me very well. I'd have found candor rather unnatural and hard to deal with, especially from a daughter. I'm sure that children need to have their secrets. And I'm absolutely positive that they don't want to know too much about their parents, certainly not about their sex lives. For now I was happy if Dorothy and I could stay on reasonable terms and if she could refrain from accusing me of murder.

Then Dorothy said, "I know what I'm going to do tomorrow. I have a plan."

"Good."

"I'm going to sit somewhere with a phone and a phone book and a couple of trade directories and newsletters and some other things I picked up today, and I'm going to call anyone I can find—agents, casting directors, film companies, producers— and persuade some of them to see me."

It seemed like a perfectly serviceable plan, though I had no idea if it was likely to succeed. A young Englishwoman's voice, with enough warmth and passion and persuasiveness and so long as it didn't sound too desperate, might indeed open doors in L.A. Or it might not. Or it might only open doors that a father would prefer remain closed to his daughter.

Nevertheless, I decided to be encouraging. I told Dorothy to go for it, not least because (and I knew immediately this was a rather shameful thing to be thinking) if Dorothy was holed up in her hotel room all day, then I was free to see Barbara, my Hollywood conquest, my former movie star.

It was a long, long time since I'd been in the dating business but I felt sure that the same old etiquettes must still apply. You had to be keen but not *too* keen. You had to make the phone call but not too soon. In the present case, however, since I was only in town for two weeks at the most, I thought a display of eagerness was excusable. I called Barbara at her office and said I'd like to meet up with her again.

"Well, of course," she said. "We've only just started."

We agreed that I'd turn up at the office in the late afternoon. "See houses first?" Barbara asked. "Or fuck first?" I was enough of a gentleman to leave the decision up to her. She chose the latter.

We went to the mock-Tudor house again and had sex again. It was rather better this time, rather more leisurely and less unfamiliar. Afterwards Barbara got up while I stayed where I was, flat on my back in the four-poster bed, unwilling to move, and as I lay there I watched a patch of early evening sunlight form a dagger of light on the sheet beside me. I could see it slowly moving, edging onto my chest, as if aiming for my heart.

Then I heard the back door of the house open, and for a second I wondered if I'd said something wrong and Barbara was about to abandon me. I went over to the window and looked out to see her, completely naked, squatting at the edge of the swimming pool and very deliberately urinating into the water. I stepped back from the window. It felt too early in the relationship to witness such an act, whatever its meaning. A little while later she came back into the bedroom with a couple of carrier bags.

"Would you do something for me?" she asked.

"Probably," I replied.

She handed me the bags and said, "Put these clothes on."

Just for a second I wondered if I was being asked to participate in some sort of fetishistic dressing-up game, if the bags might contain masks and cloaks, leatherwear and God knows what. I would have found that hard to cope with and was relieved to find that the bags contained perfectly ordinary, if by my standards unusually stylish, clothes: a gray linen suit, a black silk T-shirt, some loafers.

"Well, these are very nice," I said, but I still thought we might be playing a game.

"Wear them," she said. "They'll help you look the part."

I did as I was told, and once I'd put the clothes on I was aware that I probably didn't look too bad, if not especially like myself. It was certainly a new experience to have a woman buying clothes for me, and one I rather liked. Caroline had never cared what I wore.

"You knew my size."

"I guessed. One of my many skills." She scrutinized me with something like fondness. "You look good," she said. "All dressed up with somewhere to go."

"Yes?"

"Come on, Henry, I'm taking you to a party."

The party was in a sixties house, longish, lowish, flat-roofed, a lot of floor-to-ceiling glass, some exotic flowering bushes rearing up against the walls. Inside there were polished wood floors, blinds, built-in furniture. The party was well under way.

One of the things I hate about Hollywood parties as depicted in the movies is the way that all the guests always look so entirely Hollywood. Obviously the major guests will be played by major stars, so of course they have to look unnaturally good, and I accept that. But the background guests, the extras, they always look unnaturally good too. They're played by young aspiring actors, or even models, and especially if it's a certain sort of movie (I find myself thinking of Blake Edwards), one or two of the girls will be dancing topless before very long, then diving into the swimming pool.

You don't have to be a believer in gritty social realism to realize that even in Hollywood there must be plenty of ordinary, lumpy, none too glamorous people at parties. This proved to be the case here. One or two were conspicuously good-looking, one or two were rather fancily kitted out, but there were plenty of ordinary-looking civilians there too. Frankly, thanks to Barbara's dressing of me, I was one of the more stylish people there. If you'd looked around the room and spotted the well-dressed Englishman in the gray linen suit, you might well have assumed he was something of a player. This thought pleased me no end.

Barbara didn't seem to know any more people at the party than I did. She went and said hello to someone who looked like he must be the host, and he was friendly enough toward her, but I got the impression that they didn't know each other at all. I felt that Barbara and I were gate-crashers, and this didn't really look like a party worth crashing.

"So what do you think, Henry?" she said.

Thinking she was asking me how I was enjoying the party, I said, not wholly truthfully, "Oh, it's fine. But who are these people?"

She shrugged grandly. "I don't know. Hollywood riffraff, I guess."

"Who do you know here?"

"Nobody."

"Then why are we here?" And then I realized she wasn't asking me what I thought about the party but how I liked the house.

"Because," she said, "I happen to know that the guy who owns this place is, as we say, motivated to sell, but he's dithering. He hasn't signed up with a Realtor yet. If we made a preemptive move and you came in with a not-bad offer, we could close the circle and make everybody happy. So what do you think, Henry?"

I said, "Well, it's rather hard to look at a house while there's a party going on in it."

"Not at all, Henry. This way you can see it in action. You can poke in a few corners, use the bathroom, whatever. You go take a look around while I get us a drink."

I suppose I was faintly annoyed. I thought Barbara had brought me to the party for, I don't know what you'd call it, social reasons? I'd been naive enough to think we were on a date, but it turned out it was just business. That seemed vaguely dishonest of her, not that I was in a position to castigate Barbara for dishonesty. But it did make me wonder if the sex and the new suit were just business too.

It might have been a good time for me to come clean, but I continued to play my part. I inspected the kitchen, the living room, the bathroom; they were all fine, and they would never have anything to do with me. I stepped out onto the patio, from where I could see the swimming pool. As yet there were no topless revelers in it.

Along the edge of the pool were three lounge chairs, only one of which was in use. A girl was on it, sleeping or drunk or comatose. She was a pretty girl, skinny, large-breasted, wearing rather few clothes, a short red skirt and a top, and both had been pulled out of shape. She looked very vulnerable, and I don't think it was only fatherly instinct that made me think someone should throw a coat or blanket over her, do something to preserve her modesty.

I suppose I might have done it myself but I saw a man walking along the patio toward her. All right, I thought, somebody else has had the same idea, my responsibility is ended. And when he got to her the man did indeed start adjusting her clothes, but instead of covering her up he exposed her even more, lifted the skirt to reveal skimpy white knickers, which he deftly (*deftly* was definitely the word) removed. Then he unbelted his trousers and lowered them a little, just enough, and then he started having sex with the girl, who continued not to stir.

Barbara came out carrying two drinks and briefly watched me watching. She said, "Is voyeurism another of your endearing traits, Henry?"

"No," I said, "really not," but I knew I was continuing to stare. "That girl's unconscious. This is a rape that we're watching."

"Rape can be a tough thing to define," said Barbara.

I didn't think so. "We should do something," I said.

"She comes to a party. She gets totally bagged. She allows herself to pass out. What did she expect would happen?"

"Perhaps she thought some decent people would look out for her."

"No. In L.A. she'd never have thought that."

I knew I had to do something and I was a little disappointed that Barbara didn't feel the same way. It would have been easier for two people to intervene, especially if one of them was a woman.

"Besides," Barbara said, "he *is* a fairly well known movie actor."

And she said his name, one that a lot of people would recognize, and yes, once I'd been told, I realized that it was indeed him. He looked rather different from this angle but it was him all right. And that only made it worse as far as I could see.

I grabbed Barbara by the hand and set off toward the lounge chair. She wasn't eager to come with me but she didn't resist. We were about halfway there when I saw that the girl was waking up. Her eyes opened and registered alarm. But a second later she didn't seem so alarmed at all. She looked at the man who was on top of her and recognized him just as I had. This coincided more or less with the man having his orgasm—a small, matter-of-fact occurrence, it appeared—and then he quickly stood and zipped himself up. He remained there gently preening and he gave the girl a smile. He thought he was quite the little devil. And then I saw that the girl was smiling too and she patted him on the leg and said, "OK, thanks, Jack," and he left her, and she sat up and began pulling herself together, and I was left feeling morally adrift.

"I wish I hadn't seen that," I said.

"What? Out of sight, out of mind?"

"I mean I wish it hadn't happened."

"Well, if you're to start being ethical you won't last five minutes in this town. Even if you are a doctor."

"Look," I said, "you know I have a daughter."

"Do I know that?"

"Maybe I didn't mention it," I said, though I knew perfectly well that I had. "That girl there reminded me of her."

"You mean she's a drunken slut?"

"I mean she's about that age and she's an aspiring actress."

"I'm sorry to hear that, Henry."

"And I'd hate her to be in a position like that girl."

"That girl *chose* to be in that position. And yeah, it was a bad choice. Deciding to be an actress is just about the worst choice a young woman can make."

"Perhaps you should tell that to my daughter."

"Why would she listen?"

"Well, you used to be an actress, didn't you?"

She looked at me as though I'd accused her of being a former Nazi. "How d'you know that?" she said. "Have you been sneaking around? Have you been checking up on me?"

"No, no, I recognized you." It was more or less true but she didn't seem to believe it.

"Which movie did you recognize me from?"

"*Suicide Planet,*" I said. It was the only title I could remember offhand.

She shuddered as though I'd reminded her of some humiliating faux pas she'd spent years trying to forget. "Here's a piece of advice for your daughter, Henry: if she wants to get on in Hollywood she'd better learn to give a very good blowjob."

I was rather taken aback. I thought about our time in bed together earlier that day. Undoubtedly Barbara Scott did give a very good blowjob. I now wondered how she'd perfected her skills. Our conversation got a bit sparse after that.

I was glad to see that the rumors about L.A. being an early to bed town were true. Barbara and I left the party, said our rather chilly goodbyes, and I drove back to the hotel. I wasn't precisely sure what had happened between us. Had we fallen out? What was so wrong with my knowing that she'd once been an actress?

At the hotel I had rather less time to ponder this, since I found Dorothy impatiently waiting for me, looking distraught once again.

"Bad day?" I said.

"Yes," she hissed.

"Your phone calls didn't come to anything?"

She tossed me a little magazine she'd been using. It listed talent agencies and casting directors and told you which films and TV shows were in production or preparation. Dorothy had circled and underscored many lines of print, although the meaning of each one was identical. Every agency offered the same stern command. "Absolutely no phone calls or visits." "Phone calls, faxes, and tapes not welcome." "No drop-ins." The best of them said, "Accepts photos/resumes by mail only." That seemed touchingly old-fashioned.

"Well, you could send them your photograph," I said.

"Look at me," she said. "Look at this fucking haircut. I don't even look like my photographs anymore."

"We'll get some new photographs," I said, a perfectly easy thing to do in Los Angeles, surely, but Dorothy was not consoled.

"There's only one person in the whole of L.A. who has any respect for me," she said.

"And he's right here beside you," I said.

"I meant Bob Samuelson," she said. "And he's been fired."

"Well, let's track him down then," I said. "He must still have plenty of contacts."

"I tried. He's not in the book, and the agency won't give me his home or cell phone number."

"I'll get his number for you," I said.

"If they won't give it to me, why would they give it to you?"

"I'll go there and get it," I said. "I'll find a way. It's the least a father can do."

sixteen Tonite Let's All Make Love in London

So, less than a week later I'd maxed out my credit card and I was in London, the swinging city where apparently I (or some early version of me) had lived and breathed and wandered into a murder scene about three hundred and fifty years ago, and boy, was that a mistake! Basically London was just "the horror," like I said to Henry on the plane when I was being a basket case.

Fact is, I couldn't really have told you why I was going there. Was it research for my movie? Well sure, I guess, but it also seemed to have gone way beyond research. So was I going there in order to scare myself some more? Like as if I'd seen the trailer for the horror movie and almost wet my pants and now I had to go back and prove that I was tough enough to sit through the thing itself? Maybe. Or was it to engage in some abysmal psychological quest, to investigate the mysteries of life and death, past and present, to penetrate to the heart of my own personal darkness? Yeah, you bet, though I'd never have said anything nearly as pretentious as that. And when the English immigration guy at Heathrow Airport asked me my "purpose of visit" I just said tourism because he sure didn't look like the kind of guy who'd want to hear about psychological quests and hearts of darkness.

London was just the way I'd always imagined it: gray, cold, rain kind of hanging in the air. The people looked very white, very vicious, and underfed, and the streets looked too narrow for the cars, which looked too small to be real cars. You wouldn't have wanted to make a movie there.

I'd booked myself into a crummy, way overpriced hotel that might have appealed to a serious history buff because my room told me a whole lot about the people who'd stayed there before me. They were a messy bunch, and I learned way more than I wanted to know about their personal habits, what cigarettes they smoked, what gum they chewed, what color their pubic hair was.

Needless to say, the tourist guides didn't list Alsatia as one of London's must-see attractions, but obviously I knew where it was, where it had been, and off I went to explore. I got there, wandered through the area, looked around, and of course it was basically a big, big disappointment. For one thing it was way smaller on the ground than it had looked on the map. You could have seen all there was to see of it in about ten minutes. And what was there was way less interesting than I'd been expecting. The streets were just streets. In some of them there were multinational coffee bars, like I could've been in Seattle for Christ's sake. And the buildings were just buildings; some of them were good and old, but some of them looked like they'd been built last week, and every one of them had security cameras clamped all over the outside just like any other office building. And OK, some of it was a little bit quaint: I came across a place called the Protestant Truth Society. There were some squares and courtyards that had picturesque potential, but they were full of law offices and there were all these young guys in pinstripe suits like they should have been going to some fancy expense-account restaurant, but there they were sitting on benches, eating their sad little English sandwiches.

I took a few photographs but my heart wasn't in it. Nothing

about Alsatia was any less gray and cold than the rest of London. The streets had no magic. There was nothing there that corresponded in any way to what I'd experienced in my regression. Where were the cobblestones and the overhanging eaves, the hunchbacks and the ostlers, the quacks and the serving wenches and the fencing masters? Where was the threat, the darkness, the promise and stench of death? Just in my imagination?

This whole English escapade was looking like a complete bust, a very expensive waste of time, the kind of thing some rich idiot L.A. movie guy would do. And I was not rich. I felt like your basic dumb American, one of those tourists who go in search of authenticity and then get all disappointed because the real thing isn't nearly as cool as the version they saw in the movie. I felt I'd been cheated, but I'd cheated myself.

I'd been hanging around the area most of the day, getting depressed and gloomy, and suddenly the jet lag hit me and I'd had it. I felt crazed and tearful and hot, like my skin didn't fit me anymore. I needed to sit down and I needed something to eat. English food—don't get me started. I found a pub. It was on the corner of a nice little square, which was picturesque again, very English and old-looking, even if most of it was being used as a parking lot for BMWs.

I went into the pub and I kind of knew what to expect; a friend of mine had taken me to some fake English "tavern" in Santa Monica—not as fake as all that, apparently, because this place looked pretty much the same. I ordered a beer and a plate of curry (just like a native), but the place was packed, and I thought people were probably looking at me, so once I'd got my food I went to sit outside in the cold on a wooden bench at a table pressed up against the parked cars. I felt just terrible. The beer was warm and tasted like medicine. The curry didn't taste like anything at all. The only slight consolation was that I was too out of it to start feeling sorry for myself.

I'd been there for ten minutes when a man and a woman came along and asked if they could share my table. I figured this was a quaint local custom so I didn't say no, though I wanted to. They were English, and they didn't look like tourists, but they didn't look like they worked hard for a living either.

The man was, I don't know, late thirties. He was heavy and thin-haired, bearded, bookish, a bit tweedy and frayed, a very American idea of what English men are supposed to look like. He might have been a teacher at a fancy school or an antique dealer or something. He didn't match with the woman at all.

There was nothing tweedy or bookish about her. She was a lot younger than him and looked as though she was dressed up for a wedding, the kind where everybody gets drunk and starts fighting, and she wasn't wearing enough clothes for the climate. She had on a floaty, flowery dress, black seamed stockings, and chunky high heels, and she had a lot of overarranged blond hair and oxblood lips, and her nails were too long and painted metallic blue. I mean what can I tell you, I know these things are culturally specific but basically she looked like your average young slut.

You know how it is, you can always tell when somebody wants to talk to you. You can feel them working up the energy to say something. Not that these people had any lack of energy, or at least *he* didn't. He was the one who did all the talking. Wasn't it a miserable day? It had been a rotten summer, hadn't it? Did I come here often? Where was I from? What did I do for a living? What was I doing here?

This wasn't what you're told to expect from the English. Weren't they supposed to be cold and reserved? In fact I was the one who held back. I didn't tell them why I was there any more than I had the immigration guy. I stuck with the tourist story. I said I was a pool cleaner on vacation.

"You're rather off the beaten tourist track, aren't you?" he said.

"Yeah well," I said. "I thought the changing of the guards was getting old."

"Very wise," he said, "very wise. And how is the old country treating you?"

"I haven't been here long enough to know," I said. "Right now I'm feeling kind of deranged." Was I imagining it or did their eyes light up?

"Oh," he said, "a London virgin. We'd be happy to further your education."

What was I supposed to say? That I wasn't a virgin? That I didn't want my education furthered?

"Oh, you'll find plenty of anti-American prejudice in London, I'm afraid," he said. "A mixture of envy, ignorance, imperial ambivalence, and memories of the Second World War. On the other hand some of us are doing our best to make up for it. Some of us are distinctly Americophile. Here, what are you drinking?"

I was only about halfway through my first beer and I didn't think I wanted another, but he insisted, and he also said I'd made a bad choice of beer (which I was happy to believe) and that I should have some of the "local brew." I said OK.

While he was at the bar, the woman, who still hadn't said a word so far, opened up her purse and worked hard at her makeup, and when she was finished and satisfied, she gave me a smile that was so friendly it scared the hell out of me. In order to have something to do I messed around with my camera, and I was still doing that when the guy came back from the bar.

"That's a very swanky-looking camera you've got there," he said.

"Yeah, it's pretty good."

"Well, that opens up all sorts of possibilities, doesn't it?"

"Yeah?"

"I'd say so."

We swapped names. He was Brian. She was Angela. He was a "writer." He actually said it like that, in quotation marks. She was a legal secretary.

"Though sometimes she's positively *illegal*," Brian said, and he laughed more than you'd think anyone could have at such a lame joke.

I didn't bother to ask what kind of writer he was. From looking at him I thought I could guess—one of the failed variety: too literary, too wordy, too out of touch.

"This area we're in was once known as Alsatia," he said, "after Alsace in France . . ."

And then he told me more or less what I already knew, but I didn't feel I could say, "Yeah, yeah, yeah," because obviously it was pretty unlikely that the average tourist would know this stuff. I guess I did find it a little surprising that he should be telling me at all, but not as surprising as all that. He was a writer; writers, even failed ones, have a habit of knowing stuff, especially about their own neighborhood, and Brian kept talking about the "lovely little townhouse" round the corner where he and Angela lived. I knew that sooner or later he'd suggest that we go back there, and he did. He said they had some good port and Stilton. I felt like I'd walked into a Dickens adaptation.

"Angela isn't the kind of woman who cooks," he said, "though she has many other talents."

I already knew this was going to end in some kind of weirdness, but hell, hadn't I come to England in search of weirdness? The house was no distance away, still within the boundaries of what would have been Alsatia, and it was a strange place, unwelcoming, lots of cramped little rooms all elbowing one another.

There were a lot of books, a lot of dusty drapes and heavy furniture, lots of old maps and prints on the walls, a lot of smells: bodies, old perfume, mildew.

Brian got out the port and Stilton. He ran around doing things, getting glasses, turning on lamps, putting some general-purpose classical music on the stereo. Angela sat in a chair by the cold, empty fireplace doing nothing except trying to act the part of a cool, detached beauty.

"So you, like, know about history," I said.

"It's one of my passions," Brian said.

"Have there ever been any famous murders in the vicinity?"

"What a curious question," he said, and he looked at me conspiratorially, as though I might be planning one and he kind of liked the idea.

"I'm just, you know, interested," I said. "Like in L.A. they have death tours where they drive you round in a hearse to see where movie stars died."

"How quaint," he said. "Well, stop me if I begin to bore you, but Alsatia, naturally, was the site of all manner of historical transgressions—"

"Let's not talk about murders, eh, Brian?" Angela said.

Brian looked like a guy who in general wouldn't have appreciated being interrupted, much less told to shut up, which was what her line amounted to, but he just nodded in agreement, as though she'd caught him indulging a bad habit. And maybe it was also a signal between them. Angela put down her drink and came over to me and started massaging my shoulders.

"Oh yes, I can feel a lot of tension there," she said, and she was damn right.

Brian watched her, and he watched my reactions even more closely. I had a feeling I knew what was coming next, and I wasn't too surprised when Angela lowered her face to mine and kissed me. It was a big, wet French kiss that tasted of port and Stilton and a few other unidentifiable things.

Brian was really liking what he saw. The young, good-looking blond stranger was messing with his wife (or whatever she was) while he watched. It seemed a lame old fantasy in some ways, but I have to tell you I was kind of into it. Sometimes it's good to embrace the weirdness of other people's lame fantasies. And Angela was a really good kisser. I mean, taken as an overall package, she wasn't that attractive, but I think men are often way too critical of women. They watch movies and they complain that Audrey Hepburn's too thin, Gwyneth Paltrow's too bland, Kathleen Turner's too lantern-jawed, but in the real world we're turned on enough by someone like Angela who's a good kisser. And available.

Just to be sure I was following the plot properly I said, "You two have like an understanding, right?"

"Oh, we do," said Brian, "we most certainly do." And then Angela's hands were all over me and Brian said, "Shall we all go up to the bedroom?"

I hesitated for a second. "Well, you know, I *am* straight," I said.

"That's fine," said Brian. "So am I. Bring your camera."

The stairs were narrow and dark and the carpet was frayed. Angela led the way and I followed, with Brian directly behind me. I already felt like something in a sandwich. As we got to the top of the stairs I saw a framed print on the wall. It showed a dodo, sitting all alone on a little islet, surrounded by vast expanses of ocean, looking totally forlorn. The print was very old, maybe even seventeenth-century. It seemed a hell of a coincidence to find it there, but by now I was getting used to coincidences.

"That's a cool picture," I said.

"Oh, don't get him started on the dodo," Angela said. "We'll be here all night."

"It *is* one of my pet obsessions," Brian said, and he looked like he might be about to give me a lecture, which I wouldn't have minded, but then he decided he was hotter to get into the bedroom.

So one way or another I had sex with Angela and Brian, and it was really OK. It wasn't *great*. It wasn't going to be one of the great erotic highlights of my life, and there was a moment when I thought, did I really come to England for *this?* But on balance it was OK.

Brian had a pretty broad definition of what counted as "straight." He rubbed my back, which I couldn't really complain about, since I was mounting Angela at the time, and when he started stroking my balls I did think about asking him to stop, but by then it would have seemed kind of redundant, so I didn't. And between us we took a lot of photographs. We passed my camera back and forth, and sometimes set it to automatic, and snapped away like crazy, over and over again. I felt just a little uncomfortable with that but in the end I thought, what the hell, everybody needs holiday photographs.

Once I'd done what I'd been brought there for, Brian said, "I wonder if you'd excuse us," which was his way of telling me to vacate the bedroom while the two of them got on with some private business of their own. Go figure.

"Help yourself to more port downstairs," he said.

So I picked up my clothes and camera and left the bedroom. The door closed behind me and I could hear giggling coming from behind it. I guess the smart thing would have been to get the hell out of there and go back to my hotel, but I wasn't feeling smart, and maybe I was also feeling that I wanted something more out of this thing.

I got dressed on the landing in front of the dodo print, and I'm ashamed to admit that I seriously thought about stealing it. It would have made a neat souvenir. But I didn't take it, not because I was afraid of being thought of as a thief, more because I was afraid of being thought of as a prostitute.

So I went downstairs, and yeah, I thought I was owed a little something, another drink at the very least, but when I got down to the hallway I saw a door leading into a room that was obviously Brian's office. There was a desk with a big, out-of-date computer on it, and all around the walls were books and more framed prints: old medical illustrations and scenes of old London, as well as a couple more dodo prints. This was getting interesting.

It was occurring to me that maybe I could use Brian as an unpaid consultant for my movie. I thought he probably knew way more about Alsatia and the dodo than I did. Once he'd finished upstairs with Angela I'd ask him some questions, maybe we'd do some brainstorming.

I sat in his chair at the desk and waited, but that got boring real soon, so I started going through the drawers. There was nothing much of interest until I got to the bottom left and found a manuscript with the title page *The Restoration of the Dodo* by Brian Braithwaite; until then I hadn't even known the guy's last name. I took it out and looked at it, discovered it was a novel, or at least part of one, and started to read it.

William Draper walks through the stew and babble of London's Alsatia: a place named after a war zone, the quarter for squatters, criminals, cutters of purses and throats, for whores of various hues, for fencing masters, for writers and artists (the less pecunious sort). Above all, Alsatia is the place for mountebanks, for those who profess an arcane knowledge of physic and surgery, for charlatan alchemists, for the hawkers of astrological tracts and prophetical almanacs: a home to all manner of natural philosophers and Empericks, of seventh sons and circulators, in a word—quacks.

This was seriously weird, seriously creepy, and it felt like something more than just coincidence. And another thought crossed my mind: was Brian going to be competition for me? Did the world need two guys working on two different dodo projects? In the interests of research I thought I'd better find out what Brian had written. I also figured that this manuscript would do fine as my souvenir. I grabbed it and ran off into the night.

seventeen The Secret of My Success

William Draper makes a brief visit to his father's house in Holborn, where he is admitted by Barnes, his father's right-hand man. William has with him all the relics of his university days—his books, his instruments, his caged dodo—and he secretes them all in a shed in a dim corner of the rear courtyard, where he knows his father will never stoop to go.

He expects his father to be enraged at this enforced departure from the university. For all the injustice, for all William's self-perceived innocence, he expects his father will consider him the wrongdoer, hold him culpable for his own humiliating expulsion. He fears that even the scars on his body and face will be insufficient to assuage his father's wrath.

And true enough, when William first encounters his father in the study of the house, where the old man sits transfixed at his desk examining some paper samples from a Kentish supplier, the condition of William's skin—blatantly visible as it seems to William himself—goes quite unremarked. He knows better than to expect sympathy from his father, and he also knows better than to prevaricate. So without hesitation, though with considerable trepidation, he tells his father that he has been sent down from Oxford, and he is about to launch into a defense of himself, an explication of the whys and wherefores and how wronged he is by the university, by Dr. Clayton, by—if you will—fate. But his father's manner, against all anticipation, suggests that explanations will not be required.

"I am sure it is for the best," his father says.

William thinks perhaps the old man may be too preoccupied with the samples before him to have heard properly or that he's losing his hearing or has fallen into a sudden senility. There's little else that would explain such equanimity.

"Yes," his father adds, sounding positively philosophical now, and not remotely like himself, "we should trust that everything that happens is for the best. To believe that we control our destinies is the worst of folly and vanity. We must accept the divine plan and so forth."

William had thought he would be able to deflect some of his father's expected anger by stating that he was to become an agent of the Royal College of Physicians. He is much taken with that word *agent*. But now that, in the face of his father's fatalism, such pacification is unnecessary, the news falls rather flat. Flatter still, since his father shows no evidence that he is surprised or intrigued or even interested. He greets the news of his son's changed destiny with a benign and sluggish nod. One might almost think he was relieved. He wishes William well in his new venture and says, unconvincingly, that he will have his full support.

William had hoped that this support might have a financial component to it. At the very least he thinks a good father might agree to give him an allowance that is equal to the sum no longer being spent on his education. But nothing is offered and William knows better than to ask. And it occurs to him that money may be at the root of his father's apparent indifference. Perhaps he is too anxious about his own fate, his business, some anticipated losses, to have any anxiety regarding his son. Still, it is not a matter on which William can interrogate him. If the father shows no concern for his son, it scarcely behooves the son to fret about his father.

"You have accommodation?" his father asks.

Again it does not sound as though the question is rooted in any great concern for his son's welfare, but William is glad that his father accepts the impossibility of their living under the same roof. In any case, the answer is yes. Dr. Lloyd, William's contact at the Royal College, has arranged, or at least caused to be arranged, some lodgings for him in Alsatia.

"I am sure you will find it a most wonderfully colorful and entertaining place," his father says.

As a matter of fact this is precisely how William feels too, but he can't suppress the childish desire that his father should demonstrate a little more concern and trepidation on his behalf.

"London is a great lifter of the spirits," says William.

And yet establishing himself in Alsatia has quite the reverse effect upon him. He would not say that his lodgings are a disappointment, since his experience in Oxford has already taught him to put aside high expectations; nevertheless, his new home depresses him profoundly. It consists of a single, stark room, up in the eaves of a house that looks too precarious to stand. At ground level there is a print shop, and between that and William's quarters are many rooms filled by the printer, his wife, and their tumultuous family. They are not hospitable. They find William an inconvenience and would much prefer that he were not there, or rather they would prefer that they did not need his money. But alas they do, and it is not every lodging that will countenance the presence of an exotic creature such as William's dodo.

The printer's family is vast and protean and clamorous. Of

course, William never thought Alsatia would be a quiet place, yet he is amazed by the noise from this family of, is it eight or ten children, he cannot keep track, and there seems to be a fluid number of aunts and cousins who flow through the house, sometimes staying the night, sometimes longer. And they seem intent on making all the sounds, if not the actions, that would accompany a murder. Such muffled cooing as William's dodo makes passes quite unnoticed. William tells himself to be cheerful. He tells himself that this is only a temporary arrangement. London is a city of opportunities, of many accommodations. He thinks he will soon be moving on.

He also thinks, at first, that he will be out of place here in Alsatia, that his youth and naivety will set him apart, make him an easy mark, and for a time he walks the villainous streets accompanied by a certain collared timidity. Yet he is not molested, nor robbed, nor even stared at. Largely he is ignored, and he can scarcely believe how much that pleases him.

There is an alehouse situated not twenty yards from his lodgings, and the first time he goes there it is in search of food, rather than drink. The aroma of mutton stew draws him in, but naturally he orders a mug of ale to go with it. He had thought he would quickly feed himself and then scurry back to his own room, his books, and his dodo. But once the first pint of ale is inside him, he feels content to stay a while longer, to drink another couple of pints. The warmth and darkness of the tavern is sustaining, and besides there is plenty to look at, lots of life to observe. Humanity here is not perhaps in its most perfected form—there are visages here that make his own much-maligned face look positively cherubic—but that makes them all the more fascinating. They bring out the scientist in him. He wonders what can be read in these faces, what bodily conditions, what arrangement of humors. He also wishes that perhaps he was something of an artist and might record some of these faces by sketching.

He gets to bed late, and he is not quite sure by what method, but come the morning he's awakened by the printer's eldest daughter, who is holding a letter for him. He is certain that she cannot read, yet the seal of the Royal College of Physicians communicates itself to her eloquently enough. The missive is from Dr. Lloyd, outlining William's first task. He reads his orders, washes, dresses, feeds his dodo, then hastens to an inn called the Golden Fleece, where he is to seek one Dr. Hartshorn, a man with dubious Dutch connections, begetter of Hartshorn's Omnium Oil, a substance that the Royal College views with the utmost suspicion.

William's mission sounds simple enough: talk to the doctor, if doctor he be, get him to describe the qualities and powers of the oil he is peddling, induce him to make grand medical claims for it so that he condemns himself out of his own mouth. Then William is to make a purchase of the stuff and take it away for inspection and analysis, so that if necessary—and Dr. Lloyd is sure it *will* be necessary—there will be evidence against the man when the church court prosecutes him.

William considers what subterfuges he might employ, but in the event his task is made easy, laughably so, by the man himself. Dr. Hartshorn has erected a makeshift stall outside the door of the inn, and above it is a banner proclaiming Omnium Oil for Everyone. And Hartshorn stands before it, a rotund, hot-faced fellow in a dense brown suit, and he has something of the preacher about him, although for now he stands silently, and unlike so many quacks, he makes no crowd-pleasing speeches.

There are a few moochers standing about, in expectation of

something or other, hoping that Dr. Hartshorn will put on some sort of a show, but Hartshorn seems to be waiting too, so William also waits, joins in the general lingering, until he can stand it no longer.

"Dr. Hartshorn," he says, "I wonder if you would take a look at my face."

"I saw it plainly enough from a distance. A closer inspection will not be necessary, I think." The voice has the clip of the Low Countries, and the manner is dismissive, if also self-protective.

"Then can you say what ails me?" William asks.

"No, sir, and it matters not. Whether the cause is in the blood or in the constitution or in the stars, Hartshorn's Omnium Oil will surely right the problem."

"Really, sir?"

"I said so, did I not? It clears the head, dispels the stone, disperses agues, banishes all distempers whether common or particular. In fact it is my firm belief that this oil will cure diseases that have not yet even been suffered, that God has not yet seen fit to inflict on his creation. So why would it not cure you?"

"Indeed," William says, and he would have to admit to being impressed by Hartshorn's rhetoric. "Then I should certainly like to buy some. But tell me, what are the ingredients in this marvelous stuff?"

"Only the most costly, precious, and natural ingredients. All rightly prepared."

"Prepared how?"

"With skill and science."

"But . . ."

"You would not expect me to share all my secrets with you on so limited an acquaintance. Besides, the layman would scarcely have the knowledge to comprehend such matters."

"And is it to be applied internally or externally?"

"Either," Hartshorn says.

"Does it contain mercury, for instance?"

"It may."

"You do not know?"

"Of course I know, but why would I reveal such knowledge to you?"

"To put my mind at ease perhaps."

"Your mind is your own affair."

"I do not think it unreasonable that a man should know what he is buying before he parts with his money."

"Sir, it is your own decision. If you so choose, you may keep your money and your disease. In fact now that I think of it, my oil might be too refined a substance for you."

And so William finds himself pleading with Hartshorn to get him to sell a bottle of his very, very expensive oil, a substance that at best may be useless, at worst malign. William sees that there is more art in being a quack than many might suspect. But at last, as was no doubt inevitable, Hartshorn does indeed condescend to make a sale. William pays over money, which he hopes the Royal College will be swift to reimburse, and takes away a small bottle.

He finds a quiet corner and opens it up. It has no great smell, perhaps just a hint of parsley. It looks thin and a little cloudy, and as for whether it contains mercury, his instinct is that Hartshorn would not go to such expense. He tastes it and it seems weak, innocuous stuff, yet he can't quite forbear to take a smear of the liquid on his fingertips and gently work it into the skin of his scarred cheeks, hoping for what? The best?

As per his instructions, William reports to Dr. Lloyd's chambers at the Royal College of Physicians and after a long wait is shown in. He hands over the small bottle of oil, and the doctor weighs it in his hand as though it were a pebble picked up from the beach. He seems more interested in William than in the oil.

"Your impressions of our Dr. Hartshorn?" he asks.

"A sham, but a somewhat clever one. A rogue but not a blackguard."

"On what basis do you make the distinction?"

"I think the bottle contains nothing more than oil infused with some herbs: a very expensive medium for the frying of eggs."

"No mercury, no lead? No other toxins?"

"I cannot be certain, of course, but my instinct tells me that Hartshorn wishes to fleece his clients, not poison them."

"And if you are correct, how would you deal with him? The courts? Jail? A good whipping?"

"A very small whipping perhaps. Or an arse kicking. And let us smash all his foolish little bottles and tell him not to show his face in these parts for a good long time."

Dr. Lloyd smiles but William does not dare smile back. He is afraid he may be the source of amusement.

"I see you are a pragmatist rather than an idealist, Mr. Draper. Be careful you do not turn into a cynic. You are much too young for that."

"I shall do my very best, sir."

"And how is your accommodation in Alsatia?"

"Modest."

"Still, I expect you will not be spending much time there. The whole of London beckons."

"Yes, sir."

"You should take yourself to Lambeth, to the Ark."

"The Ark, sir?

"It is a pleasure ground of sorts, also a kind of museum, a

world of curiosities, set up by the senior John Tradescant, now inherited by his son. Their Ark is a place of many wonders, of art and science. Why they even have such a thing as a dodo." The doctor looks smug. He thinks that William will never have heard the word *dodo*, and he will take great, complacent delight in demonstrating the extent of his superior knowledge.

"I know very well what a dodo is," William says. "I know all about the dodo."

eighteen Scream

Here's another thing you might hate about the movies: the fact that the central character always has to be what movie people call "proactive." He has to go out and *do* things; he can't simply sit still and have them done to him. It's not enough for things to happen around him; he has to be the one who makes them happen.

I can see how this is good for movies but it seems to me that this is almost the exact opposite of the way most of us conduct our lives. Certainly you'd *like* to be in charge of your own fate, but no sensible person ever really thinks he is. Most of us try to hang on, endure and survive, sit tight and do nothing, hope the sky doesn't fall on us, and only when it inevitably does do we run around performing crisis management and damage limitation exercises. I suppose this isn't terribly filmic.

A detective is the ideal proactive hero. He knocks on doors, he does things, he seeks things out. And in truth I did feel like something of a dick as I went up in the lift to the Caswell Agency to extract Bob Samuelson's home or cell phone number. I was also going to employ some creative subterfuge, which is always the stuff of movies.

I knew it would take some restraint on my part not to go in there and tell Bob Samuelson's boss that she was wrong about everything, wrong to tell my daughter she was too fat and plain

165

and yellow of teeth. There would be the temptation to tell her she knew nothing, to tell her that if she couldn't see Dorothy's entirely obvious gifts, then there was clearly something wrong with her. If I wasn't careful I might even tell her she was a damned fool to have fired Bob Samuelson, although obviously I was on shaky ground there. But for Dorothy's sake I knew I would say none of the above.

And so I presented myself at the Caswell Agency's reception area and told the spry young man behind the red lacquered desk that I was Henry Cadwallader and that I had an appointment with Bob Samuelson. It was one of the few occasions that I was glad Dorothy and I had different surnames.

"Oh dear," the receptionist said, and he rolled his eyes, which I took to mean that I wasn't the first person to have come there in search of the departed Bob. "You'll have to see Ms. Ricardo."

"Who's that?" I asked.

"Bob's boss. Former boss."

This was going quite well. Someone whom I took to be a schoolgirl, there to meet a parent perhaps, stepped into the reception area. She was small and bouncy and looked about fourteen, wearing heavy-framed spectacles, perhaps to make her look older, but they added all of three months to her apparent age. This, need I say, turned out to be Georgia Ricardo. She sat down beside me, shook my hand, and I felt as though a daffodil stem had been pressed into it.

"You had an appointment with Bob?" she said.

"Yes," I said. Then thinking I was being suitably guileful, I added, "Is he around?"

"How well did you know Bob?"

"Oh, reasonably well," I said. "At least professionally." Obviously I couldn't say he was a great pal because then I'd have known his home and cell phone number.

"I'm afraid Bob's no longer with us."

I feigned surprise.

"Bob has passed away," she said.

Now I showed real surprise. Did she really mean that he was dead, or could she possibly be using "passed away" as an elaborate corporate euphemism for fired?

"Oh God, I'm sorry about this," she said, and she burst into tears. I didn't know what on earth to do.

"This is terrible," I said, still not absolutely sure what I'd been told.

"Like I don't really blame myself," she said. "He deserved to be fired. He had substance abuse problems. He was a big drunk. A big, lovable, good-looking drunk. But a drunk. And he was having problems with his wife and having to sell his house. But then he had to go and die."

So, no euphemism after all. "That's genuinely awful," I said.

"It happened in his own house. He was on a bender. He fell, hit his head, died in a pool of Bud and vomit. We're trying real hard to keep it out of the media."

"I see, well . . ."

There was no longer any need to procure his phone number. I wanted to get out of there, but Georgia Ricardo had more that she wanted to unload.

"And frankly, Bob had lost his touch. You wouldn't believe some of the losers he'd wanted the agency to take on recently. *You* on the other hand . . ." She was giving me the once-over, moving her head around so as to view my face from different angles. "Yours is a face we might be able to do something with."

For a moment I felt as if I were being considered as a suitable case for plastic surgery, possibly even taxidermy. Georgia Ricardo was saying a number of things but I really wasn't listening. I was, inevitably, wondering what were the chances that the man

I'd knocked to the floor in his own house in the Hollywood foothills was actually Bob Samuelson? Small, surely, I told myself. And even if by some bizarre chance he was, what were the odds that the fall I initiated was the one that killed him? Even smaller, if you wanted my medical opinion. He'd been looking just fine when I left. And if he was the serious drunk that Georgia Ricardo was describing, he could certainly have fallen down again without any help from me. Nevertheless, I still had a movie-inspired vision of some idle, corrupt cop putting two and two together and making me a murderer. This being a possibility (however remote), I thought it best to get out of the Caswell Agency very quickly. I also felt the urgent need to talk to Barbara. And, of course, I would have to break the bad news to Dorothy.

"Would you like to step into my office?" Georgia Ricardo said.

"No, really, I think I should go, I'm really thrown by this. Poor Bob."

"We're all thrown but life has to go on. Come into my office. That's what Bob would have wanted."

I hesitated a moment too long and Georgia Ricardo swept me off into her office. She sat at her desk beneath a poster for *Metropolis* and said, "You really do have a face, you know."

"Well, yes."

"It's expressive, it's fresh, it's likable but there's some pain there. Do you think you could read something for me?"

"I really don't think so," I said, "in the circumstances. Bob dying and all that."

Georgia Ricardo transformed herself, became durable and fierce, and she said in a loud stage whisper that could probably be heard outside the office, "Do you know how many people in this town would kill for the chance to read for this agency?" I shook my head, she softened and said, "I see you as being able to play the innocent slob, but then you could also play the innocent slob who turns out to be the murderer. Please read for me, Henry. If you won't do it for me, then do it for Bob."

I thought I was about to scream. I was handed a movie script open at a page of dialogue between a villain (my part) and the leading actress, to be read by Georgia. My character's Englishness wasn't specified in the script but was no doubt in keeping with Hollywood views of the perfidiousness of the English. He had done, or was about to do, something unspeakable to the other character's children.

I made my reading as perfunctory as possible, a performance that I felt sure would guarantee my swift departure from the premises. However, when we got to the end, Georgia Ricardo said, "Nicely underplayed," and then she rooted around in her desk, got out a yellow legal pad and some official-looking forms as though she was about to sign me up there and then. It was time to call a halt.

"So tell me a little about yourself," Georgia Ricardo said. "What have you done?"

"Studied medicine at Oxford," I said. "I did my clinical work at Guy's and then—"

"I mean in the business. I'm guessing a lot of stage work back in England."

"No," I said.

"TV then? English TV? I can see you in a country house murder mystery."

"No, no TV."

"Not film work I know, because I'd have seen you."

"No, not film."

"What then? Stand-up comedy? Performance art? Experimental video?"

"I'm not an actor."

"Yes, you are. If Georgia Ricardo thinks you're an actor, you're an actor, buddy."

"I don't think so."

"Then you think wrong."

"But really, I'm a doctor. A real doctor. I just came in here because . . ."

Georgia Ricardo started to laugh, and although there was nothing very spontaneous or natural about it, it was a sign that she was starting to believe me. "So why exactly did you come here?"

"I wanted to talk to Bob," I said, which was by no means a complete lie.

"About what?"

"About my daughter."

"You have a daughter? Well, bring her in too."

"She's already been in. You told her she wasn't right."

"Then I'll bet she wasn't," Georgia Ricardo said.

This would have been a hell of a good time for me to deliver my denunciation, but the need to make speeches had been entirely blown out of me.

"Actually, this is wild," Georgia said. "This is actually very cool. You walk in off the street. You have no experience. You just come in to see Bob Samuelson, the late Bob Samuelson, not for yourself but for your daughter, and you just blow us away. This is good stuff. This is showbiz legend territory."

"I have to go," I said.

"You *are* crazy. If you walk out that door you'll regret it, maybe not tomorrow . . . blah, blah, blah."

"Well, I can't think any further than tomorrow right now."

I could see she was baffled by my behavior, and I thought she might be about to shout at me, something about my never working again in this town, but then she decided on a different approach.

"It's OK," she said, "we're all acting weird since Bob died. It does you credit." She looked like she was about to cry again. "I'll tell you what," she said, and she handed me a black-edged card, an invitation of sorts. "I'll see you at the funeral. We'll talk. You're not getting away *that* easily, buster."

Once out of the Caswell Agency I immediately called Barbara, and choosing to disregard the way things had ended the previous night, I said, "I think I need to see you."

"That's very sweet of you," she said.

"That house we looked at where the chap was drunk," I said.

"You're interested now?"

"What was his name?"

"I don't remember offhand. Why?"

"Can you please check for me?"

"You're being mysterious, Henry. This is about what?"

"Probably nothing. I hope. But it's very important. So please check for me, please."

There was a long and terrible pause, as Barbara put me on hold and some vigorous Spanish music trumpeted down the line. At last the music cut out and Barbara's voice was there again and she said what a part of me knew she would say, "Samuelson."

"Oh God."

"Whassup, Henry?"

"Now, I *really* need to see you."

"Well, that's even sweeter but you're going to have to give me a clue here."

"Samuelson's dead."

"Is he? How do you know?"

"It's a long story, but apparently he died after a fall."

"Well, that's a drag as far as you buying that house goes, because—oh right, oh shit, OK, I hear you, Henry. Oh wow. I see. Do I? Meet me at the Tudor house in half an hour."

A rendezvous at the mock-Tudor house seemed unnecessarily dramatic. Why couldn't we have met at my hotel, or her office, or a Denny's restaurant? Or anywhere? Nevertheless I drove there, arriving some time after Barbara. She was already in situ, wandering through the house in an insubstantial black lace bra and knickers, an indulgence by the costume department, it seemed to me, and a terrible distraction, and a madly inappropriate bit of behavior since we were there to discuss a man's death.

Nevertheless, Barbara listened carefully enough as I told my story, and really there wasn't much to tell, and afterwards as she posed elegantly and uncomfortably in front of a vast baronial fireplace, she said, "Well, I don't think there's a court in America that would convict you. An English doctor protecting a respectable realtor against some drunken Hollywood loser—people like that don't go to jail, Henry."

"So do you think I should go to the police?"

"You really haven't grasped the nature of American justice, have you, Henry?"

"Probably not," I admitted. "Only what I've seen in the movies."

"I said they wouldn't convict. I didn't say they wouldn't arrest you, put you on trial, and ruin your life."

"Wouldn't going to the cops confirm my innocence?"

"*What* innocence?"

"What *innocence?*" Was I really going to have to defend myself to Barbara? Evidently so, and perhaps it would be good practice. "I mean, it's very unlikely that the death had anything to do with me," I said. "Samuelson was drunk and getting drunker all the time, and I didn't do more than push him—"

"Who are you trying to convince, Henry. Me or you?"

"Medically I suppose it is just about possible that he died as a result of the fall I inflicted, a blood clot perhaps, but—"

"I'm going to pretend I didn't hear that. Henry, you're forgetting one very important thing. You and me are the only ones who know you knocked him down. We're the only ones who even know you were there. As far as anybody else is concerned he was alone, he was drunk, and he fell. End of story. As long as neither of us says anything, who's going to be any the wiser?"

"It sounds so morally dubious," I said.

"And yet so sensible."

"Perhaps."

"It also sounds like you're going to have to be extra specially nice to me, Henry."

She unhooked her bra, peeled off her knickers, and I was indeed very nice to her. Having sex felt like the last thing in the world we ought to be doing, but Barbara was insistent, and she also reacted with more energy and vehemence than she ever had previously. My sudden brush with death and potential criminal culpability aroused her powerfully. This struck me as very trashy indeed. We finished up exhausted, half on the floor, half inside the hearth of the fireplace.

After we'd got dressed, and after she'd assured me that everything was going to be just fine, she put a document in my hand. For a moment I thought it must be something to do with Bob Samuelson, but it turned out to be a printed sheet containing the details of the mock-Tudor house, complete with a couple of skillfully composed photographs. I saw that the house was worth, or at least priced at, roughly four million dollars more than I could possibly afford, i.e., four million dollars. On the bottom of it she'd written instructions on how to disarm the security system. Then she also handed me a set of keys to the house.

"I think you're going to have to be very nice to me very often," she said.

On the way out to her car Barbara squatted down beside the swimming pool and urinated in it again.

❀

"I have some bad news for you," I said to Dorothy as I walked into her hotel room.

"I've got some for you too," she said, so I let her go first. "You're probably not going to believe this, but Bob Samuelson's dead. They just reported it on TV."

Don't you hate it in movies when people turn on the radio or television and immediately they hear a news bulletin concerning the very thing they want to know about? Corny, eh?

"What did they say?" I asked. "Was it an accident or murder or what?"

"Why would it be murder? You've been watching too many movies."

"Very possibly," I said.

"So," said Dorothy, "one less contact in Los Angeles. Which is to say one hundred percent less contacts in Los Angeles. And what's your bad news?"

"Exactly the same," I said. "Bob Samuelson. They told me at the agency. I even know when the funeral is."

"I suppose we have to go."

"Do we?" I could think of compelling reasons why I shouldn't be there.

"Perhaps I'll be able to do some networking," said Dorothy,

then seeing my aghast expression added, "I'm being ironic, all right?"

"About which part?"

"Not about going to the funeral. I mean, when you've slept with a guy a couple of times, you really ought to go to his funeral, don't you think?"

"You slept with Bob Samuelson?"

"Only a couple of times."

"And he didn't even give you his home or cell phone number?"

Dorothy gave a big shrug, "Welcome to *my* world, Dad."

So, I might have killed a man who'd slept with my daughter a couple of times. That was undoubtedly a new and rare experience, though surely one that a lot of fathers might have envied.

Dorothy gave one of those throaty, harsh, rather actressy laughs. Then she said, "Do you think fate's trying to tell me something?"

"Such as?"

"That I'm doomed here in L.A., that I should go home."

"No," I said. "No. There's no such thing as fate. There's only what happens. Or if you're being proactive, what you *make* happen."

Dorothy looked at me with a certain amount of surprise but also some admiration. "Are you giving me a pep talk?"

"I'm saying you shouldn't give up quite yet."

"But apart from networking at funerals, do you have any bright ideas about what I should do next?"

"Yes," I said. "We'll call Rick McCartney, auteur of the future."

nineteen Bringing Up Baby

Next morning I was on the train to Oxford. I was going there to the Museum of Natural History to see the Oxford dodo: not a real dodo exactly, but about as real as you can get. I knew there were two dodo fragments there—a beak and a foot that had come from a living creature, preserved over the centuries by dehydration. I was hoping that maybe they'd inspire me.

OK, I was grasping at straws, but these little chunks of dodo did have some history of inspiration. If you believe the story (and why wouldn't you?), Lewis Carroll—whacked-out math genius, photographic pioneer, and lover of little girls—had stood in the museum in Oxford and been inspired to write the dodo section of *Alice in Wonderland,* you know, the part where the dodo organizes a "caucus race" and they all run round in a circle, starting where they like and carrying on for an unspecified amount of time and then the dodo says, "Everyone must have prizes." I wasn't inclined to see anything too totally symbolic in this, but I did feel the need for some sort of prize, and although I could see that a lot of people might think that sex with Angela wasn't such a bad prize, for me it wasn't nearly enough.

The whole nightmare of the dark room and the murder hadn't exactly disappeared, but it was seeming way less real now that I was in England than it had back in L.A., and that was probably a real good thing. If I'd found some place in modern London, some kind of force field, some locus of energy, somewhere that felt like the very scene of the crime, well, wouldn't I have been feeling a whole lot worse than currently I was? What would I have *done* with that feeling? What would have been the *use* of it? More and more, that "remembered" event was feeling like a hallucination, some mental state I'd got myself into, *talked* myself into. It was like I'd seen a movie and thought it was the most amazing thing I'd ever seen, and then I'd watched it again on DVD and it was no good at all, it didn't even feel like the same movie.

And no doubt Carla Mendez had some pretty vital part in the process, but at this point I wasn't thinking of her as a past-life therapist anymore. Now I thought she was a crackpot hypnotist or some low-grade illusionist, or maybe more like an executive producer. She'd helped put the thing there in my head but she really had no idea what she was doing. She was unleashing stuff she knew nothing about, and that was pretty damned evil of her, but blaming her wasn't going to do me any good, not now. Was there some Institute of Past-Life Therapists I could report her to for unethical behavior and they could tear up her membership card? Seemed unlikely.

At least I had something to read on the train, Brian's opus, *The Restoration of the Dodo*. Can't say that I felt too bad about stealing it. In these days of fifty-dollar inkjet printers all those old plot devices about missing manuscripts and precious originals kind of goes out the window. And maybe you'd say I shouldn't have been going through Brian's desk in the first place, but you know, maybe he and his wife shouldn't have picked up some strange American guy and brought him back to their house for weird sex. Hell, I could have murdered them in their beds.

Can't say, either, that I was expecting much from Brian's writing. Brian just didn't look like the kind of guy who'd write the great English dodo novel. But I sat on the train, wedged in between a skinhead and an old lady reading a beekeeping magazine, and I started to read Brian's work, and oh, crap! Oh, holy crap!!

The Restoration of the Dodo is the story of a guy called William Draper who lives in seventeenth-century England, and he gets obsessed with dodos and decides he's going to fill the world with them. And as I read the first chapter, I thought, shit, Brian and me have both had the same damn idea. Not so unusual really, happens all the time in the movies. It's not about plagiarism, not even about lack of originality; maybe it's more about picking up something that's floating in the air. The zeitgeist or some shit like that. And you know, once I'd got over the immediate holy-crap factor, I thought maybe there was an upside to this. If this novel of Brian's was any good, then maybe I could find a way to option the damn thing and then at least I'd be going into pitch meetings with a "property." Then, if I got some development money, I'd do a wall-to-wall rewrite and make it my own, just like any novel that gets turned into a movie.

So then I read the second chapter and it seemed to come off the rails as far as I was concerned. The guy gets some weird skin disease, and to me that looked like a liability in a movie. OK, so there are some good-looking stars who like to play roles that involve a bit of facial deformity, to prove that they're not just pretty boys, like Mel Gibson in *The Man Without a Face* and Tom Cruise in *Vanilla Sky*, but it's still a liability.

Then in the next chapter they're trying all these insane ways to cure him, and even though I guess they were authentic, and even though they were sort of visual in a way, I couldn't really see an audience sitting through scenes where the hero has to get naked and sit in a tub of ice and get covered in gold leaf and have his whole body rubbed with stinging nettles.

But then in the fourth chapter, oh my God, the dodo hauls out the guts of the dodo keeper and then William Draper slits the guy's throat in a mercy killing; well, that was *my* scene. My fucking scene! That was the dark room I'd been in. I'd stood there, smelling the dodo shit, the blood, the death. But I read to the end of the chapter and there was no me there. No stranger appeared in the room. I felt cheated, like I'd ended up on the cutting room floor.

Now this made no fucking sense at all, right? I mean, I hadn't ever really believed in the whole past-life reincarnation circus, but it was way easier to believe that I'd regressed into a past life than it was to believe I'd regressed into some English guy's fucking *novel!*

I came up with two possible explanations. One, that maybe Brian's fiction was based on a true account, a diary or letters or something, written by someone in the seventeenth-century who'd witnessed the scene with the dead dodo keeper, and that's where I'd gone back to. Of course, that scenario meant that Carla Mendez's skills were for real and that I was maybe the reincarnation of that seventeenth-century dodo-owning diarist. OK? Sounded like crapola to me, but I preferred that to the other explanation.

The second possibility was simply that Brian had made the whole thing up from scratch, "based on an original idea by Brian Braithwaite." That could mean that I hadn't dropped into Brian's novel but into his head. It meant that Carla Mendez wasn't doing past-life therapy, she was doing some kind of weird telepathy act, putting one brain in touch with another. If Brian's brain and mine were both being tied in knots by thinking about dodos, then maybe it was just possible that they'd made some kind of psychic hookup. That made Carla Mendez quite the queen of the ether, though it still didn't mean that she knew what the fuck she was doing.

Do you buy either of those explanations? Do you want to? No, me neither, not really. But did I have a better idea? Nope. I decided to read on. There were only two more chapters and I got through them as quickly as I could, looking for clues, more stuff about *me*. But there wasn't anything as far as I could tell, just a lot of crud about this William Draper guy getting kicked out of college and going to London to be a kind of quackfinder general, and the last one had him running off to some place called the Ark. It might have been good stuff but I couldn't tell. My critical faculties had taken a bit of a beating. In fact by this point my head felt like there was a small mammal performing gymnastics inside it.

But then the train arrived in Oxford, and I had a museum to go to, exhibits to see, and you'd be amazed how easy it is not to think about stuff when you really put your mind to it. What else was there to do but put one foot in front of the other? I went to the museum.

I thought I'd have to go to some really dark, obscure corner of the place to find the dodo remains, but hell, at first it looked as though they'd made it too easy for me. I just walked in and there was a big glass case with a dodo display in it. But it turned out the preserved foot and beak weren't there. I guess they were too delicate to put on display, so they'd made plaster casts and put them in the case instead. They were kind of interesting; the beak looked like some primitive weapon, and the foot looked like some old lady's glove, but they weren't the real thing, and a guy might have felt cheated, but I didn't especially, because there was some other cool stuff in the case too.

For a start there were some prefossilized bones that had been dragged out of a swamp in Mauritius, and they seemed pretty authentic, but they were nothing compared to what was next to them. There was a dodo skeleton, a real one as far as I could tell, and that was seriously cool, and right next to it was what looked exactly like a stuffed dodo. OK, I knew it had to be a fake, a replica, something made using (I'd guess) turkey feathers, but somehow that didn't make it any less impressive.

It looked just great, this replica, exactly the way a real taxidermied dodo would have looked but better probably because this one was pretty new and fresh and not three hundred and fifty years old. There side by side were the skeleton and the replica, the real and the fake, as if the skeleton were an X-ray of the created object. And what can I tell you, I was suddenly, incredibly moved. They were there and they were fantastic and I felt connected and swept away and suddenly kind of tearful. So I guess it was cool. Intense. Inspiring. An epiphany, I guess. A moment in and out of time. It didn't take too long. I didn't know what I was going to do with that feeling, but I had a real sense that I could do *something*.

Then it was over. I'd seen the Oxford dodo. I'd seen more than I'd expected to see. I'd had my perfect moment and now I could get on with my life. I bought a couple of dodo postcards at the museum store. They were selling all kinds of dodo junk: mugs and key rings and cuff links and whatnot. Seemed kind of disrespectful, but that's merchandising for you.

I went outside and sat on the low wall surrounding the big lawn in front of the museum, and even though my brain was turning itself inside out—Carla Mendez, Brian Braithwaite, murder, thought transference, plagiarism, taxidermy, threesome sex—I still thought, hell, maybe I did something right for once by coming to England, to Oxford, and seeing the dodo remains.

I hadn't found what I was looking for but maybe I'd found something else instead.

That was when I saw Brian pounding toward me along the street. My first reaction was to get up and run, but I guess I was also intrigued as to what was going to happen next, what he'd say or do—a new plot point—so I stayed there waiting for him. He was hot and out of breath when he got to me. He was carrying a briefcase and he was smiling like he was very glad to see me, which was a surprise. I guess he looked at home there in a college town, amid the ivory towers. He sat down carefully on the wall next to me and said, "You took part of my novel," but he sounded hurt rather than angry.

"I figured you had another copy," I said.

"I did. I do. But that's not the point."

I wasn't going to play into his hands and ask what *was* the point.

"The point is, I'd gladly have given it to you," he said. "The point is, you shouldn't have left like that."

"Well, you and Angela seemed kind of occupied."

"Only temporarily, I assure you. I thought you and I had quite a few things still to discuss."

"Alsatia?" I suggested. "The dodo?"

"For a start, yes. Then I hoped to move on to other things."

"And your book. We really should have talked about that."

He gave a shrug of modesty. "I hope you like what you've read. But you've only read a part of it. There's plenty more where that came from," and he slapped his hand on his briefcase to show that it contained more of his work.

"Tell me, Brian," I said, "where do you get your fucking ideas?"

I was being sarcastic, but I guess in this case I really did want to know. And Brian obviously wasn't sure if I was screwing with him or not, but he wanted to tell me anyway.

"They just come," he said. "Inspiration. Like visions. I close my eyes and there they are, like movies running in the screening room of my imagination. Like dreams."

He got a misty and idiotic look in his eyes and that made me less embarrassed about asking my next question. "Have I ever figured in any of your dreams?" I said.

"Well no, not you personally," he said.

"But impersonally?"

"Not you, but someone like you."

"And are there murders in these dreams of yours?" I asked.

"Why yes, sometimes."

He didn't know what I was talking about, and neither did I, not really. Then he said, "You should have this," and he opened the briefcase and took out more pages of manuscript. "Here, take it. I know I'll never do anything with it. Completion anxiety. Fear of failure. Fear of success. Do what you will with it."

I took the extra pages from him, five more chapters.

"What exactly do you think I'm likely to do with them?"

"You're a filmmaker, aren't you? Don't look so surprised. There's nothing psychic about it. One of your business cards fell out of your pocket while you were getting undressed. I know you're not a pool cleaner. 'Auteur of the future.' How impressive it sounds."

"Look, what the fuck is this about, Brian?" I demanded. "How come when I regressed into a past life I found myself in a version of your fucking novel?"

"What?"

"You know what I'm talking about, don't you? A dark room, a mutilated corpse."

He looked at me as though I was deranged, which I was. "Have you been taking drugs, Rick?"

"Don't be dumb."

"You should see a doctor. Angela and I would both be very supportive."

I thought that hitting him might make me feel better, but I didn't do it, I really didn't.

Somewhere in the course of the conversation Brian's sweaty hand had taken hold of my forearm. I knew from the previous night that Brian was a touchy-feely sort of guy, but he was gripping me so hard he was stopping my circulation.

"Hey, Brian, enough with the tourniquet."

"Sorry," he said, but he didn't let go. "Please come back with me."

"What?

"Back to London, to the house. Angela's there waiting for you. For us both. She'll be so glad to see you again. You could stay with us for a few days, for a while. Cheaper than a hotel. We could come to an arrangement. Something long-term, possibly something permanent. Angela would love a baby. You appear to have good, strong genes."

"What are you talking about?"

"I'm not the jealous type. I'd treat the child as my own."

"This is ridiculous, Brian. This is insane. You don't know me."

"But I do. I feel like I've known you all my life."

I started to get up and so did he. I shook his hand off me but then he lunged as though he was going to hug me. I put out my hand to keep him at arm's length, nothing more than that, and I guess my hand must have made contact with his sternum, nothing more than a light push, but he fell backwards and the wall acted as a sort of pivot and he tipped over it, and his head hit the sidewalk on the other side and there was a horrible snapping sound, and he went out like a light. Oh shit.

The first thing I did was look around, and there was nobody there, nobody to turn to, and nobody (as I instantly realized) who was a witness. Thank God. Nobody had seen anything. I mean, there was nothing to see, it was an accident, all right, but still . . . I bent over Brian and felt around for a pulse. I couldn't find one. I listened to his chest and tried to see if he was breathing, and I couldn't find anything, absolutely nothing.

I needed some help. Or at least Brian did. I picked up the briefcase and ran into the museum and told the lady behind the desk of the souvenir counter that there was a man lying on the sidewalk outside and he didn't look so good.

"Is he drunk?" she asked.

"I don't know," I said. "I've never seen him before."

Maybe that was more information than she needed from me, like I was being too obvious about covering my tracks, but she treated it as a normal answer, and she called for the museum's first-aid guy, a dapper little bald dude who came jogging down the corridor with his first-aid kit, and we all went outside to administer to Brian.

And Brian had gone. There was no absolutely no sign of him. Had he been spirited away? Had he been teleported to another dimension? Hell no. I chose to think it meant he was alive and well and that I'd been wrong—hey, I'm not a doctor—that he hadn't been dead, only stunned, and that he'd gotten up and walked away while I was inside. The two people from the museum obviously thought I was a nut job, but so what, I could handle that.

I put Brian's briefcase under my arm, slipped away, headed for the station. I didn't read any more of the novel on the train journey. I wanted to save it for the flight. I got back to London, went to the airport, paid an arm and a leg to change my ticket, and got the first available plane out of there.

The flight was pretty empty. I spread myself out and settled down with the second half of *The Restoration of the Dodo.* At first I thought the story kind of lost its way: a lot of stuff about quackery, executions, taxidermy, a love story that never quite happened, and nothing more about the murder scene I'd witnessed. But then—I don't know, I guess I was feeling vulnerable or sentimental or something—it suddenly occurred to me that this dodo I was reading about was going to die. And why should that have been such a big deal? Like I always used to say in pitch meetings, everybody dies. But for some reason I got hit with all these feelings about death and mortality and extinction, and I just lost it completely.

And that's why I was having a major panic attack on the plane and why I was so pathetically grateful to Henry Cadwallader for telling me I wasn't going to die. And that was why I gave him my card and said we should get together for a smoothie, but I didn't really mean it. It was just one of those things you say.

Tom Brewster met me at LAX, which was real good of him. Even then I knew he was one of the good guys, and he asked me what kind of trip I'd had, and I stuttered something about it being "interesting" and immediately he said, "You got laid, didn't you?" And I didn't deny it, though I didn't tell him the circumstances. And Tom laughed and said, "And did you make any progress with your damn movie?"

"Not progress—regress," I said, which seemed kind of bitterly funny to me, an in-joke that only I was in on.

"What?" said Tom.

So I decided to tell him the whole story, although I guess it wasn't really a *decision,* it was more of a thing I had to do, that I couldn't control, something I had to get off my pecs. I just vomited it all out, like I'd been given some verbal and psychological emetic. By this point I didn't care what Tom or anybody else thought of me. If he thought I was crazy or stupid or criminal, so what?

Tom drove and he listened, and he grunted quietly in disbelief from time to time, but at least he took the story seriously, which he had no obligation to do, and he didn't make a detour to drop me off at a nearby funny farm. It took most of the drive for me to purge myself and by the time I'd finished we were pulling into the driveway of Tom's studio.

"You really think you went back into a past life?" he asked.

"I don't know."

"You think maybe you went into this English writer guy's head instead?"

"I don't know. Maybe."

"And he wanted you to impregnate his wife?"

"Seemed that way."

"And then you hit him and he disappeared."

"It was just a push. And you know, I don't think he like *dematerialized*. I think he just got up and hailed a cab or something."

"So he wasn't dead?"

"Not if he hailed a cab. Hey, there are times when I can't even find my *own* pulse."

"And you had an epiphany in the museum, and then you had intimations of mortality on the plane."

"Yeah, that pretty much sums up my vacation," I said.

We sat there, neither us knowing what we were supposed to do next, and at last I said, "So, Tom, what have *you* been doing?"

"Working," he said. "Just working."

For the next few days I played the slacker and hunkered down in Tom's studio, spent a lot of time in front of the TV, vegging out on the leather couch, which was also my bed, smoking a little weed, drinking a little beer, watching a lot of *Powerpuff Girls* episodes that Tom had recorded. I thought about calling Carla Mendez but what would I have said? "Hi, bitch, did you know that between us we've totally fucked up my life?" But maybe she was psychic enough to know that already.

Oh yeah, and I downloaded the pictures of me, Brian, and Angela having sex. OK, I know I was probably a pervert for hanging on to those pictures, but the fact is, they were really pretty hot. Very real. Very dirty. You might even have thought I had a talent for this shit.

So then, a few days later, Henry Cadwallader called me up, and obviously I'd pretty much had it with English guys at this point. But this one *had* kind of saved my life, or so it had seemed at the time, and even if he hadn't really, he'd still done a good job of helping me deal with my panic attack. So I guess I thought I owed him something: not much, but something. He said he needed advice about the movie industry, and I thought, oh boy, is he ever asking the wrong guy. But hell, I went ahead and set up a breakfast meeting. I'd seen people do that in the movies.

twenty **Stealing Beauty**

William Draper sets off from his all-too-humble lodgings, headed for the rural splendors of South Lambeth, to see the Tradescants' Ark, to see the Ark's dodo.

He travels in a coach with a pair of festive old scholars who throughout the journey talk much about science and nature, but there is something in their mood, an excitement, a playfulness that is anything but scientific. They are on a jaunt, and while William shares some of their excitement, he finds himself looking down on them, regarding them as triflers. His errand is of a far more serious nature.

They arrive in due course, and as William descends from the coach, the so-called Ark looks like not much more than a farmhouse, though a large one that has been extended and elaborated, given a new wing with a turret. It is set in a patch of land smaller than he had imagined, no more than a couple of acres, though it is clearly a most marvelously abundant and fertile plot.

William is in general not much given to being impressed by flowers and foliage; they seem too mundane to him. Yet even from outside the boundary wall he can tell that here is a rare collection of outlandish and exotic flora: creepers, climbers, gaudy and sensuous blooms, leaves shaped like knives, like feathers, like fleshy organs.

He pays his sixpence and passes into the grounds. He had expected the dodo to be given pride of place, to be the very first thing any visitor would see. He cannot understand how collectors, and certainly not those with the reputation of the Tradescants, could fail to have the dodo as centerpiece of any collection. And yet there is no immediate sign of it. Instead the first thing to catch his eye, leaning against a tree, is a set of gigantic bones, like an archway or some piece of discarded architecture. The custodian who takes William's money, and who stays close by as though he distrusts his visitor's intentions, explains that these bones are from a whale's ribcage. William pretends to be impressed.

In fact William's intentions are unambiguous, at least to himself. He intends to view the dodo kept here, to satisfy himself that it is a healthy specimen and of the appropriate male sex, and then he will seek out someone in authority, the surviving Tradescant for preference, and make a simple offer. "Let us breed our dodos," he will say.

How could anyone refuse? This Ark is a place where nature teems, where miracles of horticulture, husbandry, and art are performed daily, where wild, foreign nature is ordered and perfected, made to conform to the temperate laws of the English climate. Why then would its keepers decline to be part of a plan to raise a flock of dodos?

The custodian presses on with a tour of the grounds, pointing out wonderful living specimens, some from as far away as America: tulip trees, bear's breeches, staghorn sumac. They step inside the orangerie and William breathes in the queasily perfumed air while above his head the glass roof seems to focus and concentrate the light. William is eager to get to the house. The dodo must surely be there.

Once he is in the house, however, there is still a great deal the custodian insists on showing him first, again much that comes directly from nature, though here it is preserved rather than living: shells, bones, dried seaweeds, the husks of exotic fruits and vegetables, malign-looking skulls, a toad in amber, a mermaid's hand, a serpent suspended in spirits.

William tries to suppress his impatience but only becomes more frustrated when they move from naturalia to artificialia. William is shown into the room of rarities. He is dazzled by the polished, wide-planked floors, battered by the clarity of the Venetian glass in the windows that allows light to flood into the room. All about him he sees dense clutter: coins and medals, shoes and boots from many lands, a crowd of faces carved into a cherry stone, many weapons of war and execution, a knife used by the Jews to perform circumcision, paintings done in unfathomable alien styles.

Only the most glum and melancholy of spectators could fail to be impressed by the glut and superfluity of wonders, and yet William is not happy. He did not come this far merely to look at pictures, and the custodian senses that all is not quite well with William.

"Do you find our display lacking in some way?" he asks, not without mockery. "Is it less than you expected?"

"No, sir," William says. "In some ways it is far, far more. But chiefly, nay solely, I have come to see your dodo."

"Ah," says the custodian brightly, "'Tis easily seen."

All eagerness, William begins to follow the man. Perhaps a sighting of the dodo is reserved for those visitors who show themselves to be connoisseurs, only those who have the wit to ask to see it. He feels sure the custodian will lead him outside to some special place, to a gilded cage or artfully constructed pen, but in the event he moves only to a shadowy corner of the room of rarities, where the light doesn't fully penetrate, to a glass case, a glass coffin as it will seem to William, and the custodian points to a dead thing, a misshapen pile of feathers and skin, stretched out on a crude armature, a dead dodo, looking nothing like itself, looking like nothing at all.

"It is dead," William says, and the custodian looks at him as though he were a dimwit, a village idiot, not fit to appreciate the wonders of the Ark.

"Ah, sir," says the custodian. "I see you are a scientist."

Well, that is one name for it. And certainly it is in the name of science that William continues with his duties on behalf of the Royal College of Physicians. He continues to find and inform against the worst sort of quack.

He is sent to Haymarket on an errand that promises him little by way of drama or even satisfaction. He goes to see one of the area's "beauty specialists," a female quack, a "wise woman," if you will, a certain Mrs. Hendrick. There are many of her kind in London, and they seem to him to be harmless by and large. They chiefly serve other women, supplying them with beauty powders, face washes, night masks, lotions, and unctions to hide the effects of pox and age and hard living. They also offer palliatives for women's courses and remedies to soften the pains of childbirth.

It strikes William as innocent stuff, yet the college has told him of a serious complaint brought against Mrs. Hendrick by an unnamed gentlewoman. The matter is a discreet one, and in William's opinion both trivial and embarrassing, but he is in no position to pick and choose his errands. He is certainly in no position to decline one. The offended gentlewoman claims to have paid a substantial sum to Mrs. Hendrick in exchange for a cream that promised to enlarge and whiten her breasts but instead merely caused her to break out in a rash.

William thinks that if he had been gulled in such an intimate and humiliating way, he would have kept his silence on the matter, though he understands that this may be precisely what the quack intended and is therefore potentially all the more pernicious. But even so . . . Mrs. Hendrick, he has been told, claims to be the wife of some deceased physician, a familiar and generally improbable claim. Sometimes there seem to be more late doctors' wives in London than there were ever living doctors.

He arrives in Haymarket, at the lady's lodgings, which look both respectable and civilized. A small sign by the door says, "Mrs. Mariette Hendrick, Herbalism and Natural Science," a modest enough claim. He knocks; a maid opens the door, looks him over, and immediately leads him inside to a small waiting room. She has evidently drawn her own conclusions from the sight of his face.

The waiting room is simple, quite bare at first sight, cleanly swept, as though to emphasize that there will be no deception or trickery here, though again he sees how that in itself may be a form of deception. The room has two doors, the one by which he entered and another, washed a pale green, that leads deeper into the house, into a back room. There is one thin, lightless window.

Against one wall of the room is an oak chest, with an elaborate, indeed ostentatious, lock upon it. Across from the chest is a glass-fronted case, a miniature ark, a personal cabinet of curiosities, only some of which he can identify: strangely mottled birds' eggs, the spine of some creature, chunks of rock streaked through with veins of aquamarine crystal, a stuffed or at least dried baby crocodile. There are two wooden chairs at the center of the room, set at an angle, pointed toward each other, one grander and higher than the other. He chooses the smaller, sits down, and waits.

In due course there is noise behind the green-painted door. It opens and for a second William is afforded a glimpse into a strange, dark world, a workroom perhaps or a laboratory. He sees outlines and shadows, glass vessels shaped like pears, metal pots, an astrological chart on the wall, something that might be a small furnace, something alchemical, a skull that looks just slightly less than human. Then Mrs. Hendrick enters—walking with a slight limp, he notices—and determinedly closes the door behind her.

Although William knows that widows come in many styles and varieties, she nevertheless confounds his expectations. First, she is young, only a little older than himself. And she is beautiful. If her appearance owes anything to her own products, they must be effective indeed. She carries herself with confidence and dignity, with something of the aristocratic, though she is more natural, more informal than that word suggests.

Certainly her complexion is as clear as any milkmaid's, though her eyes and mouth show evidence enough of artifice, henna on her eyelids, the lips freshly crayoned. Her hair is thick and sleek and black. Her fingers are much beringed, and round her throat she wears a necklace of amber. A petticoat hemmed with elaborate lace peeks out beneath her velvet skirt. Her jacket is edged with black-and-white fur from an animal William cannot identify.

She greets him and assesses him with her frank, clear eyes. William has the feeling that she sees deeply into him, far deeper than he would wish.

"Mr. Draper," she says, and she settles in the chair opposite him, "what may I do for you?"

"I am not here for myself," he says, cleverly as he thinks, "but on behalf of my wife."

"She is too distempered to come herself?"

"Yes, partly that, and because she is a very modest woman, and this is a somewhat delicate matter."

"No need for embarrassment within these walls."

"It concerns . . . her . . . bosom."

"Oh, is that all? Why should a woman be embarrassed by a pair of breasts?"

"Why, why indeed?" he says, and then thinking that he is dissembling rather skillfully, he adds, "Nevertheless, my wife is embarrassed by hers."

"How so?"

"Their bloom has departed," he says delicately. "They have become loose and pendulous and have lost much of their whiteness. I have heard that this is an area where you have some expertise."

"Indeed? So tell me more about your wife."

He had not anticipated this and now realizes that he should have. "Well, she is a plumpish woman, dark-haired, not tall, essentially healthy . . ." He wonders why he is devising such a plain wife for himself, but at least his creation sounds plausible.

"Children?" asks Mrs. Hendrick.

He casts about hopelessly before inventing a daughter for himself and his mythical wife. "Just the one, a baby girl, two years old or so."

"Still suckling?"

He has no idea whether a two-year-old child should be suckling or not, and yet since she is bothering to ask the question, both yes and no must be possible answers. "No," he says firmly, then fears he may have said it *too* firmly.

"And have your wife's breasts shrunk since she stopped suckling?"

"Yes," he says. It seems the obvious answer.

"And this displeases you?"

"It displeases us both."

"And what do you imagine I might be able to do for you?"

"I hoped there might be some lotion or balm that can be rubbed into the affected areas and . . ."

"Would that there were such a substance," Mrs. Hendrick says wistfully. "I should truly make my fortune."

"And is there not?"

"If so, then nature and science have not yet revealed it."

"Then you can do nothing for me. What shall I tell my wife?"

"I would tell her to eat well, not to shrink from exercise or moderate labor, to choose her bodices with care. And above all else I would tell her, which is to say I think *you* should tell her, that you are a great admirer of small and pendulous breasts."

"I fear my wife will be most vexed if I come home empty-handed. Are there really no pills or liquors you can sell me?"

She looks at him with pity and he can feel only shame. "No," she says, "but if you wish to be gulled, there are many less trustworthy traders hereabouts who can. Knock on any door in the street."

"But you come so highly recommended. And my wife's wrath is formidable."

"Wrath is certainly to be avoided. Perhaps there is something I could offer."

He smiles, inwardly, he hopes. He thinks he has played this well. He has forced the quack to reveal her true nature. She goes to the chest at the side of the room, unlocks it, and reaches in for a small packet which she offers him. It appears to contain dried leaves.

"What miraculous thing is this?" he asks.

"Nothing at all miraculous. It is a tisane, made from fennel, monarda, and mint. It is neutral and harmless. You may ascribe to it whatever powers you like, and if your wife has belief and confidence in *you*, then she may indeed derive some benefit. Certainly she shall receive no injury."

"And how much shall I pay you for this wonder?"

"Nothing. Making tisanes is an interest of mine. If your wife finds it agreeable, I shall happily give her the exact recipe."

He opens the packet, smells the mixture, pokes around in it with a finger. He detects nothing untoward.

"You look so disappointed, sir. You were hoping for more in the way of spells and incantations? You imagined that I was a deceiver, a mountebank? How might you have come by such an idea? And having come by it, why visit me?"

Now he seems not to have played this so well after all. Suddenly she has him beaten. He finds himself annoyed, not with her but with himself. For her he has a sort of grudging admiration.

"It is an odd thing, sir: you do not strike me as a married man."

"Why else would I be here?"

"Oh, I can think of explanations. I wonder if perhaps you are a rather shy young man who enjoys talking with women such as myself about intimate matters, such as breasts, as a substitute for the thing itself."

"Why, certainly not," he says with all the hauteur he can summon.

"It is not such a terrible thing," she says. "Sad perhaps but not terrible."

"I am insulted, madam."

"Or another explanation might be that you are one of those wretched informers employed by the Royal College of Physicians."

His silence tells her almost everything.

"But as you see, Mr. Draper, I make no false claims, sell no magical elixirs."

"On this occasion, at least," he says, and realizes that he is sounding pompous and petty. He adds, "I am most glad to have been proved mistaken."

"Do you know how to rid this world of quacks?" she asks, and indeed he does not. "Let the college abandon its monopoly. Make physic free and freely available, in every city, in every street, paid for out of the public purse. When the physicians themselves abandon their own taste for mystification and self-aggrandizement, then the common quacks shall have no models to copy. Nor will they have a market."

"Madam, you have said a mouthful."

He looks at her lips and realizes that if he stays a moment longer, he will be impelled to kiss them. He makes his excuses and departs. Later he reports to Dr. Lloyd at the Royal College, with perfect honesty and considerable understatement, that he finds Mrs. Hendrick to be nothing but admirable.

twenty-one **The Breakfast Club**

I suppose that by any reasonable standards, contacting Rick McCartney, auteur of the future, would have to be considered grasping at straws. He was a young man about whom I knew next to nothing. Pinning any hopes on somebody you'd just met on a plane, especially somebody with a penchant for panic attacks and sudden intimations of mortality, was being at best optimistic. Dorothy was even more skeptical than I was. She had only seen him for a few moments at the airport while picking up her luggage, but that was enough to convince her that he was a complete waste of space. She was quick to make such decisions, and on this occasion I couldn't have said she was being entirely unreasonable. And yet, who else did we have to turn to? We were beggars in this town, not choosers.

We met Rick McCartney at a diner close to the corner of Hollywood and Vine. Despite everything, these names still had a considerable magic to them as far as I was concerned, though there was nothing very magical about the diner. Rick McCartney was already seated in a booth when we arrived. "Hi, Doc," he said, and he sounded weary, but he summoned the energy to stand up and give me a floppy handshake, a strange mix of formality and looseness. "Saved any good lives recently?"

No point repeating that I hadn't saved his life at all. "No," I said. "Had any more panic attacks?"

"My whole life is one big, ongoing panic attack."

I hoped he was joking, though I suspected otherwise. Dorothy said hello in a cold, neutral way. She really didn't want to be there, and she was doubly resentful because she had nowhere better to be. And frankly I suspected that Rick McCartney didn't much want to be there either, but he at least felt some need to be civil, to play the game. Dorothy did not and preferred to be mean, moody, and not especially magnificent.

I sat opposite the two of them, since it would have been a tight squeeze to get anyone in beside me on my half of the booth. We ordered breakfast, and while Dorothy hid silently behind her sunglasses, Rick and I made some rather stilted, needlessly polite conversation. It was hard going. Rick was the one who finally decided it was time to get down to business.

"So what exactly can I do for you, Doc?" he said.

"Well, that's rather what we wanted you to tell us," I said, and I gave a brief recap of Dorothy's less than triumphant adventures in L.A. I put a copy of her CV and one of her now out-of-date headshots on the table. Rick looked and listened but didn't seem to be giving the matter his full attention, and when I got to the part about Bob Samuelson's death, he said, rather caustically, "An agent dies. I wonder how many people are going to show up at the funeral."

I didn't care to think about that, even though Dorothy was continuing to insist that we should be among the mourners. Somewhat pathetically I tried to make Rick concentrate on the matter in hand. "So, Rick, I ask you, what should Dorothy be doing in order to get ahead in this town?

He thought about it for quite a while, seemed to lose his train of thought, and then said, "Well, she could learn to give really good blowjobs."

This piece of advice was no more acceptable from him than it had been from Barbara. I thought it was incumbent on me to do something stern and dramatic. I said, "I think this conversation is at an end," and I got to my feet and started rooting around in my pocket for some money that I could drop cavalierly onto the table on my way out.

"Oh shit," Rick McCartney said. "Did I really say that? Look, I'm really, really sorry," and to be fair, he did sound genuinely sorry. "I really am. It slipped out. I didn't mean to piss you off. I didn't mean to insult you. Neither of you. I'm going nuts here, OK? I'm sorry. I don't know why I said that. I don't know what's wrong with me. Or maybe I do but I don't want to talk about it."

He began to breathe heavily; he was demonstrating the first signs of another panic attack.

"It's all right, Rick, calm down," I said.

He clutched his head in his hands and brought it down onto the table top next to Dorothy's headshot. It was at this point that the waitress delivered breakfast. The arrival of food imposed a certain calm on us all. I sat down again, though with a decent show of reluctance, and we tackled our breakfasts in silence for a while. Rick McCartney, however, continued to look as though he might be about to have a relapse, so I thought it best to try to talk to him.

"Do you know one of the things I really hate about movies?" I said.

He shook his head.

"When people do what I almost just did. They get up and they drop a couple of notes on the table and they walk away, leaving their food or their drink untouched. In real life nobody ever does that."

The fact that I had very nearly done it didn't make it seem any more authentic. Rick McCartney nodded in agreement.

"And you know what *I* hate?" he said. "When people have

robbed a bank or committed a murder and they're on the run, and they turn on the TV or the car radio, and right away they hear a news report about the murder. Man, I hate that."

I might have told him that in the case of Dorothy's recent experience with the report of Bob Samuelson's death this was not so improbable after all, but instead I said, "And I hate weight improbability," and rather surprisingly Rick McCartney understood exactly what I meant.

"And airplanes in movies," he said. "The way that whenever you see an airplane in a movie it's always so roomy and quiet and brightly lit. Man, I really hate that."

"Rick," I said gently, "I have a strange suspicion that despite everything you may turn out to be a man after my own heart."

He nodded in only partial agreement. Eager to keep the ball rolling, I said, "What exactly does your card mean when it says you're an auteur of the future?"

"Well," Rick said, "the term *auteur*, or more specifically *la politique des auteurs*, comes from a bunch of French dudes who worked on a mag called *Cahiers du Cinéma*, and basically they were trying to make a distinction between *auteurs*, who were like artists, and directors who were just hacks, who they called *metteurs en scène*..."

It seemed to me that he was making a very fair stab at explaining the auteur theory, though perhaps as for the benefit of a not especially bright child. Dorothy appeared to be stifling a yawn.

"What I think I was actually asking," I interrupted, since I knew perfectly well what the auteur theory was, "is what it means to be an auteur in Hollywood today, or in the future."

Rick McCartney's face took on a severe, static quality and he said, "It means that I don't get to make movies."

"Well, I suppose not many people do," I said.

He found this a terrible provocation. "Oh, some do, man.

Some do. Some incompetent, brain-dead forms of scum-sucking sewer life, they get to make their movies. Just not people like me. Not anybody who's got an imagination and a vision. You think Resnais could get a gig in Hollywood today? Or Buñuel? Or Godard? Or Rivette?"

I would have had to look it up to be absolutely certain, but as far as I knew those directors had never had a "gig" in Hollywood at all. Also, the mere fact that they wouldn't get one today and that Rick McCartney apparently couldn't get one either didn't seem, to me, to mean much. I decided not to point this out.

Nevertheless, after this display of intensity, the conversation got easier, at least between Rick and me. We ate and we talked about movies. We found that we shared many of the same filmic enthusiasms, although occasionally I had the feeling he might be pandering to what he thought were my tastes. Did he really like *Last Year in Marienbad* as much as I did? Or *The Swimmer*? Did he really think Helen Mirren was as glorious an actress as he claimed? Perhaps not, but if he was exaggerating his own enthusiasms for my benefit, I could see no harm in it.

Inevitably Dorothy was rather left out of this conversation. She likes movies but not in the way of a movie buff. Then out of the blue she said, "Look, Rick, all I want to know is, what can you do for me?"

He looked surprised, though I didn't entirely see why he should have been. Wasn't L.A. the city of the forthright and the self-obsessed? We were only there talking to him because we wanted something from him, and the sad truth was we were ready to accept just about anything.

"Well," he said to Dorothy, "I guess the one small thing I could do is take some new headshots of you." He picked up her photograph from the table and compared it with the reality.

"Could you do that?" Dorothy asked.

"Sure," he said. "I mean I've done it before. I have the equipment. I'm a pretty good photographer."

"*When* could you do it?" Dorothy demanded.

"As soon as you like, I guess. The place I live is a little weird, but it's good for taking pictures. We could go up on the roof there."

"I think we should do that," said Dorothy. "I think we should do that right now."

I was rather surprised by her sudden enthusiasm for Rick McCartney. No doubt she only wanted him for what she could get out of him, but I was amazed that she wanted him for anything at all.

"That's what we'll do then," Rick McCartney said.

A truly good father probably wouldn't have let his daughter drive off into the hinterlands of Los Angeles with some strange man she hardly knew, even if, to a large extent, he (the father) had brokered the arrangement. This theoretical good father would no doubt have wanted to ensure that Rick McCartney actually did have a place to take photographs, not just some dank basement where, for instance, he chained up girls. (Did L.A. have dank basements? Surely it must, though no doubt the dankness would be muted by English standards). But Dorothy assured me I was entirely surplus to requirements and insisted that she didn't want to be watched while having her photograph taken. I knew there was no point arguing.

I paid for breakfast and saw Dorothy and Rick McCartney drive off in the same direction though in separate cars, Rick leading the way. As I headed for my own car, parked beside the diner,

I wondered how I was going to spend the rest of the day. Another visit to the Beauty Vault? Another session with Barbara?

As I was considering this, a woman came running toward me across the car park. The run was a mite unsteady—I suspected a prosthetic foot or leg—and she was in some disarray. A cascade of blue black hair bounced and trailed behind her, and her eyes looked ferocious.

"Sir," she said, "excuse me, sir."

The politeness naturally made me assume she was going to demand something from me, money most probably, but what she said was, "That guy you were with, Rick McCartney—how well do you know him?"

"A little better now than I did an hour ago," I said.

"He's in grave danger," she said, sounding both terribly over-dramatic and terribly stilted.

"Is that right? What kind of danger?"

"Physical," she said, not relenting on the drama. "Grave physical and moral danger."

"Well, I'll tell him when I next see him."

"He needs to know *now,*" she said. "And who was that young woman he was talking to? Where is he going with her?"

I wondered if perhaps that was what had really got her so worked up. Perhaps this was Rick McCartney's girlfriend, or ex-girlfriend, jealous because she'd seen him with Dorothy.

"That woman is my daughter," I said. "They're going to his home, his studio, to take photographs." I realized this might sound rather sleazy, but it did happen to be the truth.

"OK then," the woman said. "Tell me the address. I'll go there. I'll speak to him there."

"Look," I said, "I don't have a clue who you are. Why would I give you that sort of information?"

She may have been desperate, she may have been awash in cheap dramatics, but she could see my point. "What do I have to do to convince you?" she said.

"You could start by telling me who you are."

"I'm Carla Mendez. I'm a psychic. I'm Rick's past-life therapist."

That was enough for me. I was not going to spend any more time arguing in a car park with some ludicrous female quack. I turned my back on her and headed more determinedly for my car, but she limped along beside me.

"Just a second," she said. "Please, you're English, aren't you?"

"Indeed," I said dismissively. Detecting my Englishness was no great evidence of psychic ability.

"And your name is . . . " She thought about it, reaching down into some psychic reservoir, "Is it Harry?"

"No," I said, but I slowed down a little.

"Henry," she said. "Your name's Henry. And you're a doctor. And your wife recently died."

I admit I was a little surprised by this, what I took to be an inspired piece of guesswork, but I was not exactly impressed. I put on my best authoritative doctor's voice and said, "What kind of party trick are you playing, madam?"

Her face was now pinched in concentration, and then her eyes suddenly widened, as though she'd "seen" something. Determined not to fall for any of this stagecraft, and I made a rather showy effort to get my car keys out of my pocket. However, her long elegant hands had now grabbed both my wrists, and I was reluctant to push her away. I knew where that could lead.

"Rick isn't the only one in danger," she said. "I see that you are too."

"Physical?" I suggested. "Moral? Mortal?"

She shook her head, in confusion rather than denial. Her hair shimmered around her shoulders. "It's more complicated than that. Death is involved, but not yours necessarily. It's something worse than that somehow, I think. I can't tell exactly, but I feel that something terrible is going to happen. The word that's in my mind is . . . *corruption.*"

"Enough," I said. "This is terribly, terribly stupid," and I broke free and got into my car. Mercifully, she wasn't desperate enough to try to get in with me or climb on the roof, as I'd feared she might. She decided to let me go, but I saw that she was making the sign of the cross in my direction as I departed.

You might imagine that doctors are the least superstitious of men, but it is not precisely so. Naturally we believe first and foremost in science and probability, in what we can see, touch, and measure. But most of us soon realize these things aren't the whole story. We constantly make educated guesses, play our hunches. We "know" things that we cannot possibly know by any scientific method. In surgeries and sickrooms and operating theaters we endlessly see the power of faith. Even the most skeptical of us regularly witness miracles. So even though I was more than eager to dismiss Carla Mendez's doomy and unwelcome intuitions, I couldn't quite do it. She had known, or at least accurately guessed, my name and profession. More surprisingly, she had known that Caroline had recently died.

How might a person know things like that? Did I look like a Henry, like a doctor, like someone whose wife had just died? Well, possibly so. A man does carry his being around with him. It didn't seem impossible that someone might be able to glean these things through simple (whatever that word means) intuition, and perhaps this woman did have a gift of sorts in that direction.

That, however, was rather different from foretelling the future, which she was also claiming. Intuition is not the same thing as second sight. Furthermore, believing that something terrible is about to happen may be a sign of an incipient panic attack rather than psychic ability. And yet the truth was, my intuition rather meshed with hers. I hadn't felt that I was in any specific danger, but now that some complete stranger had said that it was so, a part of me was inclined to believe it. She'd said it was a matter of corruption, and now that this idea was in my head, perhaps the truth was that I already felt corrupted.

It wasn't anything so simple as "I might have killed a man," since on balance I still tended to believe that I hadn't. But I was aware of other more local corruptions, from lying to Barbara about who and what I was (if she'd been Carla Mendez, would she have seen right through me?), to standing by while a girl was raped at a party, even to letting Dorothy drive off with Rick McCartney. Perhaps Carla Mendez had not been predicting the future after all, merely describing the present.

I called Barbara. Given the Bob Samuelson situation it seemed necessary to stay in touch, to keep talking, and yet I must say I was rather hoping I might get her voicemail. I didn't. I got Barbara and I was summoned to the mock-Tudor house again, where I was now able to let myself in with my own keys, and I was there ready for her when she arrived. She had driven there wearing nothing but a pair of scarlet high heels.

twenty-two **Head**

Was I trying to exploit Henry Cadwallader and his daughter? Hell no. No way. Well, not for anything more than a free breakfast, and it wasn't even like I was trying to get a *fancy* free breakfast out of them. They asked me to suggest a place and all I could think of was a diner where I sometimes went. I didn't have enough balls to insist on the Polo Lounge or somewhere expensive, and that just felt like another example of my lack of killer instinct, another reason why I hadn't gotten ahead in this town.

When they arrived at the diner, the daughter didn't look anything like I remembered her. She'd done something weird to her face and her hair, and she was kind of sulky and silent, but I didn't see that it was my job to cheer her up, so me and the old man did all the talking.

He seemed to have changed a little too. He'd looked like a real slob on the plane, wearing tweeds and corduroy, like your old math teacher, but now he was looking pretty good. He had a cool suit on, which helped, but more than that he had a kind of glow of self-confidence about him. Maybe *he'd* got laid too. Or maybe it was Hollywood's magical ability to change people. Even so, I still didn't think he was the kind of guy I'd have had a lot in common with.

So he told me the full story of what had been going on with

Dorothy, how she'd had just one contact in Hollywood, and he'd gone and died, and then she'd been calling around trying to get someone to see her, and I could have told her what a waste of time that was going to be. And then I went and made some dumb crack about blowjobs and he got all offended and I had to do a lot of apologizing, but the weird thing was, that kind of broke the ice and after that we had a conversation about what we hated in the movies and it was pretty good. And then I got to talking about making my own movie, and in one way that probably wasn't such a good idea because it showed that I was so *not* a player, and I got a little carried away with the passion and the, you know, bitterness, and I probably sounded like a sarcastic nerd, but I could tell he found something impressive in what I was saying, and I think even the daughter did too. I wished I could be that impressive in pitch meetings. And then Henry and I had a movie buff conversation and that was just fine.

So then, out of the blue, Dorothy suddenly says, "So what can you do for me, Rick?" And it was weird because suddenly I really did want to help. I didn't want to come across as a complete noncombatant, and you know I'd been sitting on Tom Brewster's couch all these days, doing nothing, obsessed with myself and past-life therapy and whatever, and it felt good to be asked to do something for somebody else. It wasn't exactly about feeling "wanted" but it was something. So I found myself saying that I could take some new headshots of her. That was the only thing I could think of. And she went for it. Maybe it was only to get away from her dad; I figured they'd probably had enough of each other at this point, like who takes their father with them if they're going off to conquer Hollywood?

So she got in her car and I got in mine and she followed me home. Like I said before, Tom Brewster's studio is a real passion killer for most women, but Dorothy really dug the place. She walked in and she lit up. She found it creepy and funny and weird and obsessive, and she really liked that, she said. She waltzed around picking up deformed brains and alien organs and heads with open-topped brainpans, and she was in her element. She looked alive, like she was having fun, not at all the way she'd been with her dad.

"This is a very cool place," she said.

"Yeah, we're hoping to get it featured in *Architectural Digest.*"

"Really?"

"No, not really," I said.

"Oh, I see. You're quite a comedian, aren't you?"

"Am I?"

"Yes. In the diner, that was quite a funny line, that I should learn to give good blowjobs."

"Your dad didn't find it very funny."

"He would have if it hadn't been about his precious daughter."

I got my photographic gear together and we went up on the flat roof of the studio and I took a bunch of pictures of Dorothy. Right away I could tell they weren't going to be great. I knew they'd be competent and in focus and well lit and all that, but there was something about Dorothy's face. In real life it was a good face, an attractive face, but the camera just didn't love it. Once you looked at it through a lens it turned blunt and dead. It was a real shame.

I didn't tell her that. I told her she looked great, fabulous, sexy, hot, gorgeous; I was just like a photographer in a movie, like David Hemmings in *Blow-Up.* And she believed me. It made her real happy. I guess there's nothing wrong with lying to people to make them happy but I was surprised at just how desperate she was to be liked and how easy it was to flatter her.

After we'd done the job and I was packing up the gear, Dorothy said, "I didn't tell Daddy the absolute whole story about the phone calls. When I was ringing round there was just one person I spoke to who didn't immediately tell me to get lost."

"Yeah?" I said. I had a fair idea of what might be coming next.

"This person said come right over, and perhaps if he'd been the first one I'd called, I'd have gone, but by the time I got to him, I'd been rejected by so many people I knew there had to be something dodgy about him."

"Good thinking," I said.

"I wonder if you know him. He's called Jack Rozin."

"Yep, I know Jack Rozin. By name anyway," I said wearily. It was pretty much as expected.

"Well, that's a coincidence, isn't it?"

"Not really. A lot of people know about Jack Rozin."

"Is he all right? Should I go and see him, do you think?"

"You want to be in porn?"

"Oh, I see."

Dorothy was new to this town, but she wasn't a complete hayseed. I didn't have to spell it out for her. It all made perfect sense to her now.

"He sounded quite nice on the phone," she said.

"Yeah well, anyone can sound nice on the phone."

"Mmm."

The way she stopped and thought about it made me wonder if maybe she *did* want to be in porn. Dorothy didn't look like your typical porn star, but from what I'd heard, the Jack Rozin product line was diverse enough that he could probably find a place for just about anybody.

"No," Dorothy said after a while, "I don't suppose you do porn until you're really desperate, until you've been in L.A. a couple of years and you don't know what else to do. I've not even been here a week yet. That's not enough time to get really desperate, is it?"

"Desperation comes in all shapes and sizes," I said. "Short term, long term, by the hour."

"Then I guess I'm hardly desperate at all," she said.

"Good."

"And as a matter of fact, I don't have to *learn* how to give a really good blowjob. I give a very good one already."

I'm guessing she probably *did* want to have sex with me, though I didn't know why. Because she found me attractive? Because I'd made her feel good about herself when I was taking the photographs? To piss off her dad? Because she was a slut? Because we'd had sex in a previous life? Well, possibly all these reasons, but maybe for some other reason too. In any case, I didn't take her up on the offer. I played dumb, pretended not to know what she was talking about, and I suppose the bottom line was that I was being respectful to her dad. He seemed a good, honest guy and if he trusted me with his daughter, then I thought I probably shouldn't just leap on her the first chance I got. I felt protective. Go figure.

So I said let's smoke some dope, drink some beer, and watch some junk TV instead, and we sat on the couch (my bed) and saw a couple of *Texas Justice* episodes. How's that for morality? Beer, drugs, and junk TV—yes; sex—no. But I'm guessing we had more fun than we would have done if we'd had sex. And if we'd been having sex, Tom Brewster would have walked in on us right in the middle of it, which would not have been cool.

So we were sitting there on the couch and I heard the front door clank open, obviously Tom coming home.

"That's Tom," I said, "the maniac who's responsible for this chamber of horrors."

"Gosh," she said, "I really want to meet him."

But he didn't come into the part of the studio where we were sitting. I could hear him moving around in the kitchen area, lifting something, unpacking something, pretty standard behavior for Tom, always bringing home some new weird stuff. I called out, "Hey Tom, you've got a fan here who wants to meet you," but he still didn't say anything and he still didn't appear, and then I heard a noise, kind of mechanical but also kind of feathery and then . . . and then a fucking dodo walked into the room.

I thought I must be going insane—I mean *more* insane. A full size dodo, with its big gray body and its sad, stupid face, came through the door, ambled across the floor toward me, moving slowly on its big leathery feet, curling its neck from side to side, trying to flap its helpless, stunted little wings. It was way more lifelike than the one I'd seen in the glass case in Oxford, but I guess that was because it was moving. I nearly peed my pants. If I'd had a gun I'd probably have used it, tried to blow the thing to smithereens, though it crossed my mind that maybe the dodo wasn't even really there. I thought maybe my nightmares had come to life, that my head was so full of dodos that I'd started projecting them outwards, making my hallucinations strut around in the real world. But then I heard Dorothy giggling and saying, "That's a smashing toy you've got there," so obviously she could see it too, and that felt like a reprieve. I couldn't be totally mad if Dorothy shared my madness, could I?

And then Tom Brewster walked into the room carrying a remote control that he was operating, and he pressed a couple of buttons and the dodo responded and he made it walk right up to me and peck me on the hand. It hurt like hell. That beak was a vicious thing. I looked at Tom and I didn't know if I wanted to kill him or hug him. I didn't know whether this was the nicest thing anybody had ever done for me or the very worst.

Tom Brewster said, "There's your dodo. Now go and make your fucking movie, man."

So yeah, right, like I said to Brian Braithwaite, where do people get their ideas? It's not such a bad question. For me, the easy, glib (and true) answer is anywhere I can. And you know, one idea is never enough, you need at least two or three big ideas to come together and then a bunch of smaller ideas. And that's exactly how it was with me.

Big idea number one: let's make a dodo movie. OK, that one had been sitting on the table for quite a while and we'd seen how far that had gotten me. Then I'd had a moment in and out of time in a museum in Oxford, and then fears of mortality on the plane, and OK maybe they weren't ideas but they were *something*. And maybe a robotic dodo wasn't an idea either, more of a fact, a piece of hardware. Anyway it was now a reality, a given, and maybe also an inspiration. If you want to make a dodo movie and somebody hands you a fully functioning dodo, it kind of destroys a lot of your excuses.

The next idea was more about method, something that had occurred to me while I was talking to Henry in the diner. He'd got me thinking. Till then I'd been assuming that my dodo movie had to be very Hollywood, with proper sets and costumes, naturalistic, historically accurate, with gaffers and gofers and best boys and catering trucks, but now I wondered if there was really any need for that stuff.

The moviemakers Henry and me had been talking about, they weren't like that. You could have people sitting in bed reading out texts from a book. You could have a close-up of a cup of coffee with a voice-over about . . . well, about any damn thing you wanted, so why not about the history of the dodo? Movies didn't just have to be about jeopardy, character arcs, and a big lead role for Jennifer Lopez.

So it was dawning on me that it might be possible to make a movie that was a cross between, I dunno, *The Swimmer*, *Last Year at Marienbad*, and maybe a bit of *Gummo* thrown in. I guess I was imagining something severe and formal, weird and not super-commercial but just edgy enough not to be totally *un*commercial, something spiky and a little scary and kind of sexy, though you can't really say why. That was a *very* big idea.

Then another idea came via Dorothy. Unlike her I *had* been in L.A. long enough to get desperate. Maybe it was time for me to get into porn. How about *that* for an idea? Well, not get *into* it exactly, but just do it. Shoot some porn, just enough to make some money and get ahead. Hell, Barry Sonnenfeld had done it, and he'd gone on to make a movie with "family values" in the title. And my photographs of Angela and Brian really had been pretty hot, so obviously I had some talent there, and according to Dorothy you could just call Jack Rozin on the phone and he'd say come right over, and OK, I didn't have Dorothy's obvious advantages—like being female—but on the other hand I'd been to film school.

So the plan—evolving all the time—was this. I'd go see Jack Rozin and tell him I wanted to make porn. He'd say, "Go for it, kid." I'd hire a cast and crew and some equipment and agree to shoot two days of porn, but I'd do it real fast, complete the two-day shoot in one day, and on the second day I'd take the same equipment, though with a completely different cast and crew, and make my own movie, a version of the dodo movie—a short version, something I could show to somebody to raise money, a calling card maybe. Hell, they'd have to be impressed by Tom's mechanical dodo. Or maybe it wouldn't be a calling card, maybe it would just be an end in itself. I'd just do it for the sake of doing it. That was something, wasn't it?

But the final idea, and the one that made all the others fall into place, didn't arrive until I met up again with Henry at the end of the day. I wanted him to see that I'd been taking good care of his daughter, so I went back with her to the hotel, and Henry was sitting there in the bar, but Dorothy went straight up to her room the moment she saw him, so it was just me and Henry. We had a drink and talked some more about movies, and in the middle of this I noticed he had a pile of stuff sitting on the bar in front of him, including some property details from a realtor. I looked at the house for sale, a fake Hollywood Tudor mansion, and something just clicked. Location, location, location.

"Are you looking to buy some property, Henry?"

"It's a long story, and a slightly embarrassing one. I should probably give the keys back."

"You have the *keys?*"

In that moment I could completely see a way to make my movie. I almost kissed him.

twenty-three **Face/Off**

Although he has been abandoned and spurned by the university, William Draper nevertheless feels the need to continue his education in the medical arts. It is not always easy. He learns piecemeal, an observation here and there, a conversation with an apothecary or a barber surgeon, and even sometimes a conversation with a quack who genuinely knows some physic, the kind of quack who, thanks to William's benign neglect, remains undetected and unmolested by the Royal College. Every little bit helps. But there is one spectacle that regularly furthers William's knowledge: a good public execution.

So today William finds himself at one with the London crowd, being conveyed by a wave of jaundiced, excited humanity along Tyburn toward the gallows. The streets are packed, children on fathers' shoulders, well-dressed gentlemen and ladies standing on carts, having paid for the privilege and the view. The majority is loud and drunk, full of false bravado and laughter. But William needs to be cold sober to watch an execution. He wants to see it with a scientific eye, first to observe how the victim meets his end, and more crucially to note the physical details and intricacies.

Today's is especially promising, the execution of a noted blackguard who has murdered his wife and children in a drunken, feral rage. Thus a particular end is required for him:

hanging, drawing, and quartering, a process (or rather three processes) that William finds profoundly educational, a chance to see what a man is truly made of. William likes to note what happens when the noose clenches around the neck, when the knife pierces the stomach flesh as though slitting open a bag of seed, though what emerges is much hotter, much more richly colored and textured than seed, a tangle of cords and organs, a shocking sight, yet one that has its beauty and logic. Poor Moxon.

Evisceration always rouses the crowd mightily. There is revulsion and laughter too, empathy, there but for the grace of god. And even more so when the innards are burned. Who would have guessed they would ignite so readily? Who would have thought there was need to ignite them at all? Exactly what part does this conflagration play in deterrence, punishment, or vengeance? Certainly no man relishes the idea of having his entrails set on fire, and yet William's observations have taught him that the culprit is usually dead, of shock or a broken neck, by the time the flames catch hold. And frankly William does not learn so very much from this part of the experience. But the quartering, this can be enlightening indeed.

In truth this is spectacle rather than science, yet Henry always stares hard to see the underlying pattern and symmetry, to see, for example, which tubes, cords and tendons are visible both in the neck and the severed head, to see which ones cut easily, which make work for the executioner. He sees how the limbs connect and disconnect, sees how much force is necessary to wrench them from their sockets. And these parts, not true quarters at all, but rather unequally divided portions, will remain nailed up in locations around the city for closer inspection, but like all pieces of meat they are more appealing, more themselves, when fresh.

The crowd coagulates about him, and he fears he may be too far away from the scaffold to make any detailed observations. There is one special question that has been much on his mind lately. He wants to investigate the very moment of death, a far more ambiguous thing than he would ever have imagined. Often he has been deceived, has thought the hanged man to be quite dead, only to see him then open his eyes or say some extra, inscrutable curse or prayer. William thinks it should not be so difficult. The soul's departure, the extinction of the living flame should be a more obvious, more straightforward matter.

The sky is bright, the heat blistering. William keeps his collar up, his hat pulled down, like a man with much to hide, yet this is one of the few days he can pass inconspicuously enough through a crowd. He is not enough of a spectacle for them. He feels like a prisoner in his own skin, and there are times when he would happily be rid of it. He has heard that in Turkey and in China, when it comes to executions, the state favors flaying the condemned man alive; to watch this would surely be a great revelation. How staid and dull his English countrymen sometimes seem.

She sees him before he sees her, before he has the chance to look or slip away. It is the woman from Haymarket, the beauty specialist, the so-called late doctor's widow, Mrs. Mariette Hendrick. She is advancing on him, her smile both welcoming and gently mocking. He can hardy believe she is pleased to see him, since she knows what he is and what he does, yet she shows no disquiet or abashment.

She comes up to him, looks at him evenly, and says, "Why Mr. Draper, what brings you to these nether regions?"

It is a question that would scarcely seem to require an answer, and he knows that the more complex answer he would give—that he is here to contemplate life and death, the mysteries of body and spirit, and the connections between them—would drop foolishly from his lips. So he thinks it best to pretend he is just another crass, gawping spectator, and he says, "Not the best part of me, I'm sure."

"Which *is* the best part?" she asks, another question without an answer. She is amused by his embarrassment and she says, "And how is your dear wife?"

"Do not mock me, Mrs. Hendrick. I think you know that I am a single man."

"Well, that is a great shame."

A ripple in the crowd presses in on them, moves them closer to the gallows and to each other.

"My late husband always used to say that a man might learn more at a public execution than in all the anatomy theaters of Europe."

"There really was such a husband?"

"Why certainly. You think I would invent a spouse for myself? And how else would a woman have gained her medical knowledge? At a university?"

"He taught you physic?"

"Yes. And in plain English."

"Yes," says William, "that would be a great help."

"I found it so."

"And how precisely did your husband die?"

"Precisely, I do not know. He was in Holland furthering his studies. The reports I received of his death were woolly and contradictory. One said it was plague. Another said it was a fall from a horse. It would be good to know, though I realize that knowing would do me little good."

William is inclined to ask more, about her husband and his life and work and just how much of his knowledge he imparted to her before his death. And the realization creeps over him that

Mrs. Hendrick may know more of physic than he does. He may well be in no position to judge her. Indeed he sees that this woman might be able to teach him something.

She raises her hand as though she is about to stroke his face, run her fingers over his scars, explore the length and breadth of his affliction. But she stops herself. Her hand flutters a few inches away from his cheek. To go further would be an assault.

"I believe I could help you," she says simply.

William does not react. He fears mockery and treachery. Help him how? Is she perhaps suggesting they join forces to combat quackery? But it is not that.

"Your face," she says. "I cannot be certain, and I make no promises, false or otherwise. But if you were to come to my lodgings again, we could examine the possibilities."

Is she flirting with him? It seems improbable. Does she see something in him that he has always wanted some woman to detect? Then there is a spasm in the crowd, a shift and a cleft, and the two of them are parted, and she is swept away, and simultaneously there is a roar and a cheer from the mass around him; the executioner has begun his work. William finds himself pressed into the sweaty back of a huge, immobile laborer, tall and wide as a door. He will see nothing of the execution, but it has still been a most educational day.

Some weeks later William sits in the dusty gloom of his quarters: a man and his dodo, sharing the same melancholy space. His life seems all too mean. There is work, there is the tavern, there is the apparently futile desire to find a mate. It is not enough and yet it is far, far too much. William idly scratches his cheek, dislodging some shards of skin. He feels becalmed, floating on a sea of fate's malevolent scheming. There are times when he thinks he should visit Mrs. Hendrick and see what her herbalism and natural science might accomplish for his condition, but he soon abandons the idea. What could she do for him that his Oxford tutor could not? He knows he will not make the visit. And she must know it too, since one day, unbidden, unannounced, she arrives at his lodgings.

Suddenly the printer's house is bedlam. The many children and relatives are everywhere at once making all the noises and motions of a revolution. A female creature of scarcely imaginable exoticism has arrived in their domain, come to see their strange yet most unexotic lodger. In a flurry of fur and satin Mrs. Hendrick ascends the bare wooden stairs, while William tries to rearrange himself to welcoming effect. A moment before she enters his room he throws a blanket over the dodo's cage. It is enough that she should find him here in these grim, paltry surroundings. Surely she would not understand his feelings toward this sad, flightless bird.

She steps over his threshold, leaving behind a train of wide-eyed, giddy children. William shuts the door to keep them at bay. If they choose to interpret a closed door as a sign of lewdness and immorality, so be it. The chance would be a fine thing.

"I came to you because I knew you would not come to me," Mrs. Hendrick says. "I have been thinking about you and I have brought something for your skin."

William is amazed. "I appreciate your concern, but alas, I feel that I'm incurable."

"Oh yes, I feel that too. So I am not here to cure but to disguise." She hands him a glass vessel containing a creamy ointment, thickish, oily, pale pink in color. "Smooth this into your face," she says. "It will form a sort of mask and also a shield. It will cover the rough blemishes of your skin and will protect you from the sun."

"You are offering me makeup?" he says. "You think I should paint myself like a harlot?"

"I think you should paint yourself like anyone who has something to conceal. It is a simple matter of practicality."

Across the room there is a stirring under the blanket, an ineffectual flapping, a cooing sound, something that does not wish to be concealed.

"You have a pet, Mr. Draper. Of what sort? I should like to see it. Please."

Reluctantly he pulls the blanket away, prepares to make all manner of arcane explanation, but Mrs. Hendrick says, "Why, it is a dodo."

"You are familiar with the breed?"

"I saw one once a few years ago."

William's heart leaps. Perhaps fate has brought this to him. Another bird, seen by this wise woman. She will tell him its whereabouts. He will track it down. All shall be well.

"It was displayed by a Yorkshireman, a Mr. Moxon, who called it the world's most disgusting bird. That was an excessive description I thought, and quite unnecessarily cruel of him."

"This is that very bird," William says, with a fatigued disappointment he knows she cannot understand.

"You do not choose to display it as Mr. Moxon did."

"I have other, grander plans."

"How so?"

He tells her everything, his dream of a new world populated by dodos.

"Why dodos?" she asks. "Why not chickens? Or pigeons? Or vultures?"

He decides to take the question seriously. "Because those creatures can fend for themselves," he says. "The dodo needs a friend and a champion. I have selected myself for the task, though there are times when certainly I feel I have had little choice in the matter."

"You are compelled by a higher power?"

"Or my own nature."

"You are a curious man, Mr. Draper, but not a dull one."

She takes the ointment and begins to administer to William's face. He flinches at first. It is the sort of thing a mother might do, not that he knows much about mothers. She works diligently, her fingers exploring the battered contours of his face as though remodeling them. William stands still and stoic, eyes closed, patiently enduring.

When she is finished, she shows him his image in a small looking glass she has brought for the purpose. He stares at himself. He is not transformed. It is not some wholly other face, not even his own face perfected, but it is a face made serviceable, made better, made ordinary. Above all, to his infinite relief, he does not look like a man wearing makeup.

"You have great skills, Mrs. Hendrick," he says.

"Yes, and not only in this area."

This time he does not prevent himself from kissing her, and she does not resist him.

twenty-four Family Plot

Of course I was a fool to let Rick McCartney have the keys to the mock-Tudor house. In my defense I would say that he undoubtedly had a very persuasive manner. He pointed out that certain producers financed entire movies just so their daughters could get a part. I was luckier than that, he said. I didn't have to hand over any money, just a set of keys. So yes, I could say I was doing it to help Dorothy, as indeed I was, and I suppose I could also say that I didn't really see great harm in letting Rick use the house. It wasn't quite honest, and it probably wasn't quite legal, but isn't that how a lot of movies get made? I could even tell myself I was part of a great Hollywood tradition. But I still knew I shouldn't have done it. And equally, I probably shouldn't have attended Bob Samuelson's funeral. At the very least it was in appallingly bad taste, but Dorothy insisted that she had to go and that I had to go with her. So I went.

I suppose all good actors can portray two emotions simultaneously, and so it was with Dorothy. As she sat beside me in my car (having decided that her own vehicle was a bit gaudy for the occasion) she expressed a mournfulness appropriate to attending a funeral, but simultaneously she conveyed an underlying excitement at having been cast in her first Hollywood movie, though personally I felt that "Hollywood" should be in quotation marks. I'm not one of those film buffs who make broad general pronouncements about fashions and trends in the film industry, but even I had strong suspicions that a movie, any movie, about the extinction of the dodo wasn't likely to be packing them into the multiplexes of America.

As we drove to the cemetery, I in my dark linen suit, Dorothy somber yet stunning in a new black outfit, I found myself asking her, "When you slept with Bob Samuelson . . . was it . . . ?"

"Was it what?" she demanded, all prickly, daughterly outrage. "Are you asking me if it was *good?*"

"No," I said. "No, I'm not asking that."

I suppose I was actually trying to ask whether it was meaningful, caring, whether there was mutual affection and respect, whether his intentions were honorable. Of course I couldn't ask that directly. Even I wasn't enough of a square to do that. And I suppose what I really wanted to ask was whether she'd just slept with him because he could advance her career. But I can't imagine the father who would ever be able to ask his daughter that.

"No," I said, "I was just wondering whether he seemed . . . in good health."

"What can I tell you, Dad?" she said. "He really wasn't that good in bed, OK?"

We drove in silence after that.

In general I'm rather taken by the trappings of death, by graveyards and headstones, tombs and mausoleums. They're so much neater and more enduring than the messy provisionalities of the human body. In England I frequently wandered around churchyards, reading inscriptions, noting family connections, calculating ages, speculating about causes of death. It seems to me a perfectly respectable and comprehensible activity for anyone, not least a doctor, and although I can see that many patients might not wish to think that their GP was much possessed by death, I actually think it would be rather surprising for a medical man not to be.

Of course I've seen the movie of *The Loved One* (not one of my favorite movies, though the performance by Liberace is certainly a cherishable, bravura oddity), so naturally I had some received ideas about the American way of death. Bob Samuelson was not being buried anywhere so grand as Forest Lawn, and yet there was certainly something profoundly L.A. about the cemetery, called Hollywood Forever, seeking after a kind of immortality, I supposed.

I had a certain amount of trouble finding it, because I had the notion that a cemetery would have to be located in some wide open, underpopulated location. In fact this one was wedged in between the bustle of Santa Monica and Melrose Boulevards. The cemetery entrance, when I eventually found it and parked, was opposite a carpet warehouse.

Once inside, however, I saw that the place was certainly expansive enough, a sort of grand, walled park. The sun shone, the day was calm, the colors were intense. Death's coldness and darkness, those qualities that go with the English version of mortality, were quite absent. The boundary walls were reassuringly distant, though the roar of traffic was close at hand. At the center of the cemetery were elaborate graves with ornate statuary, Egyptian- and Roman-style mausoleums, ludicrous yet undeniably impressive, and beyond them I could see a lake with ducks and herons, and a temple on an island at the lake's center.

The area where they were burying Bob Samuelson was comparatively modest, a rather distant corner. Dorothy and I had quite a walk to get there, though plenty of other people had driven into the cemetery itself. We could see some shiny black cars clustered around a grave in the distance. Dorothy took my arm and we strode on but not far before she said, "What are those two men doing over there?"

A short distance away two men loitered beside one of the graves. The headstone was a white marble chunk, and leaning against it, as it were, was a female figure carved from the same stone. She was more or less naked but was made decent by a few wisps of chiseled fabric that clung to her body. As a personification of death and mourning she was very appealing and undeniably sensual. It was a statue you might be tempted to touch, and one of the two men had succumbed to temptation. He was running his hands over the head, the bare shoulders, and back of the statue.

"That's appalling," Dorothy said.

"Well, I don't know."

"Go and tell them to stop. Go on."

I didn't intend to do anything quite so authoritarian. The fact was, I knew both the men. The one doing the touching was Duane, from the Beauty Vault; the other was Perry Martin, who expressed no surprise whatever at my sudden appearance beside him but simply said, "So how's the quest for Bibi Scott going?"

The question may have been innocent enough, though Perry Martin seemed the least innocent of men.

"It's not a quest," I said.

"What then?"

I felt I owed him no explanation, but I said, "Just idle curiosity, I suppose."

He wasn't satisfied with that answer. "Maybe we should all go down to her real estate office," he suggested, "and see what her story is."

"Whatever it is," I said, "I'm sure she's entitled to her privacy."

"Aren't we English and snippy today?" he said. "Are you here for a funeral. Is it anybody famous?"

"An agent called Bob Samuelson," I said.

He looked blank and bored. "Not exactly A-list, then."

"No," I admitted. "And why are *you* two here?"

"I'm feeling this fine piece of marble statuary," Duane said.

And then I realized something. "You're blind," I said.

"Oh?" said Duane. "Does it show?"

Perhaps he said this to embarrass me, but if so, he failed. "Actually no," I said. "It certainly didn't show when I met you at the Beauty Vault."

And he'd known where Barbara's photograph was: a good trick. Or something.

"The statue," Perry Martin said, "is supposedly carved from life. Louise Brooks. I'm mad about her. And since she's a silent star, how else am I going to give Duane an idea of what she's like?"

"I see," I said.

Duane stopped feeling the statue. "It's Perry's passion, rather than mine," he said. "But since I love Perry, I love what he loves. We go to the movies. We sit. He watches and listens. I just listen. Afterwards we compare notes."

"I'll bet you've usually seen a better movie than he has," I said.

"Oh, he's sharp, isn't he?" said Perry Martin.

Dorothy had had enough of waiting for me. "Daddy," she called out loudly, "we have a burial to catch."

We scurried on and I was left thinking that in other circumstances I might have had a lot to ask Perry and Duane, not least about what went on behind the green baize door of the Beauty Vault.

"What were you doing there?" Dorothy demanded when I returned to her side. "It looked like you were befriending them."

"No, no, I was just reasoning with them."

Need I say that I could hardly go to a cemetery without thinking about Caroline, my wife, my late wife? And this seems as good a place as any to tell the story of her death.

Caroline, incidentally, has no grave. She was cremated. In the circumstances we decided that was the best thing to do. By "we" I mean Dorothy and I. Perhaps if we had to do it again we'd come to a quite different decision, and there were times when I thought it wouldn't be so bad if there was a grave where I could go and place a few flowers, though no doubt there are people who'd think that was the height of hypocrisy on my part.

The simple fact was that I did not make Caroline happy. For a long time I tried and failed, and then I stopped trying. Her own attempts to make herself happy were equally hopeless. They consisted of drinking too much, taking too many prescription drugs, and having affairs with unsuitable men. She was always threatening to leave me, but apparently none of her men was ever prepared to steal her away.

Initially I was hurt by her unfaithfulness, though I feigned indifference, and eventually the indifference became genuine. Caroline stayed with me. She had nowhere else to go. Neither did I for that matter, and in any case there was Dorothy. We stuck it out. As far as the world was concerned we were an ordinary married couple, and perhaps there was nothing so very extraordinary about us.

I couldn't have said that I was pleased with the arrangement but I certainly wasn't unhappy in the way that Caroline was. As a matter of fact I suspect that the amount of happiness we're capable of experiencing is determined at a very early stage of our development, and Caroline simply wasn't programmed for happiness. Gradually she got more and more miserable. I offered to arrange some counseling for her, an action which in retrospect I see was guaranteed to prevent her from going.

She continued to suffer. She began an affair with a local builder. From the circumstantial evidence it appears to have been a boozy, bruising, passionate affair, which I'd have thought was the kind that suited her best, but something about it caused her brand new forms of despair. I was less inclined than ever to be sympathetic. She was drunk one night when I came back from the surgery. Her anger and self-pity threatened to overwhelm us both. She said she was contemplating suicide. Glibly, sarcastically, hatefully, I said that sounded like the solution to all our problems. Two days later she was dead: slashed wrists, an appallingly lurid way of doing it.

So, was I a monster? Yes, probably. Was I a bad husband and a bad human being? No doubt. But despite whatever Dorothy said or thought, I was not a murderer, at least not in the case of my wife. Bob Samuelson might be a different matter.

After Caroline's death, her lover came to my surgery to talk. He wanted this, not me. The nurse and the receptionist had gone home, so we would be alone there. He was late and I thought perhaps he was trying to prove something by that, but then his white van pulled up across the street. He looked younger than me, though I suspect he wasn't.

He came into the surgery and stood in the outer office, where I was waiting for him. He seemed to have dressed up a little. He had on workman's trousers and dirty sneakers but also a clean white shirt and a knitted tie, which I guessed he'd put on specially for the occasion. He looked uncomfortable and I was content with that. He made several attempts to speak but couldn't quite manage it. I said nothing either. I could stand there as long as he could.

At last, clumsily, boyishly, he said, "Is one of us supposed to hit the other or something?"

"I have no intention of hitting you," I replied.

Another interminable silence, then he said, "I'm really sorry, Doc."

I thought it best to accept this as a blanket apology for a whole sequence of events, and I replied, "Yes, aren't we all."

It seemed a safe and banal enough reply, but what he said next threatened all notions of safety. He said, "Do you think she loved you?"

I managed to keep my composure and I said, "Well, I'm assuming not, otherwise she wouldn't have slept with you, would she?"

"But she didn't *leave* you, did she?"

"Oh, I rather thought she did. I thought she left me in a big way."

"How do you mean?"

"By dying," I said.

"Oh, well, all right, but in that case she left us both. And if she'd loved either of us, if she'd loved anybody, like even your daughter, then I don't see how she could have killed herself, do you?"

It was not an entirely new thought, but I hadn't expected it to be shared by this man. "Oh, I'm sure she loved as well as she could."

I realized that might sound consoling. I had no desire to offer this man consolation but I suppose it was force of habit. Consolation is one of the most powerful drugs we doctors dispense.

"Yeah, well, I'm sorry anyway," he said, and he started to edge away, then stopped. "Before I go, Doctor, I wonder if you could give me something for my stomach. It's been giving me real gyp lately."

If I had been going to hit him, that would certainly have been the choicest moment. And it did occur to me that I might easily have inflicted some painful and humiliating examination on him, prescribed violent laxatives or emetics. But I resisted. I told him to see his own doctor. You see, I wasn't wholly corrupted in those days.

There were perhaps half a dozen mourners around Bob Samuelson's grave: a pair who must surely have been his mother and father, a woman I took to be his estranged wife, a couple of young men in shorts, and then Georgia Ricardo. A female priest in cowboy boots officiated.

A burial is always and only a burial. The coffin goes into the dark hole. Earth is thrown in after it. People stand and watch, as though they're waiting for something very special to happen, and when it doesn't, they gradually, reluctantly depart. That's the way burials are. There just isn't much scope for originality.

I noticed that nobody was weeping, not the parents, not even Georgia Ricardo, who'd wept so freely in her office, and soon it was all over and the mourners were leaving. Only Georgia Ricardo lingered. She had other business on her mind, and I was that business. She approached me looking purposeful and far too friendly. If she remembered Dorothy she didn't let it show, though Dorothy clearly recognized her as the woman who'd told her to abandon hopes of an acting career, and she duly slunk away, pretending to be absorbed in some nearby gravestones.

"Glad you could come," Georgia Ricardo said.

"It was the least I could do."

"Why haven't you called me, Henry?"

It seemed easiest to say, "I've been busy."

"You know, Henry, if you sign with another agency I'm going to be heartbroken. You don't want to break hearts, do you?"

"No, I don't," I said.

"So call me. Please."

She'd done her part, her professional best, and was walking away when something struck me. "I suppose you have a fairly encyclopedic knowledge of actors and actresses, don't you?" I said.

"They're all called actors these days," she said.

"So do you know, *did* you know, someone called Bibi Scott?"

Without hesitation she said, "Not personally, but I know who Bibi Scott is. Or was. Why?"

"I met her."

"Yeah? What she's doing now?"

"Real estate."

"Just as well. She's one of those people who'll never work in this town again."

"Why not?"

"Oh, I could tell you," Georgia Ricardo said, "but then I'd have to kill you."

This seemed like a very poor joke to make in a cemetery.

"What's the *matter* with you?" Dorothy demanded when we were in the car driving away. "How do you know all these people? You've been in L.A. no time at all and it's like you have a secret life or something."

"I have no secrets from anybody," I lied.

"This trip is all about me, not about you," she said.

I knew exactly what she meant but by this point I also knew she was wrong. "My whole life is about you, Dorothy," I lied again, and I think she more or less believed me.

twenty-five

Back to the Future

I guess I imagined Jack Rozin was going to be a big fat guy. I guess I thought you had to be kind of porky before they'd let you into the pornographers' union, and in any case he *sounded* fat when I talked to him on the phone, when he said sure, come up to the house in Encino, let's talk.

So I went to the house, which was Spanish-style, very nice, very expensive, and very nonporn it seemed to me, and I was met at the door by a guy who introduced himself as Tony. He looked like a bodybuilder gone to seed, and he described himself as Jack's "right hand" though he snickered when he said it. He showed me out to the pool where I couldn't believe that the strange, old, lean, hippie-ish guy under a sun umbrella was really Jack Rozin. I guess I'd also imagined that the house would be full of flunkies, and maybe a few stray porn actresses, but as far as I could tell it was just me, Jack, and this Tony guy.

Rozin looked like he should have been working in a head shop or a comic book store, and frankly he looked pretty unhealthy, like he was in some sort of pain and was hiding from the sun. He was sitting at a glass table, reading, and there was a pile of books in front of him, some of them art books, but others looked like heavyweight stuff; I saw that one was a biography of Bismarck.

He looked me up and down, like he might have been checking me out for star potential. I said hello and he just nodded, and

241

when I tried to shake hands he waved it away, as though that kind of activity was way too exhausting. Then he motioned for me to sit down in a director's chair that had been positioned in the full sun just outside the umbrella's shadow. He slammed his book shut and held it very carefully in his lap, to show that I had his full attention but that I was also kind of an irritation.

"So you want to make movies, Rick?" he said.

"Yes."

"Well, that's a very good start, because a lot of people in this town just want to *talk* about making movies. Or they want to have *meetings* about making movies. Or they want to make *deals* about making movies. Or they just want to make money and they couldn't care less about movies at all. Or they just want to get laid. But you want to make movies."

"That's right."

"OK. What kind of movies?"

"Really good movies."

"Don't we all, Rick?" he said and he got up, wincing slightly in the process and he came over and patted me on the arm in a way that you could have thought was pretty damn condescending if you'd wanted to.

"How's your back, Rick?"

"Fine," I said.

"You're a very lucky man, Rick. Don't get me started talking about my bad back."

He walked away from me, looked out over the pool as though it were a huge stretch of ocean, and he clasped his hands to the base of his spine and massaged it, but that evidently didn't help.

With a well-rehearsed air, he said, "In the Jack Rozin media mansion, there are many houses. Many product lines. Which is just as well, because this is the age of the specialist. Once upon a time sex was sex. People would sit there and look at the screen, and say, 'Oh boy, this is so great, it's naked people fucking.' That was enough. That was all it took. The actors could be plug-ugly, the lighting could be lousy, the camera could go in and out of focus, but the subject matter was all that counted. Those were the days, eh, Rick?"

I wanted to say, "Before my time, dude," but I just nodded.

"And that wore off pretty quick," Rozin said. "The public was really fast to get over their amazement at watching sex on screen. So then the people had to be more attractive and there had to be some professionalism, some good lighting so people could see what the fuck was going on. But that passed too. That was too generic, too one-size-fits-all, and the market divided and subdivided and divided again: fetish, mature, interracial, gang bangs, watersports, S and M, gonzo, bukkake, whatever. Small markets, small budgets, small profits. But small is beautiful, right?"

I didn't really know what he was talking about but I said, "Right."

"And which genre will you be operating in, Rick?"

That sounded kind of encouraging. He'd said "*will* you be operating in," not "would you like to" or "do you hope to." It might only have been his way of speaking but I liked it.

"Fantasy," I said.

"Great," he said, and it sounded surprisingly heartfelt.

"Historical costume drama, with a bit of time travel thrown in," I said.

"Wow," he said. "Not many guys come in here with a pitch like this," and he smiled fit to bust. "Go on."

"Well," I said, "we take two or three women, very modern, very good-looking—tattoos, silicone, stripper shoes, all the modern accessories—and they go back into the past—to England in the seventeenth century—and they have sex with the locals, Cavaliers and Roundheads, Puritans, peasants, and the thing is the girls are clean and scrubbed and glossy and the people back there, the ones they're having sex with, are real grungy and dirty and—"

It's not often you see a grown man clap his hands in glee, but that's exactly what Jack Rozin did, even though it seemed to hurt him, and he immediately started rubbing his back again. I was amazed. The truth was I hadn't really expected him to go for this costume drama bit. I was only trying my luck. I figured that if he went for it, then the cost of hiring the costumes could be included in the porn budget, and then they'd be there free for my dodo movie, but I'd thought it was a long shot. I'd expected him to say no to the historical bit and then I'd move on to some more obvious ideas, sloppy amputee facials or whatever tiny market segment he wanted me to cover.

"You think costumes are sexy?" he asked.

"If they're done right," I said.

"They'll take them off at some point?"

"Of course."

"Yeah, yeah, I like this. You've got a vision," Rozin said. "And let me see if I'm following this. These beautiful clean, scrubbed, sexy, modern girls are going to get fucked by a bunch of dirty, smelly guys with bad teeth and bad skin and so on. Are we on the same page?"

"Sure," I said.

"Yeah, I think that's kind of hot," he said. "So we're talking about degradation, humiliation, about having sex with disgusting people because . . . well, who needs a reason? Everybody can relate to that."

"Right," I said.

"And how long are you going to need to shoot this movie?"

"Two days," I said.

"You sure that's long enough?"

It took all the restraint I had, but I said it would be plenty. Things were going well. I didn't want to push my luck.

"And it's got to be shot on video, not film, right?"

"Sure," I said. That was a disappointment but I'd expected it.

"And you can start shooting day after tomorrow?"

"Well, I . . ."

"Yes, you can."

Jack Rozin came over to me again, to the director's chair. I thought I should probably stand up but he put a hand on my shoulder and kept me in place. He stuck his face close to mine so I could smell his breath, very sweet, very recently mouthwashed, and he said, "Are you sure you want to do this, Rick?"

"Sure," I said.

"Shooting porn isn't too good for the inner man, you know."

"I'm cool with it," I said.

"Standing there in a room with some people you don't know, telling them to do things to each other, asking them to perform intimate acts that have been stripped of all intimacy . . . it's kind of a corrupting process."

"Hey," I said, trying to sound breezy, "I'm already fully corrupted."

He gave me a look that, in retrospect, I think said, "This kid knows nothing, absolutely nothing," but all he said was, "Fine," and he patted me on both cheeks, and maybe it was playful or maybe it was sexual, or maybe it was both, but it was also a kind of handshake, a way of sealing the deal. It looked like I'd managed to get myself in business with Jack Rozin. Maybe I should have been more surprised, but the fact was, I'd started to *believe* in myself. I could see why he might believe too.

My new employer or partner or producer, or whatever the hell Jack Rozin was, returned to the shade, to his book and his back pain. He'd finished with me, at least for the time being. There was no paperwork (I guess the porn world isn't big on paperwork), nothing to sign, though obviously there were a lot of details to figure out. Rozin wasn't concerned with any of that. He said Tony was "at my disposal," though Tony didn't look like he'd ever be at anybody's disposal except his own. Jack Rozin's last words to me were, "It would be really great if you didn't totally fuck this up," and I was dumb enough to tell him there was no chance of that.

Tony was waiting for me in the hall and, in a bored way, he told me how all this worked. Basically he gave me a list of phone numbers for people, agencies, and equipment rental places that owed Jack Rozin a favor or two. I just had to mention his name, doors would open, and I'd get what I needed. Then Tony pressed a couple of hundred dollars in cash into my hand for "running expenses."

I walked out of Jack Rozin's house, and it all seemed perfect. It all seemed too good to be true. Which of course it was.

twenty-six **Mask**

William Draper scarcely knows how to thank Mrs. Hendrick for her several generosities. They bring about changes in him that are more than merely cosmetic. The gift of the skin potion is only the first step. Now that he is unembarrassed about his face, he can move through London with a new, untrammeled confidence. He looks unremarkable, and this is surely an asset for a man who wishes to spy. A new round of particularly unscrupulous quacks is rapidly put out of business.

The gift Mrs. Hendrick made him of her body is generosity of a different order, but it achieves a surprisingly similar effect. If she can find him an object of attraction, then he feels there must be something in him that is attractive. Consequently, the new William Draper who walks the streets of Alsatia has a spring, a bounce, that is pure novelty. He looks people directly in the face, and they look back and see another perfectly ordinary face. It seems a sort of miracle. And this newfound *amour propre* has other uses and consequences besides the hounding of quacks. William's search for a second dodo now becomes far more active.

If he were a different kind of man, a Tradescant for instance, he might take to the highways or the seas, making his search in person, pressing into dark corners of the land, through distant continents and new worlds. From what he hears, America is a place stocked full of every kind of wonder. Surely he might procure a dodo there.

But he knows himself. He is not that kind of adventurer. His confidence is only skin deep. Foreign lands are places of exposure, of burning suns and godless light. He knows he will, and must, stay close to home. And yet, since London is his home, a venue for chance meetings and fateful encounters, a conduit and a crossroads, his hopes remain alive.

In his explorations of the streets and taverns, he now meets all manner of men on equal terms: seekers, sailors, travelers, merchants, freebooters. He talks to them, hears their accounts of wonders and strangeness, and then casually brings the conversation round to the natural, to fauna, to birdlife, to the matter of the dodo. It is a name many are familiar with one way or another. Some curse it as a devilish bird, some mock it for its gullibility and stupidity, a few say they have seen one, and in due course William meets a Belgian spice trader who claims to have eaten its flesh and found it rather more palatable than its general reputation.

William puts it about that he is a collector of curiosities. He exaggerates his means but also understates his desire. He does not wish to appear desperate and push the price too high, knowing where that got Moxon. Equally he does not let on that he requires the dodo for breeding purposes. Quite why, he cannot say. Perhaps secrecy and deception have become a habit.

Many months pass. Sometimes a stranger tracks down William and comes bearing what he thinks, or at least states, is a dodo. William is always open to such approaches, though less so as time goes on, since the proffered creature will invariably prove to be a parakeet or a lovebird, or in one case a kind of horribly stunted Chinese dog. The stranger swears it is the thing itself, says that William is an ignoramus for declining it. Voices and fists are occasionally raised.

Sometimes a fertilized egg has been proffered, a dodo in the making. These are harder to identify and harder to resist, and William accepts one or two of them, only to find himself to be, after the hatching, a keeper of a newborn turkey or turtle or salamander. Sometimes dealers think he is more of a generalist and they bring him common or garden wonders: fossils, strange bones, grotesque plants. These he rejects out of hand.

However, what all these wanderers and hunters, these travelers and adventurers, whether sincere or duplicitous, whether honest or conniving—what they never bring him is anything that in any way resembles a dodo.

He was not quite foolish enough to believe that Mrs. Hendrick's sudden desire for him was anything more than a fleeting passion born of sympathy and the moment. He knew that was how it would be, but he is still disappointed. He is still bereft.

He sees her at regular though infrequent intervals, when he visits her house in Haymarket to obtain more of the facial potion, but she makes it clear that all she wants from him is conversation, a chance to philosophize. In this matter at least, he accepts what he is offered, what he can get.

"If you will have my opinion, William," she says, as she sips one of her more earthy tisanes, "God is something of a follower of whims and fleeting fashions, though I suppose they are all of his own making. I think he has enthusiasms, brief obsessions into which he launches himself with alacrity but then abandons because of fickleness and fecklessness."

William finds himself in uneasy admiration of this casual blasphemy.

"Strange that the Bible makes no mention of the dodo," she continues. "For surely there must have been a pair of dodos in Noah's company, else they could not have survived the flood. No doubt God wanted it that way. But why? Why destroy what he had so painstakingly created? I believe I know why."

"You do?"

"I have been considering your face, William, and its condition, and I have come to some tentative conclusions. I imagine that one morning God got it into his head that it might be a fine scheme to modify the complexions of his human creatures with a kind of impermeable layer, something like that of a tortoise or an armadillo. Your face was his first attempt. To that extent, there was a divine plan. But then he became distracted. With a shrug he forgot his purpose or decided it was not such a grand scheme after all, like a gardener who determines that he will make a knot garden or a parterre, then decides it is too much like hard work.

"And so I think it may be with your dodo. God made it and for a while it amused him. And perhaps it also amused him when the shipwrecked sailors pounced upon the dubious-tasting bird as their only means of survival. But then . . . well, God has many pressing engagements. Some projects simply fall by the wayside. It is, no doubt, a wasteful process, but perhaps wastefulness is not of much concern when you are omnipotent, omnipresent, and have all eternity before you. But we humans alas, do not. The Bible tells us that everything has its season. Perhaps the season of the dodo has passed. Perhaps mankind's season is similarly prescribed."

"You think we are doomed to extinction?"

"We are certainly doomed to death. After that the matter is in God's hand, and as I say, he seems the most contrary of old parties."

Naturally William tells her about his work for the Royal College. He would not choose to deceive her even if he could. He assures her that he is doing good and important work, defeating the villains, protecting the gullible. He is responsible for running out of town an Irish rascal who sells pills that are mostly sulphur. A Cornish woman who in her ignorance or malice recommends the inhalation of pure mercury as an infallible remedy for aging is put behind bars, and deservedly so.

Other cases may be less severe. A Frenchmen is found selling a mineral solution that proves to be nothing more than sparkling water. The product may be harmless but the price he demands is dangerously high. Then there's a Moorish fellow selling some leaf that promises medical benefits but seems only to induce dreams and a lack of will, and so he is run out of town too.

Whatever their story, whatever their intention, London is surely better off without quacks like these, William insists. Quacks like Mrs. Hendrick are, of course, another matter. The more he sees of her, the more impeccable and transparent her practice seems to be. There is no unnecessary pomp or obfuscation. She does good as simply and effectively as she knows how. The only bugbear is the matter of what she gets up to in that back room of hers, behind that green door. Sometimes when he arrives to see her, she emerges from there looking flustered and preoccupied, wearing unusually plain and protective clothing. Is it alchemy or magic or abortion that she practices back there?

None of these, he hopes, but he cannot come up with a more innocuous explanation, nor can he summon up the courage to ask.

"Let me simply put this thought into your head, William," she says. "Perhaps your Royal College is as concerned with driving out the genuine but untutored physician as it is with driving out the complete quack. Monopolies are achieved by driving out the close competitors, not the rank outsiders. Just think about it."

William promises that he will.

twenty-seven **Home Alone**

Rick McCartney's plan, as he explained it to me, was to shoot his entire movie in one day, a Sunday. Again, this suggested that we weren't involved with an epic project here, but that was all right. I like short films; I think the short is a much neglected genre.

The whole of Saturday, he told me, and I could quite believe it, would be taken up with dressing the set, arranging the lights and whatever other technical things they had to do. Dorothy assured me she would be spending the day on her own preparing for her role: getting a massage, doing voice exercises, and so forth.

Therefore my function at this time, though in due course it would change out of all recognition, consisted of no more than making sure Barbara Scott didn't turn up at the mock-Tudor house at any point in the weekend. This didn't really seem like such a big job. Sunday I assumed would be no problem. She'd be involved with an open house somewhere else. And even Saturday didn't seem like that much of a problem. She'd already told me she thought the house was unsellable, so why would she waste her time showing it to clients? In fact the only reason I could imagine her going there was to have sex with me, and in order to prevent that I decided to make a couple of preemptive strikes.

I called her up and said I really wanted to get serious about house hunting. I said I wanted to spend the whole of Saturday looking at properties, that I was prepared to look at absolutely anything and everything. She was delighted.

So on Saturday Barbara showed me condos and co-ops, town-houses and bungalows and cottages, duplex and triplex apart-ments, penthouses and even guest houses—the works. It was a long, exhausting, and strangely depressing process, no doubt made worse because I was involved in yet more deception here, and because I had to keep coming up with reasons why none of these properties was good enough for me. And when at some point in the late afternoon Barbara suggested we call it a day, buy some champagne, and go back to the mock-Tudor house, I had to deceive her still further. I said I wanted to do things differently for once, to go somewhere special, somewhere unusual.

"Like where? The Chateau Marmont?" she said.

"Possibly," I said.

"Or Palm Springs?"

"Well, I don't know."

"Or Vegas? Or do you want to go to Griffith Park and we'll do it outdoors in sight of the observatory?"

I grunted unenthusiastically.

"All right," said Barbara. "You make a suggestion."

"How about *your* place?" I said. "That would be special and unusual as far as I'm concerned."

I suspected I might be asking too much, but Barbara was un-expectedly willing. "All right Henry. You asked for it."

She lived off Los Feliz Boulevard in a bungalow court that had a lot in common with a motel: it consisted of a series of what looked like small rustic cabins arranged around an enclosed courtyard, with a fountain and a couple of lemon trees. It was modest, yet funky and very appealing.

"When I was growing up," she said, "I always promised myself I'd live in a bungalow court."

"Like Jane Fonda in *The Morning After*."

"Whatever," said Barbara. "I don't bring many people here. Only the ones I trust."

Well, that didn't make me feel especially good, but we went inside, into a small, warm, burgundy interior: heavy curtains, thick rugs, and some art deco furniture. There was a framed poster in the hall for an Italian movie called *L'Estremità dell' Amore*, with the name Bibi Scott billed as the third lead. Now that she'd invited me into her home, I thought she could hardly be quite so cryptic about her movie career. I thought we'd taken quite a step forward. There was also undoubtedly some erotic potential in being on Barbara's home territory. I felt included and accepted, and also, of course, guilty. Then we had sex, and it was spectacular.

"Henry, don't you ever get bored with the human body?" Barbara asked me afterwards.

"What do you mean?"

"In your job, being a doctor, you must see thousands, maybe hundreds of thousands of bodies. Don't they all start to look the same after a while? Don't they seem interchangeable?"

"No," I said, with complete honesty. "They look more and more different. And very few of them look as good as yours."

"You're a very sweet man, Henry. Did you always want to be a doctor?"

"Yes," I said. "Did you always want to be an actress?"

"Who said I *ever* wanted to be an actress?"

"Well, didn't you?"

"I don't know why you're so fascinated by this, Henry."

"Well, partly it's because of my daughter," I said, which was true enough. "And partly it's because I don't get to meet very many Hollywood actresses. And I get to sleep with even fewer of them. With just one of them."

"Yeah well, what a thing to tell the boys back home."

"And you haven't told me why you stopped being an actress."

"It happened. Shit happens, right? You ask too many questions, Henry, you know that?"

"It's what doctors are trained to do."

"Yeah well, maybe you should stop. Maybe you'll find out something you don't want to know."

"I want to know everything," I said.

"No, you don't, Henry. Believe me, you don't."

She got up from the bed and wrapped a dressing gown around herself as though for protection. "Are you really a doctor, Henry?"

"Of course I am. Do you think I'm not?"

"I don't know. It crossed my mind. Everybody in this town is pretending to be something they're not. Why should you be any different? You know, it's OK, it's not terrible. I'm not even sure I'd hold it against you."

"I'm *really* a doctor," I said.

"OK, so you're really a doctor. So why do I still think there's something fake about you?"

"Perhaps because you've been in Los Angeles too long."

"Good answer, Henry," she said. "But I think there's more to it than that."

"Think what you like," I said.

"Well, oddly enough, Henry, I will."

"And stop trying to be so bloody mysterious. Just because *you're* obsessively secretive, don't assume everybody else is."

This was, of course, the most terrible humbug, and it didn't make for a very satisfactory end to the evening, but at least we'd got through Saturday and I'd managed to keep her from the mock-Tudor house. That much of the plan had worked, and Sunday, I thought, would take care of itself. However, the moment I got back to my hotel there was a phone call from Rick McCartney, telling me he desperately needed me to act in his movie.

twenty-eight **The Shootist**

Putting together two separate casts and crews for two completely different movies in no time at all was quite a learning experience, believe me. The porn movie was comparatively easy. There was money, there were recognizable channels, there were people who owed favors to Jack Rozin. The art stuff, the dodo stuff, that was way harder. My dodo cast and crew were going to have to work for free, with the promise of great things in the future, and a lot of people in L.A. have heard that story too many times before. That I managed it at all is some testimony to the power of my glib charm.

I don't know if you have an idea of what it might be like to make a porn movie. Do you think it might be fun? Well, take it from me, it's no fun at all. You think it might be arousing? Well, for me personally it was about as arousing as watching somebody strip down a carburetor. But if you think it might be lots of hard work in adverse conditions, battling with egos, libidos, vanity, and the limits of the human body, then you've got it in one.

The guys—there were five of them, a model of racial integration—looked exactly like porn guys, at least to start with: muscled, tan, big-cocked, with a touch of the cyborg about them (I don't know tech stuff). Admittedly they were very professional, and they tried to make themselves look grubby and seventeenth-century. They rubbed dirt onto their finely sculpted faces and

259

their finely manicured hands, and one of them blacked out a couple of his teeth, but none of them lost that glossy, hard-baked sheen that seems to go with commercial sex. On the other hand they did seem to enjoy putting on the costumes, since I guess that was a new thing for them, and a couple of them really did try to act, boy, did they try, and I found that very touching.

For the three girls it was easier, because they were meant to be girls from the present—or I guess the future. They didn't have to change their look, and they had way less acting to do. They just had to be themselves, and they could manage that, more or less, although I'm guessing that these girls' sense of self maybe wasn't all that secure.

There was one girl who I thought was just great. She was called Tawnee and she was young and skinny with big breasts (aren't they all) and her face was just amazing, really innocent and really slutty at the same time. Obviously I wasn't stupid enough to think about dating a porn actress, but a bit of me kept thinking, yeah, in other circumstances she might be just what I was looking for. Call me an old romantic.

The fact is, I can't say that I got to know any of these performers real well in the course of the day, but in lots of ways they all seemed like regular people, just plain folks, at least by Hollywood standards: friendly, outgoing, if a little bit too full of themselves. If they'd made a few different lifestyle decisions they might have been working in offices or banks or on used-car lots.

Did any of these actors display the signs of corruption that Jack Rozin had warned me about? I'd have to say no. But then it occurred to me that maybe he'd meant that it was only the director who got corrupted. The ones who performed the acts were somehow innocent and therefore immune; they just did what they did. It was the ones who directed them, who told them to do it, who had the soul sucked out of them. I didn't know why I was even thinking about this.

And you know, these porn people really didn't need much direction. They knew what they were doing, which is to say that they did what they'd done however many times before, only this time in costume, which they took off anyway. Fact is, when it comes to sex there's a limited number of variations. OK, so with a cast of eight, that number was fairly high, and it took a long time to get through them all, but the options were a long way short of infinite. Thank God. I wouldn't have said I was exactly bored watching these people go through their routines, but it got old very fast.

Did I stamp my own directorial personality on the footage we shot? Would future film historians be able to look at the finished article and say, "Yep, that's a Rick McCartney film. He's an auteur all right. His genius was apparent even then"? Well no, probably not. For one thing, even though I was there making the porn film and trying to be professional about it, in my head I was already making the dodo movie. I was watching the light, working out angles, seeing if there were any shots from today I could repeat tomorrow.

You know, somewhere along the line it crossed my mind that it might be really cool to use the same crew and cast in both movies. To have these strange and freaky-looking, nonactor porn performers in an avant-garde art movie about a dodo: that seemed kind of appealing. It might be a selling point if nothing else. In the end I didn't go for it because first, I'd have had to pay them— these weren't the kind of people who worked for free—and second because Dorothy and Henry would have taken one look at them and known that something was up.

But I did allow myself one little indulgence: Tawnee. I was intrigued by her, by her body and her face and let's say the way she looked on camera. I had an intuition that she'd bring a certain quality that I wanted, so I asked her to be in my dodo movie and she said, "Sure, why not." In fact she looked like the kind of girl who said, "Sure, why not," to just about anything.

Apart from her and Dorothy, I had to get my dodo cast where I could. Frantically I called all the people I knew who'd ever made any claims to be any sort of actor, and you know, you'd be amazed at how few of them wanted to do a day's work for no pay in a weird-sounding art movie. In other circumstances I might have had a fun few days, or weeks, looking at resumes and headshots and audition tapes and getting people to read and do screen tests and then laughing at them behind their back. But I didn't have time for that; pretty much anyone who wanted in was in.

Somewhere I got the idea that it would be really great to have a child in the movie, a little girl, to give it a kind of Alice in Wonderland, death-of-innocence feel. And it so happened I had a friend, who was a bit-part actress herself, who had an eight-year-old daughter with ambitions. I begged them both to be in my movie. The mother said OK, they'd both be in it, as long as the kid got to do some tap dancing. I said what the hey. Tap dancing, sure. I could always cut it out later. So that was two more.

I decided that Tom Brewster would be in the movie as well. He'd be there anyway to operate the dodo, so why not use him? OK, so he wasn't an actor, but hell, some directors make their entire careers out of using nonactors. Why not me?

And you know, and I realize this sounds weird, but right from the beginning something told me I wanted Henry to be in the movie. He had something going for him. He didn't look Hollywood. He had presence and gravity and a kind of European thing. I phoned him on Saturday night and begged him to do it, like it was a last-minute crisis and I was really desperate, which in a way I sure was, and of course he said he didn't want to do it, but I knew I'd be able to talk him into it, and I did. Hey, I'm a smooth operator when I want to be.

The only advantage I had with this makeshift cast was that they weren't going to be called upon to do any real acting. They too could just "be themselves," or some version of themselves. At first all they'd be asked to do was move around the rose garden and the Tudor house, in costume, and they'd walk and sit and stand, but basically they wouldn't do much of anything for the first part of the film. They'd just *be*. Anyone could manage that, right?

Then after a while—and this was the real arty part—they'd start to read out sections from Brian's dodo novel. Neat, huh? There'd be no performing, just reading aloud directly from the manuscript, and if some of them weren't very good readers, that would be OK too. That'd be way Godardian, I thought.

And these readings would be the central section of my movie, and they'd go on for quite a while, longer than most movie audiences would want. A certain amount of boredom might set in, but that'd be OK, because I had a big show-stopping climax up my sleeve, one that I didn't plan to tell my cast about, so it would be a surprise for them as well as for the audience.

When the moment was just right, the mechanical dodo would magically appear, unannounced, unbidden, looking more magical than mechanical I hoped, and he too would walk through the rose garden and house, and the actors would stop their readings and they'd stare and react and be amazed and spooked. And they wouldn't know what to do. There'd be a hiatus while they fretted and made up their minds about what they were looking at. And then (when I told them to) they'd *destroy* the dodo. They'd smash it to pieces, tear it limb from limb, make it completely and utterly *extinct*. OK? Does that sound like a movie to you? It sure sounded like a movie to me.

So come Sunday morning, I started to shoot my dodo movie, and it was just a terrible, terrible experience. Here it was, my big moment, my big day, and it was just no fun at all. And OK I hadn't been expecting it to be like a day at the beach, like I'd be running around with a big grin on my face, but I hadn't expected it to be quite as bad as it was.

The real problem was that I felt like a fraud. I felt like I didn't know what the hell I was doing and that everybody could tell. I tried to explain what I wanted people to do, mostly nothing, just posing around and then doing some reading. But every time I opened my mouth and said anything, I got the sense that they all thought I was a complete clown.

Oh, they didn't show it, not directly. In fact they were very polite, very kind. So kind in fact that I felt they were *humoring* me, treating me like some mental defective. The fact that they didn't say anything directly only made it worse.

What they did instead was ask a lot of questions that I couldn't answer. Like, what were the actors supposed to be thinking and feeling? Like, what did the dodo *symbolize?* Like, were they supposed to be *actual* seventeenth-century characters or were they modern characters dressed up in a seventeenth century costume? Like, did I want a filter on that light? Did I want a wide angle on that shot? Did I want a cup of coffee?

And I had no idea. I suddenly had no opinions, no prefer-
ences, no vision, nothing. Oh sure I managed to make some stuff
up, to say some things to hide my inadequacy but I could tell that
everybody knew I was bluffing. They knew I was a total loser. It
had been so much easier when I was making the porn movie,
which is to say it was a lot easier when I didn't care.

But anyway we started, and the performers wandered around
looking moody, looking serious, looking lost. They tried to do
what I'd asked. They worked hard. They appeared to be committed to the project. But I could tell they despised me.

Then the reading aloud started. Dorothy was kind of embarrassing, like this was supposed to be her big moment and so she
was trying way too hard, like you'd have thought she was reading
Greek tragedy. And Tom Brewster had never read aloud before
in his life, so he was pretty terrible, and it didn't seem so Godardian after all. Tawnee was just nothing—not really there. Oh
sure she said the words—kind of—but I think she was on something, so there was a major disconnect between mouth and brain,
like she'd been badly dubbed. So much for my intuition about
performers. And the kid was a nightmare. Hey, a child actor
who's a nightmare—who'd have thought it? She couldn't read at
all. She kept saying, "Can I tap dance yet? Can I tap dance yet?"
Yeah kid, go and tap dance in the swimming pool. And her
mother wasn't much better. The only one who was any good at all
was Henry. Good old Henry. He was a natural. He was a star.
But I thought he despised me more than anybody.

By midafternoon we'd shot a lot of footage, I had experienced
a lot of anguish and self-loathing, and then Carla-fucking-
Mendez arrived. Now, she was a woman who in other circumstances I might have had a lot to say to. Like, "Hey lady, why
don't you stop fucking around with forces you don't understand?"
But this was an occasion when I just wanted her to disappear. I

don't know how she even found me at the house, but there she was limping along by the swimming pool and it was like a haunting, like the witch who'd come to deliver some terrible prophecy, which she then did.

She told me I was in grave danger. And I just thought lady, you don't know the half of it. But I didn't say anything. I refused to speak to her at all. And then I did a very immature thing. I pushed her into the swimming pool. I don't know who was most surprised, me or her or everyone else. But I did notice that my cameraman was smart enough to get it on film. I guess he wanted some shots of when the despised director finally cracked.

I immediately started worrying that maybe Carla Mendez couldn't swim because of the false leg, but she started doing a dog paddle, so I guessed she was going to live, which on balance was probably a good thing. Someone helped her out of the pool and led her away. She was in hysterics, spouting some quasi-mystical claptrap, but so long as she was out of my sight that was good enough for me.

And then a little while later some other crazy woman arrived—the realtor, as I soon worked out. She'd let herself in with her own key, and she had some young guy with her, and this guy may or may not have been a prospective house buyer, but basically he looked more like a pickup, and they both seemed kind of guilty, like they'd been caught out, which was crazy because obviously *I* was the one who'd been caught. And I was thinking oh boy, this is where the cops get called and I spend a night in a cell surrounded by brothers who think it's pretty fucking hilarious that the white boy's in jail for *trespassing*. But weirdly enough it never happened. Henry stepped in.

From the way Henry and the realtor looked at each other you could tell there was quite a story there, you could tell they had a thing going, and she was demanding to know why he was at the house and what this fucking film crew was doing, but he didn't answer that, he was just demanding to know who this young guy was and what *they* were doing there. Boy, he was mad.

Meanwhile Dorothy had also worked out that her dad had been up to something with this woman and she couldn't cope with that one bit and she went totally nuts and started screaming at Henry that he was a pervert and that he'd killed her mother. Jesus.

And then I realized that I knew who the realtor was. It was Bibi Scott, Bibi-fucking-Scott, the movie star, well OK, "star" might be overstating it, but she was definitely a movie *actress*, or at least she had been. I'd even seen some of her work. She'd been pretty sexy in those movies, and she was still pretty sexy now. And again I saw that my cameraman was still filming and I thought holy crap, I'm going to have Bibi Scott in my movie. How great is that? I sure didn't know what movie we were shooting anymore but we were definitely still shooting something. Was it high drama? Was it the stuff of tragedy? Was it an avant-garde masterpiece? Nah, it felt more like the end of *It's a Mad, Mad, Mad, Mad World.* I wouldn't have been surprised if Ethel Merman had shown up.

And then a very weird thing happened. I found myself behaving like a movie director. I told everyone to shut up and grow up. And they did. They fell completely silent and I was amazed because I hadn't realized that I exerted that much authority. And then, a second later, I realized that I didn't. They weren't silent because of me. They were silent because they'd just seen a dodo, which was walking very slowly, very steadily along the edge of the pool.

Only me, Tom Brewster, and Dorothy had ever seen the dodo

before, and I have to say it looked sensational, very lifelike, very vulnerable, somewhat scary, somewhat comical, totally un-worldly. I loved Tom Brewster at that moment. His timing was killer. This was exactly what I'd been looking for. The expressions on the faces of my cast, and of the crew and of Bibi Scott for that matter, were just fantastic: amazement, amusement, alarm. And my cameraman was still on the case. This was fantastic.

I tried to reassert myself again. I shouted some directions. "OK," I said, "now move toward the dodo. All of you. Circle round it. That's right. And now I want you to kill it, destroy it, stamp on it, make that dodo fucking *extinct*."

And you know what? They wouldn't. They didn't. Maybe they couldn't. The dodo, the *replica* of a dodo, was so strange and beautiful, so precious and moving that nobody could bring themselves to harm it. It was awesome. Even through my frus-tration, paranoia, disappointment, and thwarted authority, I sin-cerely believed that between us we might just have created a very special cinematic moment. I did the only thing I could think of. I said, "Cut. That's a wrap."

twenty-nine **Hope Floats**

There is one public execution that William Draper cannot bring himself to attend, that of King Charles, a man who could not be saved, and who would not save himself. How, scientifically speaking, could it have it come to this? What plan, mortal or divine, demanded such enormity? William spent the day, the penultimate day of January 1649, alone with his now aging dodo, hiding from the world, hiding from the horror of what his fellow Englishmen were about to do. Even the drunks and the feebleminded, the most callous of villains and most mercenary of whores, the hermits and the madmen, all felt the horror and dark chill of slaughtering God's anointed. Yet the deed was still done.

The reports said that the king made a good end of it, yet an end is all it was. The royal corpse was, after all, just a corpse, his life a light that could be extinguished like any other. God chose to do nothing. Where were the thunderbolts, the chariots, the rending of the heavens? Perhaps Mrs. Hendrick was right. Perhaps he was distracted, pursuing new interests.

What now for a college of physicians that boasts the word "royal" in its title? And what employment for one of that college's more humble and least conspicuous servants? The messages no longer come. William ceases to be their agent. He ceases to be of use. There are more pressing matters than exposing the sellers of useless remedies.

William fears the worst, that a new breed of unrestrained, unprincipled men will sell poisons disguised as cure-alls. Who will denounce them and bring them to account? Who will turn over their tables and make bonfires of their stock? Not the Commonwealth, evidently. William cannot see himself as a lone, independent agent of justice and science, and yet he feels there must be a role for him here somewhere.

Then, in the midst of an age that is all dying and austerity, he receives a visit from Barnes, his father's right-hand man. He stares for just a moment at William's restored features, then says, "You must come to the house, Master William."

"My father is ill?"

"Worse than that, sir."

"Dead, then?"

"Yes, sir. I know of nothing else but death that is worse than illness."

Together they hurry toward Holborn, a short journey between different worlds, a journey they make in silence. As William enters the hall of his father's house, he sees various unknown men loading familiar belongings into crates and transferring them to wagons that stand waiting in the courtyard.

"What is going on here, Barnes?" William asks.

"Let us press on," Barnes says. "All will be revealed soon enough, I fear."

William begins to ascend the stairs and suddenly Barnes makes as though to bar his way. "Are you sure you would not like some refreshment first, sir?"

"You have brought me here to see my dead father and now you suggest I dally?"

"Then just a word of warning, sir. Suicide is a bloody business. The maids have done their best to clean up the room, but none had much stomach for it."

"Suicide?" says William, and then he forces himself up the

stairs and into the bedroom His father's corpse lies in bed, a white sheet drawn up to the chin. The face does not look peaceful exactly, but certainly his features show an absence of pain. He looks strangely florid and waxy. Chiefly he looks very little like the man William knew. Something has departed.

And then William notices the walls, where great plumes of sprayed blood have, despite the marks of furious mopping and scrubbing, left their stains on the plaster, like claret on a freshly laundered shirt. Fearing he may vomit, William staggers out of the room to the landing, where Barnes is waiting.

"A bloody business indeed, Barnes. He slashed his wrists open, I suppose."

"Carved them out with a Scottish dirk sir, presented to him by a smoked-fish merchant from Aberdeen. Three long slashes in the left wrist, just one in the right."

"That is sufficient detail I think, Barnes. But why?"

"Debt, sir. A common enough matter. The business was doomed. It had no future and thus he saw none for himself. He decided to hasten the end."

"And did not fret about the effect this might have upon his son."

"So it might seem."

"How could a man so prudent, so steady, so wrapped up in his business—how could he let his affairs come to this?"

"I think he was preoccupied, sir."

"And what were his preoccupations?"

"Loneliness, melancholy, mortality. I think he needed company, sir."

"He had an odd way of showing it."

"Quite so."

"And these men loading the wagons, are they taking everything?"

"More or less, sir."

"And the house?"

"Mortgaged to the hilt and beyond, sir. Your inheritance will be small, I fear."

"It appears that I shall be living in Alsatia for a while yet."

"I am not sure where I shall be living at all, sir."

All at once there is a yelling that comes from the yard. Barnes and William hasten to see the cause of the trouble. More drama, more blood. One of the bailiff's men has gashed his hand open on the corner of a crate.

"A kind of justice there," Barnes says.

"Of a rather mean sort," says William. "I'll see if I can help the man."

"It would not bother me if the scoundrel died of his wounds."

"But it *would* bother me," William says flatly, quite surprising himself with those words.

He goes over to the victim, a lanky, chinless, ill-constructed young man, who is pressing a filthy rag into his right palm. The rag is sodden; blood seeps out around its edges. William finds himself acting calmly and with authority. The gathered workmen, glad to have a distraction from their loading, look to him as a man of knowledge and capability and he knows he will not disappoint them. He knows too that if they could see the scars beneath the mask of Mrs. Hendrick's facial potion, they might be far less accepting.

The gash in the man's hand is a deep, ugly thing, and he will not be lifting crates again for some time. But neither, thanks to the simple procedures carried out by William—washing, disinfecting, binding with a clean rag—will his hand turn into a vile, septic, festering pudding.

And that is the start of everything: a new life for William Draper. The news of his simple and selfless act toward the workman gives him the beginnings of a reputation for ability and honesty. From his lodgings in Alsatia he begins to dispense physic. Taking Mrs. Hendrick as his model, he only promises what he can provide, but this seems to be far more than many people have ever received before.

And so they come, at first only the poorest and most wretched, but then others come too, decent men and women, people of means, eventually gentlemen and their ladies. William takes money for his services but no more than his patients can afford, and if they can afford nothing, then so be it.

Nevertheless, despite doing much work gratis, his fortunes take a considerable turn for the better; just as well, for Barnes was wrong about his inheritance. It was not small, it was nonexistent. By the time the funeral was paid for there was scarcely enough money left for a night in the ale house, which William sorely needed. He becomes known as the doctor with the dodo and resigns himself to the knowledge that the word will never be plural.

He sees more of Mrs. Hendrick now, though not on the terms he might prefer. Sometimes she is a colleague and sometimes she is a mentor, but never a lover. He consults her on matters of female health and hygiene, and together they sometimes refer to her collection of herbals and books of anatomy. They make an odd pair but a good one. They are quacks that do no harm, who have knowledge and compassion.

Finally William feels free to ask her what he might have asked much sooner, "And what precisely do you do in that back room of yours?"

She hesitates, but only briefly. She has no desire to be mysterious, and yet she teases him first. "Why, what do you imagine?" she asks.

"I'm sure I do not know."

"But you imagine the worst."

"I do not know what the worst would be."

"Then let me assuage your curiosity," she says. "I am involved in the preservation of life."

"Then we share a preoccupation."

"No, not quite in the way that you are," she says. "I am also trying to preserve an illusion, an imitation of life even after death. Something that keeps up appearances even after the spark and spirit has departed."

"Necromancy?"

"No, no, surely you cannot think that of me."

"I had not thought it till now. Then what?"

She knows already that she will take him into the back room, show him everything, but before that she must talk him through first principles. "You have seen a stuffed crocodile," she says.

"Naturally."

"And it may still have seemed somewhat lifelike. That is because the crocodile's skin is easily preserved. Its appearance is not so very different whether the crocodile is alive or dead. Much the same can be said for snakes and lizards. You follow me thus far."

He frowns for fear that his intelligence is being insulted.

"And you are familiar with tanned leather and with fur."

"Not so familiar as yourself," he says, noting her kidskin gloves and the fur trimmings at her collar.

She says, "Man has acquired some skill in the preservation of these skins, but a fur coat or stole has only a passing resemblance to the original creature. And even when the skin is stitched up and stuffed, the effect will be less than lifelike, and also less than permanent. After a while even the best preserved skins and furs begin to decay."

William remembers, how could he not, the poor remains of

the dead dodo he saw in the Tradescants' Ark. He thinks of his own dodo, aging visibly. He thinks of himself.

"I feel there must be methods," she says, "and substances that can be employed more permanently and reliably. But it is a long and difficult search. To date, for instance, we have come nowhere near finding a means for preserving the scales of fish or," and she hesitates, "the skin and feathers of birds."

William winces a little.

"And you might say we can preserve a creature by storing it in spirits, or by mummification," she continues. "But it seems to me that these are only the means of preserving corpses, and not what I have in mind at all. I want to preserve a vision of the creature as it was in life. And not just an image on paper or canvas, as an artist might produce, not even something solid such as a sculptor could make. Rather I want to employ art and science to make the creature look alive even in death. There is as yet no word for what I intend."

The implication is clear enough. Once William had hoped to perpetuate the dodo by natural means, by breeding. Now the bird is conspicuously aging and fading, nor is he even sure it is still capable of reproduction. When it dies, as it must, what will he be left with? A corpse, a heap of bones and feathers and decaying innards, elements that will all too rapidly corrupt, turn to dust and slime. Mrs. Hendrick's unperfected skills may yet prove to be his last, best hope.

"Your experiments," he says. "What stage have they reached?"

"Middling," she says. "There is trial and error. There is persistence. Like an alchemist I measure portions, devise solutions, try those things I have not tried before. It is only a matter of time. And perhaps of God-given inspiration. There is always hope."

William feels utterly hopeless.

thirty **The Last Movie**

If I shouldn't have attended Bob Samuelson's funeral, and if I shouldn't have let Rick McCartney use the mock-Tudor house, then I absolutely definitely shouldn't have allowed myself to be talked into appearing in his damned dodo movie. I could make the excuse that there was quite a lot of pressure on me. Rick seemed desperate that I should be in it, claiming that the movie would be incomplete if I wasn't. I suspected this was nonsense but since I was supposedly helping him make his movie, it was hard to justify refusing. Equally, Dorothy joined in the process of coercion, not, I think, because she wanted me to appear, but because she wanted to please and support Rick. "I'll do anything when I trust my director." So to that extent I was doing it as a favor, to keep people happy, to move the project along. Nevertheless, I definitely shouldn't have done it. Chiefly I was concerned (and not solely for my own sake) that I would look like an amateur among professionals. I feared that my presence might bring the whole project down to the level of a home movie.

In fact, prior to meeting Rick McCartney, home movies were the full extent of my involvement with "filmmaking." It's interesting, isn't it, how often the makers of "real" movies like to include sections of "home" movies within them? The best I can think of is *The People vs. Larry Flynt*, where Woody Harrelson watches old footage of Courtney Love stripping, and the home

277

movie (amazingly enough) becomes a visual metaphor for nostalgia, melancholy, transience, loss.

At home I only very rarely played the family's old home movies (transferred to video some years previously). I suppose one needs a happier family than I ever had. But I do look at them once in a great while, and I react just the way everyone else does to old home movies, just the way Woody Harrelson/Larry Flynt does. And I hate that.

I make very few appearances in these home movies since I was usually behind the camera. So there's endless footage of Caroline looking young and attractive, but not very comfortable, smiling tensely, turning her face away, sometimes using Dorothy as a kind of shield, a way of distracting attention. Which is fine by Dorothy. She wants all the attention she can get. She's deliriously happy to be in front of the camera, though she's not exactly unselfconscious. She's there mugging, performing, showing off, being a bit of a brat, not unlike the awful child Rick McCartney had managed to get for his dodo movie. Is there any sane person in the world who can bear to watch child actors on screen?

In truth, once we started shooting the movie, it became clear that I wasn't the only one who threatened to make Rick's movie look less than wholly professional. The rest of the cast (Dorothy excepted) seemed almost as amateur as myself. The child's mother was no more talented than the child. Tom Brewster seemed a very decent chap, but he had all the screen presence of a flat tire.

It was, in every usual sense, a cast of unknowns, but personally I did know one of the people Rick had rounded up: the girl he introduced to me as Tawnee. I had seen her in action before, at the party Barbara had taken me to, having semiconscious sex on a poolside lounger with a somewhat famous movie actor. Needless to say, I didn't mention this to her. I had no idea what her background was, but it soon became clear that she was not by any stretch of the imagination an actress. The inept, affected seriousness with which she performed almost convinced me that I wouldn't be the worst performer in this movie.

It wasn't really any of my business, except insofar as I cared about Dorothy, but the fact that Rick had assembled so incompetent a cast rather made me doubt his instincts. And when he explained precisely what he wanted from us, I must say I wasn't very reassured. Wandering around an empty house and then reading out a series of texts undoubtedly had some avant-garde precedents, but I couldn't quite see how this amounted to the great piece of auteurship that Rick so evidently wanted to make. Nevertheless I tried to do what I was told and to keep a straight face, both requiring some effort.

For a start I was wearing a ridiculous costume: a cloak, tights, and a fencing shirt. I don't know how authentic these things were but I certainly felt authentically idiotic. And then there was the text we had to read out. My piece described someone finding a mutilated corpse in a very dark room. I suppose it was all right, but it seemed a bit uncinematic; you don't make a movie about death and extinction simply by having someone spouting about death and extinction. Even I was familiar with the old movie rule: show, don't tell.

It was all very hard work. In fact, when Carla Mendez turned up in midafternoon, I rather welcomed her arrival as a bit of light relief. Of course her soothsaying was pretty cringe-making and I must say I rather admired Rick for pushing her into the swimming pool. It seemed as good a way as any of dealing with her nonsense.

When Barbara subsequently arrived, it was a different matter.

I was mortified. My act of deceit was utterly exposed. But then again, she was engaged in a deceitful act of her own. She was there with some man, some *boy*. Perhaps I shouldn't have been surprised. If I'd really thought about it, I might well have worked out that I wasn't likely to be the only one she took back to the mock-Tudor house. But this young man was such a cipher, such a cliché. He was young and handsome and tanned and slim, so unlike me. He looked like a male model, for God's sake! I felt insulted. I hadn't suspected that Barbara would go for anything so obvious. But again, if I'd thought about it, I should probably have known that everybody goes for the obvious if they're given half a chance.

With no conceivable justification I started to rail at Barbara. I can barely remember what I said, and that's probably just as well. I seem to think I made accusations about her "shallowness." Her reply, which I do remember, was, "You have no rights here, Henry. You've no right to be at this house. And you've no right to tell me who I fuck."

I suppose by that point everyone must have worked out that Barbara and I had been having an affair (if that's the word), and it certainly amazed some of them. It had a particularly striking effect on Barbara's young man. He appeared to feel angry and betrayed too, but he was also disgusted, disgusted by me apparently. It was all right for him to have sex with an older woman, but it wasn't all right for the older woman to have sex with an older man. "You two like . . . did it?" he said, and he pulled a face as though he was smelling stale meat. But even so, he took the news somewhat better than Dorothy did.

"You're so disgusting!" she screamed at me. "You couldn't make my mother happy and now you're fucking some piece of Hollywood trash. I'm glad my mother's not alive to see this. I bet you're so glad you killed her!"

It was the old story as far as I was concerned, though it obviously came as a bit of a shock to everyone else there. Dorothy continued to rant more or less incoherently, while Barbara's young man felt the need to berate Barbara. Barbara and I merely berated each other.

I'm not sure how this would have ended if we hadn't at that point turned round and seen a robot dodo making slow and not entirely steady progress along the edge of the swimming pool. This, quite evidently, was Rick's great *coup de théâtre,* and he was entirely charmed and transported by the effect. The rest of us were not. The dodo looked clunky, stupid, and pathetic. I felt really rather embarrassed in fact, on Rick's behalf as well as my own. He shouted some directions to us but I don't think anyone was really listening, and certainly nobody followed them. Rick duly brought things to a swift and welcome conclusion. I had a feeling there wouldn't be wrap party.

But that didn't let me off the hook as far as Barbara was concerned. She stuck a nicely manicured index finger in my face and said, "Henry. Now. With me. You've got some explaining to do," and she dragged me off into her car, the only place that promised any privacy, and the moment we were seated, she started the engine and we roared off, with me still wearing my ludicrous costume.

I felt duly ashamed, but I didn't think much actual explaining was required. Apologies, certainly, along with groveling and perhaps certain acts of abasement. But as far as explanations were concerned, events seemed entirely self-explanatory. I'd simply let Rick McCartney use the house in order that my daughter could appear in her first "Hollywood" movie.

"I am genuinely sorry," I said.

"Yeah, yeah, of course you are," Barbara said.

"Really," I added for good measure.

"This whole thing is kind of interesting, isn't it?" she said. "We spend a day apart but we both end up going to the Tudor house. I go there for sex. You go there to make a movie. That's a real Hollywood story, isn't it?" She accelerated hard, flung the car into a corner, and nearly knocked a man off his motorcycle.

"Possibly," I said. "But you were motivated by the selfish desire to make yourself happy. I was doing it to make my daughter happy." By now I wasn't sure if I believed this, and Barbara certainly didn't.

"Oh, give me a break, Henry."

"I'd have asked your permission," I said, "but I assumed you'd have said no."

"Damn right. For a very good reason. There's no way that place can work as a location."

"I thought it worked all right," I said.

"Yeah, but not if your boy ever wants to show his movie. It's a very recognizable house. If the movie ever gets distributed, the owner's going to know and not be at all happy."

"Well, yes, I suppose I can see that."

"You want to know why I gave up being an actress?"

I did, although this didn't seem like quite the right moment to find out. On the other hand I could tell there was going to be no stopping her.

"It was all because of some man," she said. "Well, two men. The first was my boyfriend. We were in love, I guess. He was cute and he wanted to make movies. And he was a cartoonist. He wanted to make feature-length animated movies, and I guess you could say he was ahead of his time. This was way before *The Lion King* and all that stuff. And we met a guy, a producer, who said he was interested, and we said great, and he gave us some seed money."

"What was the movie?" I asked.

"*Alice in Wonderland.* You know *Alice in Wonderland*?"

"Everybody knows *Alice in Wonderland.*"

"Would you give somebody money to make a movie of it?"

"There have been several Alice movies actually," I said. "One with Dudley Moore, one with Cary Grant as the Mock Turtle. And in fact there was a Disney cartoon."

"Don't be a geek, Henry."

"Sorry," I said.

"Anyway, I'm not saying there weren't precedents, but this boyfriend of mine wasn't the guy to make it. He was only into Alice because of the drug references. I guess I was naive. And maybe he was too. There were a lot of meetings, a lot of people who had to be talked to in the middle of the night in Malibu. The money just kind of evaporated. Some of it evaporated up his nose, and OK, up mine too. But I was the serious one, the one with the sense of responsibility. I was the one who kept saying to him, write a script, do a storyboard, at least do some drawings."

"*Did* he make drawings?"

"Some."

"Did he make any of the dodo?"

"Maybe. I don't know. Who cares? The point is, eventually the money was all gone and then the boyfriend was gone too. And I was stuck there. So the producer hauls me in and tells me I owe him. Which I couldn't really deny. But hell, this was the movies. This was development money. It's money the producer could afford to lose. Right? If you can't afford to lose money, then you shouldn't be a producer."

We were now on some broad, bleached stretch of freeway. Barbara was driving dangerously fast and other cars were swerving to get out of her way.

"But *my* producer didn't see it that way," Barbara said. "He wanted me work for him. *Only* for him. I said no. He said if I wouldn't work for him, I wouldn't work for anybody. It was corny stuff. And I said the most poetic words in the American language: 'Fuck that. Fuck you.' That was it. The end of a not especially glorious movie career. Easy."

"Was it easy?"

"Maybe I was surprised at how easy it was. And who knows? I was an aging actress. Maybe I wouldn't have worked much anyway. So. Real estate."

"Living well is the best revenge," I said.

"Oh sure, there are plenty of ways of getting your revenge. Like having sex in a house belonging to the guy."

"The mock-Tudor house? That's his? This producer's?"

"Right," she said.

"You're trying to sell his house for him?"

"I'm not trying very hard. Maybe you noticed. He thinks he's sticking it to me by having me as his realtor. I think I'm sticking it to him by doing a lousy job and using the house for sex."

"And peeing in his pool."

"Right."

"What's his name?"

"Nobody you'll have heard of. A guy called Jack Rozin."

She was absolutely correct. At that point I'd never heard of Jack Rozin, but I was about to hear a lot more.

thirty-one Tapeheads

I was sitting in Tom Brewster's studio looking at the rushes of my dodo movie and I was feeling great. I was so sure that I'd shot something fantastic that I was seriously tempted to come clean to Jack Rozin, tell him and show him what I'd done, and I felt sure that even he'd be able to see how great it was, that it justified my deception. And hell, it wasn't that big a deception. I *had* shot the porn movie for him. I'd just done it quicker and more efficiently than he expected. If he had any feeling for the movies at all he'd surely see that the dodo movie was something really special.

I didn't get the chance. Looking back on it, I suppose using Tawnee in both movies was always going to be a liability. It allowed her to know exactly what I was doing, but why should that have been so terrible? I thought she was cool. I liked her. And I thought maybe she kind of liked me. I guess I was fooled by her look of innocence, which I guess means I was also fooled by my own stupid male hormones. I never expected undying loyalty from her—she was a porn actress for Christ's sake—but on the other hand I didn't expect her to go running straight to Jack Rozin and telling tales, either. But run she did, or I guess she probably just got on her cell phone and told him what I'd been doing, or at least the parts she knew about, which was enough. And Jack Rozin was really pissed.

The first I knew about it was when Rozin arrived at my door, at Tom Brewster's door, and I was surprised because he didn't look like the kind of guy who made house calls, and Tony the right-hand man was with him, and the moment I opened the door I knew I was in trouble, not least because Jack Rozin belted me in the mouth. If we're talking movie genres, this part was like a cartoon. I actually did see stars, and if it had really been a cartoon there'd have been tiny little birds flying in circles round my head, maybe flying dodos—ironic, huh?

So there I was lying on the floor, rubbing my chin, and Jack Rozin was standing over me, rubbing his back. Hitting me had obviously caused him some pain. And then Tony was picking me up off the ground, dusting me off, and Rozin was explaining stuff that I could barely follow, though I knew it was real important that I try to keep up.

"This is how it works, Rick," Jack Rozin was saying. "This is how it was always going to work. You were going to make a very bad porn movie for me. That was OK. That was what I expected. Everybody always makes a bad movie for me first time out. There's no shame in it. You were going to lose me money, and therefore you were going to be in my debt. That was the plan. Then slowly, very slowly, gradually, over a certain amount of time, you were going to pay off the debt, with a lot of interest. I mean that you'd do a lot of work for me and get paid peanuts for it. Not that you'd complain. How could you? I was the guy who gave you your first break. Are you with me so far?"

I said, "OK."

Jack Rozin looked like the kind of man who had a lot of focus, but as he was talking to me I could see that his eyes were wandering, taking in Tom Brewster's collection of grotesque movie ephemera. He forced himself to concentrate.

"So Rick, when you came in spouting all that shit about the

seventeenth century, about wanting to make a costume fucking drama, well that was OK. Whatever you'd suggested I'd have said sure, go ahead. That was how this works. You make a movie and you fuck up. I couldn't lose. And you couldn't win, right?"

"Right," I said.

"And I gave you a way out, didn't I? I always give people a way out. I said don't do it. I said don't make a porn movie. I said don't get corrupted. Didn't I say that?"

He was getting excited, as though he might like to hit me again.

"Yes, you did say that," I agreed.

"I certainly *did*, Rick, not that I expected you to take any notice. You people never do. That's what I rely on." Now he was really distracted by the stuff all around him. "What *is* this shit?"

"Movie props," I said.

"Doesn't it give you nightmares?"

"Lots of things give me nightmares."

"And what the fuck's *that*?" Naturally he'd focused on the one thing that mattered.

"It's a dodo," I said. "You know, an extinct bird. Seventeenth-century."

He looked at me hard, just in case I was being sarcastic, but I'd never felt less sarcastic in my life.

"So anyway, Rick, that was the setup. Whatever you did, you were going to end up owing me. You were going to end up working for me. But it turns out you owe me a lot more than I thought you were going to."

"This is all Tawnee's doing, isn't it?" I said.

"No, Rick, it's all *your* doing. But I haven't even gotten to the best part yet. I hear you had a pretty nice location for the shoot. How does somebody like you find a place like that?"

"Through friends," I said warily.

"No," he said. "You don't have any friends. Not anymore. Not in this town. Anyway, the *how* doesn't really matter. The fact is, you shouldn't have used my house."

"*Your* house?"

"Well, I don't live in it, obviously, and on paper it's owned by a loss-making subsidiary company of mine, but as far as you're concerned, Rick, yes, it's my house."

"Oh no," I said. "Oh shit."

"Yes, Rick, oh shit. You know, the word *respect* is so overused these days, isn't it? Everybody wants respect, everybody from crack dealers up. And the word *violation;* that's overused too. But you've shown a lack of respect, Rick. And I feel violated. And I have to do something about that. Obviously."

"I can see that," I said, and I could, I really could. At that point I could easily imagine being in "debt" to Jack Rozin, up to my neck for the rest of my life. "OK, I'm really sorry. I'll do what it takes to make it up to you. I'll make porn movies for you, OK?"

"Of course you'll make movies for me, Rick. The question is what *else* will you do?"

One of the things I was thinking of doing was running away to Brazil, getting some plastic surgery, and never showing my face in L.A. ever again.

Jack Rozin said, "I think maybe I ought to see some of this movie of yours. Seems like you risked a lot for it."

So Jack Rozin saw some of what I'd shot of the dodo movie, and you know, I was grasping at straws but I thought maybe this could turn out OK. Maybe he'd see what I'd done, see how great it was, and everything would still be fine. Yeah right. He sat there and he watched, and he didn't seem very entertained, but after a while he said, "Who's the fat, middle-aged English guy? I kinda like him."

A better man than me would have left Henry out of it, said that he was a bit part actor from out of town who'd gone back to England and that I had no way of contacting him. Me, I caved in. I gave names, addresses, phone numbers, star signs.

"And who's the little fat-faced actress?"

"That's his daughter. Dorothy."

"Yeah? Well, I want you to bring them to the house in Encino, Rick. I want to talk to them. I want to do more than talk to them."

"OK," I said.

He looked like he was about to leave, like he was finished with me, but we'd got to the part of the movie where Bibi Scott arrived at the house. For the first time Rozin showed some real interest.

"Tell me that isn't who I think it is."

"It's Bibi Scott," I said.

"Fuck. Well I guess I'll be seeing her too. Man, you really know how to piss me off, don't you, Rick? You have a talent for it."

Yeah, and I didn't even have to try.

"I don't have to tell you not to do anything stupid, do I?" Rozin said.

"I'm all out of stupid," I said.

But just to be sure, he took away the footage of my dodo movie and he also took Tom's mechanical dodo, and as he was leaving he gave a signal to Tony and I got another belt in the mouth. It hurt me more than the first punch but I guess it hurt Jack Rozin less.

thirty-two

A Touch of Class

Like any other quack, William Draper fears the restoration of the monarchy. The Commonwealth, for all its many grim prohibitions, tolerates certain practices that would have sent the Royal College of Physicians into paroxysms and would have sent practitioners such as William into the courts and jails. Under Protector Cromwell there is an understanding that the better sort of medical layman is to be tolerated, perhaps even encouraged. Who is to say that the restored monarchy would permit such practicalities to prevail?

Yet the end of the Commonwealth does not quite signal the end of common sense. Something has changed. A stranglehold has been eased. The Royal College of Physicians is fully back in business, but the populace no longer holds its members in quite the elevated, mysterious esteem it once did. It has been shown that physic may be dispensed by less highly colored birds.

Soon the country will be suffering from various evils wrought upon it by Charles the Second's reign, but for now at least, he is a king in touch with his people. He lays hands on them, literally, willingly, though of course they are discouraged from laying hands on him. Charles has renewed the tradition of touching his subjects in order to cure them of the King's Evil. This seems to William to be little more than an ornate form of quackery in itself, but that is not to say that it isn't worth a try, and it is not to say that it may not work.

There is, it appears, not very much to this touching business. A certain amount of negotiation is required, with statements from clergy that the sufferer is all he claims to be, but this is easily done, and then the sufferer hobbles along to Whitehall, to the Banquet House, joins a throng of several thousand, stands in line, and waits for the king to attend him.

Charles sits on a raised platform, flanked by courtiers, hangers-on, and men of the cloth. He looks distinguished, detached, only mildly debauched. There are prayers and solemnity but also a few stray dogs and children who scamper about creating an atmosphere of festivity as well as piety. The chosen sufferers advance down an aisle lined with mace-carrying footmen, present in case one of the supplicants is more assassin than patient, and eventually their turn comes.

They kneel before the king, who touches them with a grave yet languid hand, then places an azure ribbon around each neck, from which hangs a medallion showing the king's face. His hands sometimes address the supplicant's afflicted part, though understandably he does not wish to rummage about in the sickly bodies of his subjects. A touch on the head or the shoulder is often considered enough.

Some fall into a swoon at the touch, others leap to their feet in celebration of an instantaneous cure, but most get up slowly, apparently unchanged, and amble on their way, a little bemused, a little disappointed, hoping that their cure may be a more gradual one. Nobody is delayed long. The line moves swiftly and with purpose.

Although Charles claims only to cure the King's Evil, it is clear to William as he stands waiting in the crowd at the Banquet House that many of his fellows are there to deal with quite different ailments, as indeed is he. In other circumstances he might even be prepared to offer advice on how these people might re-lieve their pains more directly, but he cannot blame them for coming here in the hope that the king's capabilities might be more universal.

And truly this puzzles William. Why should a king, and indeed the God who directs power through him, be so arbitrary as to single out this one particular disease? Why not something more general? Why not a cure for the stone, the plague, the pox? Are these diseases too much of the commoner to be worthy of a king's attentions (though the crowd in the Banquet House is common enough)? Or are they too ungodly? Are they perhaps, in themselves, expressions of God's displeasure? God has so much to be displeased about.

William does his best to fit in with this crowd of the bent, the feeble, the mad. He has come looking as wretched and distem-pered as possible. His scarred face is exposed, free of Mrs. Hen-drick's potion, and he huddles beneath the enveloping shelter of a long black cloak. He has something of the wizard or conjurer about him. The effect is both deliberate and unavoidable.

At last William's turn comes. He kneels, casts his eyes down, then raises them upwards, toward the king's face and the heavens beyond. Charles's features form a mask of serene sanctity. His hand moves toward William, who wriggles and stirs beneath the cloak, and something else stirs there too. When the royal hand is just an inch from his forehead, William ducks aside, twists his body, and from the folds of the cloak produces his ailing dodo. He moves her up swiftly, like an offering, a surprise gift, though he has no intention of handing her over, and the king's hand makes brief but firm contact with the dodo's thinning gray feath-ers. Immediately the contact has been made, William, more of the conjurer, conceals the bird again.

The faces of the king and his courtiers, of his holy men and his mace carriers, show an amazement that threatens to turn to anger. William imagines himself being dragged from the hall, being beaten and boxed as he goes, taken and chained in some dank basement cell. It is a risk he has always been prepared to run for the sake of his poor dodo. Yet the act is both so audacious and so brief that all concerned choose to ignore it. To make a fuss would only make them look foolish. William moves on, walks out of the hall, a job well done.

But kingship has its limitations. The dodo does not improve. Her gray feathers look grayer. Her sad eyes look sadder. There was always something mournful in her voice, but now it sounds like a half-forgotten, melancholy hymn. William wonders if it is a matter of faith. The king is the conduit for the Lord's healing divinity, but this is surely not a thing to be dispensed promiscuously. It is surely not, for instance, to be dispensed to nonbelievers. A bird is incapable of belief, therefore incapable of saving itself. Perhaps the dodo is simply beneath God's attention. Perhaps she is beneath contempt.

Two weeks later William Draper's dodo is dead.

He carries the dodo's slowly corrupting remains to Haymarket, to Mrs. Hendrick's lodgings, conveying them in a wooden wine crate, as close as he can come to a coffin, since he has no intention of interring his beloved bird. He presents Mrs. Hendrick with a corpse and asks (only) that she restore it, not to life—he at least allows that she cannot perform miracles—but to some simulacrum of life, to a state of vital inertia.

"Let us see how advanced is your science," he says to her.

Not advanced enough for William's purposes, of that she is sure. She will do her best, will do all she can, but William's hopes and expectations are so unreasonably high, his need so desperate, that she knows her skills must inevitably disappoint him.

She retreats into her back room, into the world behind the green door, and William, all dread and anticipation, follows her. She places the dodo on the workbench and begins by taking a series of precise measurements and entering them on a chart she has drawn up specifically for the purpose. William finds himself wonderfully impressed by this utilization of science and calculation.

She begins the delicate matter of preparing the dodo's feathered skin. She takes a large but neat bone-handled knife and makes an incision, beginning at the lower end of the breastbone and moving upwards. As various internal fluids ooze out she mops them up carefully to prevent their spoiling the feathers. She loosens the skin, pulls it away from the body beneath, and inserts wads of cotton to keep flesh and skin apart. The legs are stripped of their covering and are then cut off with a pair of scissors, leaving the feet sheathed in skin.

Similarly, the tail is separated by hacking through the last joint of the backbone. Mrs. Hendrick then introduces a hook into the lower part of the rump and suspends the bird above the bench, all the time loosening and peeling away the skin and feathers. She pulls at the wings, stretching them loose until she can make a further incision at the elbow joint.

Now she turns her attention to the head, taking pains to expose and remove the skull, while keeping the membranes around the ears and eye-sockets intact, though the eyes themselves she cuts out and discards.

Several cuts are required, through the roof of the mouth and the base of the lower jaw, before the brain can be removed. She draws it forth and for a second she holds it between her fingers, a tiny, delicate, hopeless thing.

She removes every trace of fat and muscle from the head and neck, and then begins liberally coating these areas with a preservative solution, something mysterious but with arsenic as its active ingredient. Then she moves on to the inside of the skin, coating this too.

Then more of the same, much more, stripping away more fat and muscle from the wings, legs, and tail. Then, determinedly, she ties the bird together, stringing the intact bones, drawing up the wings to a position they held in life.

Beyond this point William can watch no more. Indeed he is surprised he has had stomach for so much of the spectacle. A carcass is left behind, efficiently butchered, though a piece of meat that none would willingly consume. This body will now be boiled, the flesh will soften, coddle, melt away so that Mrs. Hendrick can then extract the remaining bones, prior to stringing these too with wire, forming a secure skeleton, an armature around which the preserved skin will be fixed.

The body cavity will be padded with excelsior, glass beads will replace the eyes, the beak will be touched with pigment to create a more realistic effect. There will be more dousing of the bird in preserving liquids: alcohol, green vitriol, corrosive sublimate, liquids to deter the parasites that would feast on the dodo's remains.

And at last, at long last, a fortnight later, she presents William with the gift he wants more than anything else, more now even than he wants her. The dodo is restored (after a fashion), resurrected, standing again on its feet, its head erect, its stunted wings clutched to its sides. It is a strange thing to see, disturbing and sinister in its way, but nevertheless a kind of wonder. The dodo is motionless but she does not look quite incapable of motion. She is lifelike in her stillness, and this seems as good an impersonation of life as any dead thing can muster. William suspects, and fears, that this may be as close to immortality as any living creature can come.

thirty-three   Do the Right Thing

I got a phone call from Rick McCartney telling me he was in the very worst trouble of his life and that he needed me, in his terms, to "take a meeting" with Jack Rozin, in order to save both his skin and his dodo movie. He told me everything, although not all of it was such news to me as he thought. He was surprised, for instance, that I had even heard of Jack Rozin, and even more surprised that I already knew he was the owner of the mock-Tudor house, though I assured him this information came my way too late to have made any difference. From my point of view, the biggest surprise was that Rick had shot a porn movie for Rozin. Barbara hadn't given me chapter and verse on who Rozin was and what kind of films he made, but his demand that Barbara work for him and nobody else now took on extra meaning.

I'm not essentially an angry person, though I thought I had every reason to be angry with Rick McCartney, and perhaps with Dorothy too since she was, in some ways, the prime mover in all this. I didn't know why Rozin wanted to see me, and neither did Rick for that matter, but I felt sure it wasn't to pat me on the head for the good work I'd done in Rick's movie. I suppose I could have simply refused to go. It would have left Rick in some difficulties, but they were all of his own making, and none of my responsibility. There was, however, the problem of Dorothy. If Jack Rozin could ruin Barbara's already established career, what might he do to Dorothy's scarcely existent one? Perhaps curiosity also played a part. I wanted to look this man in the face and see exactly who he was.

Rick, Dorothy, and I went to Jack Rozin's place, making a long, unfamiliar drive into the Valley. The house was a surprisingly elegant and understated structure; I was getting quite an eye for these things. We were let in by a large, fleshy bodyguard who seemed to know Rick somewhat, but he busied himself in a distant part of the house as soon as he'd directed us to the garden, where Rozin was waiting for us. Rozin wasn't alone. Tawnee was there too, looking infinitely less cowed than I thought she should have been, and next to her was Barbara, doing a very convincing performance of being unafraid, while steadfastly refusing to look me in the eye. Rozin sat in the shade, by a table on which was a video camera and a gun. Some ten feet away, posed precariously by the edge of the swimming pool, was Rick's mechanical dodo, looking inert and terribly endangered.

My first impression was that Jack Rozin was man of about my age, with many of the advantages I lack—good health, fitness, leanness, a tan, and so forth. But then he got up from his chair, and from the way he stood and moved, I could see he was suffering from severe back pain. This gave me a very small amount of pleasure.

"So Henry," he said by way of an opening remark, "have you been watching much porn lately?"

"No," I said.

"Well, it's a jungle out there, Henry. In the old days it used to be that good-looking girls would only do straightforward, ordinary sex. If you wanted something that involved weirdness you had to employ a less good-looking girl. The weirder the sex, the uglier the girl. But that's all changed now. These days it doesn't matter. The most beautiful women in the world will do anything, absolutely anything. Isn't that right, Tawnee?"

Tawnee giggled and said, "Yay!"

"I make all kinds of movies," Jack Rozin said. "Every kind I can think of. If somebody wants to see it, then I feel I have a duty to show it. There's a series I'm working on right now called *Age Gap:* beautiful young women having sex with disgusting old men. There's another series where beautiful young men have sex with disgusting old women, but that needn't concern us right now.

"And I use the word 'disgusting' in quotation marks, Henry. Personally I don't find these movies disgusting at all. Some of my best friends, et cetera. Sure, the guys in these movies are old, and sure, their bodies are crinkly and fat and lacking in muscle tone, but so what? That's the way it is with bodies. And these people don't do anything disgusting per se in these movies. I mean they just have sex.

"And sure I've had people on my back saying it's all about violation of the young by the old, that it's my sick revenge on youth and beauty. Smut as a memento mori, if you will, but I think that's what all movies are when you get right down to it."

I had never had a conversation with a pornographer before, so I had no standard of comparison, but even in my wildest dreams I would not have expected him to use the term *memento mori*.

"So Henry, I've seen the movie, Rick's little dodo fantasy, and what can I say? I like your work."

He looked as though he might be expecting me to say thank you. If so, I disappointed him.

"In fact I'd say you're too good to be appearing in a movie by Rick McCartney. You should be in Shakespeare. In a Coen Brothers movie. In Spielberg. But I understand how these things go. Life isn't fair. Talent goes unrewarded. Nice guys sometimes finish at the bottom of the heap."

I certainly suspected that was where I was at that moment, though I saw immediately that if Jack Rozin seriously thought I was a nice guy, then I had quite an advantage over him.

He said, "Some pornographers are in it for the sex. But not me. I'm in it for something more complicated. Yeah, OK, so maybe my accusers are right, maybe I'm in it for the degradation and corruption. Seeing some little slut like Tawnee or (no offense) your daughter being fucked on screen by some young, good-looking guy, that really doesn't do anything for me. What's degrading about that? But seeing some pregnant coed, or some desperate forty-year-old librarian who needs money for her mother's cancer treatment, now that starts to get interesting for me. And in your case, Henry, seeing some dignified, serious, middle-aged English actor having sex with some little slut like . . . oh, let's say like Tawnee here, well, that would be very corrupt. That would be very satisfying indeed for me."

That was when I decided I seriously wanted to kill Jack Rozin, but at that point I didn't know how I was going to accomplish it. I imagined, for instance, that he and I might end up wrestling for the gun that was on the table, that it would go off by accident, that he would take a bullet in the stomach and fall at my feet in a twisted heap. But that was only one of the possibilities.

"Here's the deal," he said. "I just want you to fuck our little friend Tawnee here, age and youth, the old world and the new, while I get it on film and your daughter and your new girlfriend watch. Pretty degrading, huh?"

"I'm not an actor," I told him.

"You're too modest, Henry. I've seen the results. You've quite a screen presence."

"I'm a doctor," I said as plainly as I could, and I saw he was confused.

"What kind of doctor?"

"A medical doctor. A general practitioner."

He looked at Rick and Barbara for confirmation. He apparently trusted them more than he did me, and their faces told him that, unlikely though it must seem to him, I was telling the truth.

"Then what the fuck are you doing mixed up in this shit?" he asked.

"I was doing Rick a favor. My daughter too."

"Well, that'll teach ya. Are you as good a doctor as you are an actor?"

"Rather better, I would hope."

"Well, aren't you the Renaissance man? Makes this whole thing even sweeter, doesn't it? That Hippocratic oath you sign up for. Is there anything in there that says a doctor can't appear in a porn movie?"

"No," I said. "That's one of the eventualities Hippocrates didn't foresee."

"So there's no reason why you shouldn't, right?"

"Perhaps you should clarify the reason why I should."

"Because your pal Rick owes me big time, but he doesn't have anything I want. Whereas you do."

"And if I don't agree, then Rick's dodo movie gets destroyed and he and Dorothy never work in this town again."

"Very good, Henry."

"And Barbara?"

"Well, I've been thinking about that. Right now I'm not sure of the best way to damage her, but I know I'll be able to come up with something."

I believed him, and at that moment he was as good as dead.

"OK then," I said, "let's do it."

Jack Rozin laughed. He liked my spirit, or something. Tawnee laughed too, though it seemed she was laughing at her own private joke. But Rick, Dorothy, and Barbara didn't see anything to laugh at. They looked truly mortified. But personally I thought it was a great moment, one of revelation, horror, disbelief, a moment when everything you know turns out to be false. For my own part it didn't matter. Agreeing meant nothing. It was just words. I knew it would never happen. I knew that one way or another Jack Rozin would be dead quite soon.

"OK, Henry, time to strip for action," he said.

"Daddy, you can't," Dorothy said, but I pretended I hadn't heard.

Rozin picked up the video camera but the movement caused him some pain and he thought better of the idea. "Here, McCartney, this is your job." Rick took the camera from him.

"What's wrong with your back?" I asked.

"I wish I fucking knew," Rozin said passionately. "It hurts like hell is all I know. I've had second opinions and tenth opinions and I've paid through the nose for 'em. I've seen chiropractors, naturopaths, acupuncturists, Chinese herbalists, every quack in the phone book."

"Let me look at it," I said.

In the circumstances he was understandably reluctant, but the chance of free medical advice was as irresistible to him as it had been to the poor Mexicans in the van. He took off his shirt and presented his smooth, hairless back to me, but I noticed he was keeping a careful eye on the gun. I tried to be reassuring. I put on my very best bedside manner. I ran my hands along his spine, then pushed at a few pressure points and paid some attention to his trapezius muscle.

"What are you finding back there?" he asked.

"Various things," I said.

I asked a few standard questions. Was he on medication, was he having trouble sleeping, did he suffer from panic attacks? The answer was yes in each case.

"Are you psychic or something?" he said.

"No, but I'm very familiar with back pain. Half the patients I see are suffering from it."

"So what can you do about it?"

"I could give you an injection."

"What kind of injection?"

"A painkiller-cum–muscle relaxant, with some vitamins to boost your immune system. It's basically herbal."

He turned round and looked me in the eyes, trying to decide if he could trust me. I blinked innocently and reassuringly, and he concluded that he could. I was a doctor after all. Doctors can get away with murder. I got my bag, opened it, quickly prepared a hypodermic, and then, very carefully, I injected a syringe full of morphine into him: a lethal dose.

Don't you hate it in movies, and sometimes even in real life, when people say, "He took enough drugs to kill a horse"? I have no idea how much morphine it takes to kill a horse, but I had a very shrewd idea of how much it might take to kill Jack Rozin— the amount you would find in the syringe of an aircraft's emergency medical kit. I'd picked it up while I was administering to Rick McCartney during his panic attack on the plane. I'd had a feeling it might come in handy in L.A.

Jack Rozin's reactions to morphine poisoning were the standard ones: pinpoint pupils, confusion, shallow respiration, nausea, vomiting, spasticity, and eventual respiratory failure. It was classic, textbook stuff. My long, expensive education hadn't been entirely wasted.

thirty-four **The Natural**

I wonder how many people have seen an actual murder with their own eyes. Not that many, I'm guessing. In the movies and on TV you can watch hundreds of them every day if you want to, mostly fictional obviously, though sometimes one or two real ones sneak through—Lee Harvey Oswald, that Vietnamese dude who got shot in the head—but up at Jack Rozin's house we saw the real thing, and it was way less spectacular than in the movies but also way more dramatic.

Henry just did it, and it didn't look like much but we all knew it was a very, very big deal, life-changing stuff, and not just for Jack Rozin. We were witnesses and, I don't know, maybe we were accomplices, and sure it was terrible, but you know it was also kind of magnificent.

In fact Henry was pretty amazing right from the moment we got to Rozin's house. He was a natural. He didn't seem to be acting at all. He was totally believable. I really thought he was going to go ahead and have sex with Tawnee right there in front of us all. And Jack Rozin certainly believed it, and Dorothy too, I'm sure, and probably Bibi Scott as well. It seemed a pretty bad thing to do, and way out of character, but for a moment there none of us doubted it.

But then Henry started doing his doctor act, which OK, I guess wasn't really an act, but the way he talked to Jack Rozin and then started examining his back, he looked as though he was genuinely concerned, like he really wanted to help the guy. Which obviously he didn't. It was only when he got out the syringe, that I thought OK, something's going on here, something's wrong with this picture. I thought maybe he was going to inject Rozin with tranquilizer or anesthetic or something and we'd all run out of there, though obviously that wouldn't have solved anything in the long run. But hell, whatever he injected Rozin with, it sure didn't make him tranquil. He fell over and started panting and vomiting and thrashing around, and it was obvious, even to him (maybe especially to him), that Henry had gone and pissed all over his Hippocratic oath.

Before he died, Rozin did manage to yell out and Tony, the bodybuilder or bodyguard or whatever the hell he was, came ambling out of the house, not in any hurry, like he was used to hearing a lot of yelling around the place. And when he arrived, he saw his boss crumpled on the tiles by the pool, writhing and gasping for air, and he didn't know what the hell was going on, so he said, as I guess anybody might, "I'll call for a doctor."

And then Henry was more magnificent still. Very authoritatively he said, "I *am* a doctor," and you could see Tony breathe a sigh of relief. Everything was going to be OK now because a doctor was there. Then, pretty much in his next breath, Henry said to Tony, and this was the clincher, "This man's dead. Perhaps you ought to call the police."

That was pretty much the last we ever saw of Tony the right-hand man, and obviously it was the last we ever saw of Jack Rozin. Henry had done something terrible and reckless, heroic and, like I said, magnificent.

If I'd been directing the movie, it would probably have ended right there, on a freeze frame of Henry, syringe in hand, looking rueful but triumphant, realizing the enormity of what he'd done, yet having no regrets. Instead, I knew there were going to be a lot of codas and false endings, and maybe even a whole courtroom drama. Man, I hate courtroom dramas. But the one thing we didn't do was call the cops.

I did a quick search of the house, found the tapes of my dodo movie, then took Tom Brewster's mechanical dodo and split. In fact we all split, all going to our separate lives, leaving Jack Rozin's corpse curled up under the shade of the sun umbrella, and I wondered if I'd ever see any of these people ever again, at least in the flesh. I knew I'd be seeing a lot of them all on screen when I did the editing on the dodo movie, but I suspected that the actual people were leaving my life forever.

Right before I went, I had a small movie moment with Tawnee. I got all tough and aggressive and told her that if she ever wanted to work in this town again she'd better keep her mouth shut and forget everything that had happened. She was dumb enough, naive enough, maybe scared enough, to fall for it. Or at least she said she did. Also, I thought, Tawnee was the kind of girl who was probably pretty good at forgetting most of what happened to her.

At that moment the career of Rick McCartney, auteur of the present and future, suddenly didn't look so bad. I had my movie back, and the only person who could have completely destroyed things for me was dead. I mean, I wasn't going to rat out Henry, but even if someone else did, even if I got indicted as an accessory, my movie was still going to get made, and that seemed like enough.

I thought I might leave town for a while, drive up north, find an out-of-the-way place with some cheap editing facilities, but first I wanted to do something else. I had to go see Carla Mendez. I had a small amount of apologizing to do, chiefly for dumping her in the swimming pool, but I had some other business as well.

I drove to her apartment in Venice. She wasn't exactly pleased to see me, but she wasn't surprised either. Maybe her psychic powers had told her I was on my way. She'd made one or two changes around the place. It was way less cluttered with mystical knickknacks than it had been and there were one or two signs of ordinary life. She'd pinned some photographs of family and friends up on a notice board, and there were some magazines and letters lying around.

"There's a lot I don't understand," I said to her.

"Welcome to the club," she said. "Where do you want to start?"

She was way more cooperative than I'd been expecting. I was afraid she'd get all mystical on me.

"Well, I think there's only one real question," I said. "And that's are you for real?"

She wasn't surprised or offended by the question, like it was something she'd been wondering too, and she replied, "Your guess is as good as mine."

"Did I really go back into a past life?" I said. "Or did I dream it? Or did you hypnotize me? Or did I go into a written text? Or into a writer's mind? Or what?"

"I don't know," she said. "Which would you like it to be?"

"And when you turned up at the house during the shoot, to warn me, how did you know I was in danger?"

"I just knew. All right? But I don't know how I knew. That's how it is with this stuff, I guess."

"So you *are* for real."

"I'm a real something, but right now I'm not sure what. I guess basically I'm a quack, but not a *complete* quack. I have my moments but I'm not some big-time psychic, and the fact is I've had most of my best moments with you. I'd done plenty of regressions with other people before you, had a few small successes, but nothing like what happened with you. With the others it was two-thirds bullshit and me asking leading questions, but with you it felt like the real thing. It scared the shit out of me."

"I want to go back again," I said.

"No," she said. "I really don't think so."

But she said it in a way that I knew meant yes. Look, I've seen enough science fiction movies where the hero gets in the time machine for the last scene, and the thing malfunctions and he ends up God knows where in some postapocalyptic wasteland and the machine's dead and he can't get back and he wanders around for the rest of his life as the last man on earth. It makes for kind of a downbeat ending. But I went for it. I took another past-life regression. I knew I was being an idiot, but I was being the kind of idiot who has a sense of an ending, an understanding of the dramatic necessities. I sat in a chair in Carla Mendez's apartment, shut my eyes, hoped for the best, and back I went.

But this time it wasn't seventeenth-century London, and it wasn't Alsatia. It was somewhere way more modern than that. I was inside a movie theater: a big old-style picture palace with swagged curtains, plaster angels, and plush seats. The place could have held, I don't know, a thousand people, but I was the only one there, and it seemed like it was shut, like I'd been locked in after everybody had gone home. The only light came from a few emergency exit signs, and the projection booth was dead. It was scary, not as scary as coming across a mutilated corpse, but there was something very creepy about it. I thought I heard somebody call my name, but obviously there was nobody there, and I stayed put, seeing nothing, doing nothing, feeling nothing, and after a while I got bored with the whole deal, and I was glad when Carla Mendez pulled me back.

We tried again, several times, but it was no good. Something had closed down and dried up. The only place I could regress to was this big, weird, empty movie theater. Carla Mendez told me I ought to be grateful, but gratitude wasn't exactly what I felt.

We had to give up eventually. No point beating a dead horse or a dead dodo. Carla made some herbal tea and I wandered round her apartment, looked at the photographs she'd pinned up on the notice board, and holy fuck, there was a face there that I recognized.

"Who's this dude?" I said, trying to sound calm, trying to keep it all together; I knew perfectly well who it was.

"That's Brian," she said. "Brian Braithwaite. He's an old client of mine. English. You'd probably like him. He's a writer. He just sent me something he wrote. Want to read it?"

thirty-five **The Beast**

The year is 1665. William Draper stands in the gloom of his own bedchamber, in his own house, in this plague-ridden city, and he equips himself, dons the fancy dress of a plague doctor: leather mostly, a leather hat, leather gauntlets, leather mask. He wonders if the mask needs to be quite so thoroughly grotesque, with its glass eyepieces, its long beak packed with rags and aromatics, yet he wears it with some satisfaction. He fears, indeed expects, that the plague may be too subtle and devious a foe to be defeated simply by cowhide, but he knows of no better protection, nor does anyone else, certainly not the fellows of the Royal College of Physicians, most of whom fled the city long ago, as, for that matter, did most of the quacks. But dressed this way he is finally, utterly protected from the harsh glare of the sun and from prying eyes, and that is a sort of salvation.

The stuffed dodo appears to watch him while he dresses. Can birds catch the plague? he wonders. Or spread it? Perhaps the dodo's death was a kind of salvation too. All that lives must die, but some modes of death are more merciful than others. And now there is something absurd and stuffed and birdlike in William's own appearance. Perhaps he and his dodo are now true kindred spirits, both laughable and useless, but in the streets William tries hard to be of use.

He moves through the city doing what he can. He carries a

long stick that he places on patients' wrists, to feel their pulse without touching them. This tells him little, but it is something to do. The dying are at least partly comforted to know that a doctor is in attendance. He tries to say the right thing. He tries to make his prayers sound convincing.

The sun roasts the air. The mud beneath his feet is caked and mummified. When he converses with his fellow man, the healthy as much as the sick, there is much talk of God and his wrath, and William can see that even the least vengeful of gods might have looked down on the deeds of Charles the Second, his restored and recently anointed, and found cause for chastisement. On the other hand, why would he be so slow to act? If God was inclined to visit pestilence on London and its inhabitants, why wouldn't he have sent a plague down even as the previous Charles mounted the block? Why wouldn't he have smitten the regicides with new and infinitely malevolent diseases? Why wait so long? Why choose such a common affliction as plague?

To William it feels like last days, comets in the skies, ministers driven from the church and the cities, leaving behind the weak and the corrupted. It feels like the end of something, perhaps the world, perhaps just the end of life, his own life.

He comes across a rogue Italian quack selling a fumigant, a brownish powder that he claims can be burned in the house to keep the plague at bay. To William it looks and feels very much like dried cow dung, and in a previous time, in what now feels like a previous life, he might have been moved to investigate further, to sample, analyze, and denounce. But in days such as these he is inclined to leave people to their own fragile hopes. What else do they have? Fumigants will not save them, but then what will?

He walks through Haymarket, past the house where Mrs.

Hendrick used to live. She is long gone, too canny and cunning a woman to remain still and await her fate. The house is shuttered and empty. It is a long while now since William ran out of the facial potion.

He returns home; peels off his leather finery; examines his body once again; checks the old, familiar scars made by the sun, stable and barren as a desert landscape; and then he sees new signs, new markings, harbingers of the plague. A week ago it started, marks that looked like fleabites but which rapidly spread and developed to become blotches and pustules, and now as he examines his groin and his armpits he detects hard knots of gristle beneath the skin, grown to the size of duck eggs. He could hardly say that he is surprised. There is perhaps some hint of relief at the arrival of the long-awaited, long-delayed traveler. Perhaps he has even embraced and willed his fate. In helping the plague victims of London he has put himself at risk, perhaps choosing to hasten the not quite inevitable.

No further need of protection now. He goes to his own front door and opens it for what he knows will be the last time. He has a piece of chalk in his hand. He draws a rough cross on the wood of the door and the words "God have mercy on us": an announcement, a warning, a plea. And he's reminded of some other words he saw on a sign, words written by Moxon, "The world's most disgusting bird." These days there is so very much to be disgusted by.

William Draper looks at his dodo: mounted, stuffed, a little faded, almost but not quite lifelike, and suddenly he sees a movement. He thinks at first it might be a trick of the light, a glimmer of shadow, but no, the feathers are quite definitely moving, showing what? Signs of rebirth? Of resurrection? A miracle?

He looks more closely, and the dodo's gray wings seem to be

alive, as indeed he sees they are, with worms: small, gray, lively maggots. The dodo's extremities are pulsating with life, but not their own. Mrs. Hendrick's skills were all too imperfect, as she always admitted, as he always knew. The movement is that of parasites, born of corruption, a perfectly natural process.

thirty-six

The English Patient

Perhaps you're wondering exactly why I killed Jack Rozin. Perhaps you think I behaved out of character. Perhaps you think my 'motivation' wasn't really strong enough. I disagree, obviously.

Certainly I couldn't see that the world would be in any sense worse off for the absence of Jack Rozin. I could hardly claim to know him very well, yet circumstances had given me rather a powerful insight into the man and his works. Neither was very appealing. If the punters had some urgent need for products such as *Age Gap*, another supplier would surely step forward, but I felt they could probably do without. A little less smut in the world would hardly be a tragedy. But let's be clear, I didn't kill Jack Rozin as part of some ludicrous antipornography crusade.

Certainly I was somewhat motivated by the fact that he had snuffed out Barbara's career, prevented her from working in her chosen profession. That seemed to me a terrible thing to have done. It was indefensible. The fact that Rozin was perfectly prepared to do the same with Rick and Dorothy only made it worse.

Equally, of course, I wasn't best pleased that he'd tried to coerce me into abasing and humiliating myself on camera. I thought that his enjoyment of the corruption of others was utterly rebarbative. Tawnee struck me as a sad and vulnerable creature who needed to be saved from the likes of Jack Rozin.

So, was all the above reason enough to kill Jack Rozin? Well, in my opinion it very definitely was. However, one of the main reasons I did it was simply because I could. We are all too seldom in a position where we can put our most intense impulses into action. I found myself in a situation where it was terribly easy. The mechanics, the practicalities, the actual execution of the deed—the murder, if you prefer—were all very simple. The morality was simpler still. I saw that, on balance, taking everything into account, I would be "doing no harm" by killing Jack Rozin.

And one more reason? Perhaps because I could see no other way out, no other way of resolving matters, of bringing our various dramas to a head, of providing a suitable sense of an ending.

Don't you hate those movies where, as the titles roll, there's a series of stills of the characters, and subtitles appear telling you what happened to them all after the film ended? That seems so slack and lazy to me, and somehow a cheat. Characters don't exist outside the confines of the movie; that's what makes them characters.

Then again, there are those movies where it's all over in twenty seconds: Hitchcock was obviously very fond of this. One moment our hero is clinging to the ledge by his fingertips, then suddenly he's saved, then he's in church getting married as a precondition to living happily ever after. It's very convenient for a moviemaker but it doesn't bear much relation to life as I know it. The problem with life—one of the many—is that you have to live through every single damn moment of it.

Yet again there are those other movies where, in the very last moments, somebody says something that changes everything and makes it all right. "The cavalry's coming." "For you, old man, the war is over." "What took us so long?" I really hate all those fakeries.

Inevitably, killing somebody creates a certain amount of chaos, both moral and practical. There's a desire for action, a need for rushing around. Dorothy, Rick, Barbara, even Tawnee —they all ran around like headless chickens (or dodos), trying to make plans, invent alibis, trying to make good their escapes. Dorothy, for instance, screamed that she hated L.A., hated acting, hated me, and never wanted to have anything to do with any of us ever again; she was going back to England to start a new life. It sounded like a very good scheme.

Barbara said nothing to me, but she looked tearful and I thought I could guess what she was thinking. She'd been trying to sell a house to a nice English doctor, and he'd turned out to be a cold-blooded killer. She had some rotten luck with men.

It did occur to me that I too, like Dorothy, might make a dash to the airport and flee to England or South America or wherever else it is that fugitives run to these days. But frankly I always hate scenes at airports, whether they're in life or in the movies— *Casablanca, La Jetée, Educating Rita.* So I didn't run to the airport. Very calmly I got into my car and drove to the Beauty Vault instead.

It was a long drive, but the traffic was untypically light. I heard a couple of distant sirens and I saw a police helicopter in the sky, but that was all perfectly normal for L.A. I knew they weren't coming for me. It was too soon. At that moment I felt untouchable. And perhaps, as I drove, I should have been feeling more disturbed or manic or remorseful, but I really didn't. Perhaps it was the true measure of my corruption that I didn't feel corrupted in the least.

I parked in what I had come to think of as my usual spot behind the Beauty Vault, next to the Mexican couple's van. I could hear them inside, sounding as though they were having a particularly nasty argument. I went into the Beauty Vault, and if I exuded the aura of a man who had just committed a murder, neither Perry Martin nor Duane detected it. Martin was again up a ladder rearranging his wall of feminine fame. Veronica Lake now seemed to be very much in favor.

"And what can we do for our favorite English customer today?" Perry Martin asked as he descended.

"Two things," I said. "I want to buy that animation cel of the dodo. And I want to see what's behind that green baize door of yours."

"You want a lot."

"Yes, I do. So name your price."

The one he named was even more extortionate than I'd anticipated, but I paid up, not exactly willingly, but with moderately good grace. I had nothing to lose. He made quite a show of packing the cel in a museum-quality, acid-free folder, and then an even bigger show of producing the key to the green baize door.

Had I really come to believe Perry Martin's rather ponderous promise that I would find what I was looking for behind that door? And did this mean that I now knew what I was looking for? Well, I suppose yes and no was the answer to both those questions. Perry Martin moved toward the door, saying, "Are you're sure you're ready for this?" and I said that I most certainly was.

So, what was I expecting? A small dark room crammed with the most arcane and intimate relics: dodo bones, wigs and teeth of the famous, trusses, prosthetic limbs, Jayne Mansfield's stuffed dogs? Or perhaps a very tiny preview cinema, perhaps with just one seat, the air thick with dust and old smoke, and on the screen there'd be fugitive images from the worst, most dreadful private footage? Well, I wasn't exactly *expecting* these things, but I was certainly ready for them.

In fact the green baize door opened to reveal that it was only the first of a pair of doors. The second was a couple of feet in front of the first; the space was like an air lock, with just enough room for a man to stand in, and there I stood between the two doors, alone in cramped darkness as Perry Martin closed the first door behind me. I felt like I was playing hide and seek. I hesitated to move forward and remained there long enough to notice a line of light seeping in under the bottom edge of the second door, as though there was not the expected darkness beyond it but some intense and powerful light source.

I turned the handle of the door in front of me, an abrupt and decisive gesture that only emphasized the door's flimsiness, and I flung it open and took a step forward—to emerge into the bleached brightness of the car park.

I had simply stepped out of what was now very obviously a rear exit of the Beauty Vault. There was no back room, no inner sanctum, no preview cinema, and perhaps if I'd thought harder about the layout of the building, I might have realized it much earlier. The great revelation, the thing I had been looking for, was apparently my own rental car and the van belonging to the Mexicans.

Was Perry Martin making a rather labored demonstration of some Zen paradox, or was the whole pretense of a back room simply a ruse to annoy and revenge himself upon the sort of manic memorabilia collectors who always assume the dealer has some secret stash of wonders?

Meanwhile I could still hear raised voices coming from the back of the Mexicans' van, but now they sounded alarmed rather than angry, and the rear doors were suddenly thrown open from inside to reveal both husband and wife, Carlos and Elisa, in states of high excitement and distress, the states that invariably accompany childbirth.

I did what I was supposed to do, what I'd been trained for. I behaved like a doctor. I delivered the child, though fortunately nature did most of the work for me. Chiefly I stood and watched and said encouraging words in English that the couple probably didn't understand.

The birth was swift and messy, and apparently not too painful. The baby was a little girl, perhaps slightly on the small side, but healthy enough, despite everything, with all the right bits and pieces located in all the right places. Both parents were weeping now and looking at me with a respect and wonder that I knew I didn't deserve.

"You should probably go to the hospital," I said. "Make sure everything's all right."

Carlos hung his head at the sheer scale of what I was suggesting, not least because, as he now pointed out, his van had two flat tires. Without much premeditation I handed him the keys to my own car, and he grabbed them as though he thought I might change my mind if he hesitated. Perhaps I would have. He and his wife and new baby daughter packed themselves into the vehicle, and I in turn climbed up into the cab of their van. It seemed a better resting place than most. As they drove away I didn't feel much of anything except tired.

I unwrapped the animation cel of the dodo and propped it up on the dust-caked dashboard of the van. Sunlight shone through it and revealed a mesh of scratches and flaws in the celluloid that I hadn't noticed before. And really, now that I looked at it more carefully, the cartoon wasn't very skillfully done at all. It was a crude, hurried, artless thing.

And then the passenger door of the van opened beside me and a very familiar woman's voice said, "Hey, how's it going, killer?"

It was Barbara Scott, of course. Apparently I'd been mistaken about her reaction to Jack Rozin's death. I had no idea how she'd found me, but I was very glad that she had. She climbed into the van and did a double take when she spotted the cel of the dodo on the dashboard. Her natural surprise at seeing it there was immediately superseded by the realization that after this day nothing I did would ever surprise her again.

"You OK?" she asked. "You look like you're dying."

"We're all dying," I said, and it sounded like the corniest line that I or anybody else had ever uttered. Barbara laughed and then she kissed me. We both sat there contentedly enough, and I hadn't the slightest idea what was going to happen to us. I closed my eyes and waited for the next movie to start.